"Are you all right?"

"No." The tears had stopped. Shelby was drained of everything. How long had it been since they'd abducted her daughter? "I'm not all right, Tim. I want my daughter back."

"I know you do. But Aimee is fine, Shelby. We have to believe that." Tim stared at her, his eyes filled with shadows. "The writing said she was safe."

"I don't believe that. And neither do you. She was safe here with me, Tim. Happy and healthy and loved. How can Aimee be safe away from the one who loves her most?"

"But, Shelby, you have to have faith. You have to."

"It's hard to keep hoping, Tim," she whispered. "All the terrible things you hear that happen to kids. What if Aimee—"

"No!" Tim jumped to his feet. "Don't say it. Don't even think it! Until we know differently, Aimee is fine. Do you hear me? She's fine!"

Books by Lois Richer

Love Inspired Suspense

Love Inspired

LOIS RICHER

Sneaking a flashlight under the blankets, hiding in a thicket of Caragana bushes where no one could see, pushing books into socks to take to camp—those are just some of the things Lois Richer freely admits to in her pursuit of the written word. "I'm a book-a-holic. I can't do without stories," she confesses. "It's always been that way."

Her love of language evolved into writing her own stories. Today her passion is to create tales of personal struggle that lead to triumph over life's rocky road. For Lois, a happy ending is essential.

LOIS RICHER

SECRETS
OF THE ROSE

Steeple
Hill®

Published by Steeple Hill Books™

STEEPLE HILL BOOKS

Steeple
Hill®

ISBN-13: 978-0-373-87383-8
ISBN-10:   0-373-87383-2

SECRETS OF THE ROSE

www.SteepleHill.com

Printed in U.S.A.

Be still and know that I am God.
—Psalms 46:10

This book is dedicated to Cristopher, who keeps digging until he gets the answers he needs. Congratulations on reaching your goal.

ONE

But he that dares not grasp the thorn,
should never crave the rose.
—*Anne Brontë*

Victoria, British Columbia
Monday, April 21

Perhaps it was the date—ten months to the day after Grant's abrupt, tragic death.

Perhaps it was the hour—that no-man's-land of black yawning silence in which all the world seemed to die.

Or perhaps it was simply that she wasn't yet used to being alone.

Whatever the excuse, Shelby Kincaid was wide-awake. She lay on her bed, bathed in a puddle of moon shadows that washed through her balcony doors, and ordered her mind to shut down, to forget the past and focus on the future.

It might have worked—except for the creak of one tired floorboard in the hall.

Shelby sat up, glanced at the greenish-blue hands on the gilt clock Grant had presented on her last birthday: 3:13 a.m.

Shadows danced over the walls as a shiver of wind tickled the blossoms of the apple tree outside her window.

Creak.

The hardwood's protest came again, closer this time. Just outside her door.

The phone on the nightstand sat waiting. All she had to do was pick it up and dial 911. She reached out.

Reech!

Her hand froze. The second squeak was barely discernible over the thud of her heart, but Shelby knew exactly where it came from, had vowed to oil that same hinge a hundred nights before when she'd crept in to check on her baby.

Aimee's door.

Someone was inside her house and now they were going into Aimee's room!

Forget the phone.

She twisted toward the security panel on Grant's empty side of the bed and stabbed the silent alarm. Soon the soundless summons would bring police from all directions of the city. But she couldn't wait for them. She had to go to Aimee.

Her legs, rubbery with fear, barely held her upright. Shelby pushed away from the bed, tiptoed across the thick buttercream broadloom and opened her door just a crack, enough so she could scan the hall, perhaps catch a glimpse of the invader.

No one lurked in the shadows. Which meant he must already be inside Aimee's room.

Her entire body began to tremble. Her stomach squeezed into a knot imagining her five-year-old daughter's terror waking to a stranger's face. Shelby reminded herself of her past training with Grant: Assess, then act.

She couldn't wait for the police, her daughter's life might be at risk. All she wanted to do was get to Aimee, hold her, keep her safe. Shelby slipped into the hallway, then surged ahead, pausing only long enough to wrap her fingers around the brass candelabra from the hall table, the sole weapon in sight.

Something—a squeal—made her careless and the candles fell to the floor with a clatter. Though quickly hushed, the noise galvanized her into action. She raced to Aimee's door, thrust it open, and breathed her daughter's name.

But Aimee could not respond.

Aimee was gone.

The four-poster lay empty. Only the soft organdy curtains moved, billowing in through the window, carried by the night air.

Shelby rushed across the fuzzy white rug, stared down through the glass into the gloom. The cavernous darkness of the garden lay below, silent, brooding. She could see no one.

When she turned, Shelby noticed the red letters scrawled across her daughter's mirror.

Aimee is safe.

Her brass weapon fell to the carpet.

"Not my baby, God. Please don't let them take my baby!"

Once they arrived, the police questioned her for hours.

Was the alarm functioning properly? Who would know how to disable it? Was the front door securely locked? Had she heard a car? Did she have any enemies? Was this connected with Grant's accident?

"I don't know." She recited the words over and over again. "I don't know. Please, just find my daughter. Don't you understand—they've taken my daughter!"

And she hadn't been able to stop them. The guilt burned through her like acid.

Within two hours the house was brimming with crime scene investigators, their gray-white powder covering every surface in sight. Esmeralda Peabody, who had been the housekeeper first for Shelby's grandmother and then Shelby, would be furious at having to repolish the intricately carved antiques. But Aimee would have a field day mucking through all that powder. If she ever came home again.

"Mrs. Kincaid? We really need you to concentrate. You're sure you didn't hear anything else but the footsteps?"

Shelby closed her eyes, forced herself to replay the scene in her mind, to relive the moment when she saw the bed, knew her child was gone. The moment her stomach hit her toes and her world stopped.

How could this have happened?

"Nothing else." Shelby gulped down the pain. She couldn't break down now. She had to help them find answers. "Just the footsteps in the hall, the door creaking. A muffled sound. That's all."

She looked up suddenly, her mind honing in on the last memory.

"Do you think they hurt her?" she whispered. "Is that what I heard?"

"No, we don't think that. Not at all."

The rush to reassure did nothing to ease Shelby's anxiety.

"We found a bit of material stuck in the frame. We think it was torn off something—pants, perhaps. You probably heard the thief muttering when he caught them, Shelby. May I call you that?" The lead investigator, a woman, taller than Shelby and about seven years older, kindly wrapped a blanket around her shivering shoulders, then sank down beside her.

"Call me anything." Shelby huddled into the warmth, wishing it would penetrate to her heart. "Ask whatever you need to. I don't care. I just want my daughter back. Please, can't you find her?"

Why didn't they do something, call someone? Why did they keep asking the same thing over and over?

Shelby felt her world spinning and knew she needed to reach for the focus that had kept her centered during key investigations she'd handled in the past. But she'd been out of the workplace too long, her training gone rusty with disuse these last ten months. Besides, those had been other people's loved ones.

This was Aimee, and Aimee was all she had left. All Shelby could do was silently implore God, the police, anyone who would listen—beg them to bring Aimee back where she belonged.

"Please, Detective. We need to find my daughter. She'll be afraid. She's only five."

"We'll find her. We've already started searching." The smile was grim, but it promised results. "Please call me Natalie. Natalie Brazier," she repeated, as if unsure whether Shelby had heard her say the same thing five minutes earlier. "I haven't lived in Victoria very long, so I'm not familiar with your history. I'd like to learn a little more about you, Shelby."

Detective Brazier resembled a starlet more than a policewoman. She arranged her long, lean body on the sofa beside Shelby with a natural grace and elegance, her black silk suit molding itself to every curve. Shelby recognized the designer—and it wasn't a knockoff. Whatever her job, this woman had expensive taste.

Shelby found it odd how her brain had never stopped storing details, even though she hadn't returned to work after Grant's death. Height, weight, hair color, body language. Once that had been vitally important to her job. But that was before Grant—

"I understand you lost your husband a short time ago."

The sting of reality dissolved her memory of those halcyon days in the past. Though the reminder hurt, it helped Shelby center herself, refocus. She nodded, pinched her lips together to stem the prick of nearby tears.

"Grant died ten months ago. Ten months tod—yesterday."

"Ten months to the day?" Natalie lifted an eyebrow at her nod. "Well." She made a notation. "Can you tell me what happened to him?"

What would Grant say if he knew she'd lost their precious child? Or did he already know? Was Aimee with him?

No! Please God, not Aimee, too.

Come home, sweetheart. Please come home to me.

Shelby closed her eyes, drew several deep breaths, then dashed away the storm of tears.

The policewoman studied her as if she wasn't sure what to do next, then she reached out for the tissue box and held it toward Shelby. Another detail to store—the woman was good at reading people. But then she would be, in her job.

Shelby took one, wadded the softness into a ball and forced herself to go back in time.

"I'm sure this is all in your files," she muttered, unable to quench the bitterness that always boiled up at the unfairness of it. "You'd only have to read it."

"I'd rather you told me."

"Fine." Shelby unclenched her fists and began. "We owned—I own a business called Finders, Inc. Someone asks us to recover something they've lost—stolen art, heirloom jewelry, that sort of thing. Or they ask us to find someone they need to get in touch with—a friend, a brother, heirs. We employ a team of specialized investigators who are trained to discreetly locate these things or people and, if possible, restore them to the client. At the time of his death, Grant was working on a project."

The utter silliness of those words struck Shelby as she said them. Grant was *always* working on a project. He loved nothing more than the thrill of the chase, the rush of tracking down a special order and presenting it to a buyer with that grand flourish only he could pull off. He would never do it again.

Would it be the same with Aimee?

No! She wouldn't think that. Stabs of pain radiated from behind her eyes. She squeezed them closed, breathing deeply to regain control. *Focus*, she ordered her brain.

"Can you go on?"

"Yes." Shelby forced herself to speak of a time when life had been simple, happy. "The thing you need to understand is that I didn't work Grant's case." She struggled to pull up whatever scant details her brain possessed. "Anything I say is secondhand information. I don't know many of the particulars, but that he'd been hired to find something a client had lost years ago—in Europe, I think. At one point Grant had information that the object was in Greece, but the lead never panned out. He'd returned and was following something new when the ex-explosion took place. He was killed in the fire." She bit her lip, the loss bitter still.

"I see." Natalie wrote something on her little black pad in precise letters. She tapped a pencil against the paper. "Can you tell me what the object was?"

Shelby and Grant had created two rules when they'd developed their plans for Finders, Inc. He'd insisted that in order to protect themselves, they must refuse to be involved in anything illegal. The second rule was Shelby's idea—once accepted, Finders would always finish the case. Underlying both rules lay the implicit understanding that a client's identity would never be revealed.

Finders never broke a confidence. Never.

"Why would you need to know that?" Shelby took a second assessing look at the detective who appeared more like a model. "My husband is dead. Are you implying that Aimee was taken because of something he couldn't find? Are you implying that she, too, might be dead?" She could barely say it. Only by clenching her fists could she force the unspeakable words past her lips, even while steeling herself for the worst.

"I'm not saying that. No! Not at all." Natalie's warm hand closed over Shelby's. "Please don't think that for a moment. But if we knew who his client was, what he was searching for and why, we might have an idea about who may be behind Aimee's abduction. Perhaps your client was angry that your husband didn't find his or her item. Perhaps your husband did find it and sold it elsewhere." She held up a hand as Shelby began to protest. "It's all supposition, but barring any other leads, I have to consider every angle. We want to find your daughter, Mrs. Kincaid."

Was this woman trying to smear Grant's reputation? Would that help her find Aimee? Shelby hated her sudden suspicion of everyone, of every situation. Grant would never have endangered her or Aimee. Never.

If Aimee was all right, then she was being held by someone. But there had been no ransom request. Nothing made sense. Who would steal a child from her home, from the mother who loved her beyond anything else in the world, for no reason?

"I can't imagine what any of Grant's work would have to do with Aimee's abduction. And remember, my husband died ten months ago. Why wait this long?" She saw Natalie's lips part and realized she was wasting time by arguing. "Never mind. Whatever you want to know, I'll tell you."

"Just tell me what you can recall."

Shelby thought for a moment, organizing the bits of information her brain had retained.

"I never knew exactly what my husband was trying to recover. I was busy, working my own cases. When we were home, we deliberately focused on each other and our child, not on work. I do remember that Grant said his client was an older woman—over ninety, I think." Was that what he'd said? Shelby reconsidered. "Or maybe the client hired him to find someone over ninety. Anyway, age was one reason why he wanted to conclude his investigation quickly."

She reached toward the phone.

"I'm afraid I don't know the client's name offhand, but I can find out if you must know. Though I can hardly imagine she'd be a threat."

Natalie frowned, shook her head.

"No. You're probably right, a woman that old wouldn't be involved in kidnapping. Perhaps something else connected with the business then? Some new client whom you've offended in some way?" she asked hopefully.

Shelby shook her head.

"Not me. Since Grant's death, I haven't even gone in to the office. Daniel, that's Daniel McCullough, is in charge now. He was one of our operatives, but he'd ceased most of his fieldwork and begun to fill a role as coordinator when the business grew too much for Grant and I. Since Grant's— well, lately Daniel's been handling everything. If you want to know about other clients, you'd have to talk to him."

"Okay. I'll call him later. He's trustworthy?"

"Completely." At least there Shelby had no hesitation.

"Good. Now, I have more questions for you."

Shelby rose, her mind moving into the automatic mode it would have used if this had been someone else's child she'd been hired to find.

"Yes. You'll want a picture, of course." She started toward the door, but was prevented from moving by a firm hand on her arm.

"It's okay, Shelby. We already have one. Your neighbor came over a few minutes ago. He woke up, saw the cars and was worried about you. He found a photo of himself and Aimee. We're using that. For now."

There was a look on Natalie's face that Shelby didn't understand.

"Tim? Tim is here?" She looked around, then realized that they would keep him away from her until they had all their answers. "Thank you, Lord, for Tim."

"How well do you know Tim Austen, Shelby?"

Some flicker in the detective's midnight-blue eyes added a waver of unease to the moment. Shelby frowned. There was something suspicious in her question.

"How well?" She shrugged. "As well as I know most people. Better, actually. He's lived next door for about six months. No, maybe it's been longer than that." She drew a hand through her mussed-up hair and realized she hadn't combed it, hadn't yet showered. As if that mattered.

"I don't remember exactly when Tim bought the house. But he never knew Grant. He came after that." She smiled. "Aimee loves Tim. And he loves her. Tim often used to watch her playing while I was busy arranging details for the garden."

"The garden?" Natalie stood at the window, her eyes on the newly tilled earth beyond the windows.

Shelby sucked in a breath of courage. Rehashing all these details seemed futile to her, but she supposed the police had to start somewhere.

"The rose garden. Yes." She walked to the doors, pulled them open and motioned to the area beyond. "My husband loved roses. This was his garden. I'm working on plans to make this house and its grounds a public attraction, as a sort of memorial to him. He'd want to share the beauty he and Gran planned. Grant was my grandmother's soul mate when it came to roses." She couldn't help the little smile that bubbled up at the memories.

Natalie scribbled in her book.

"The two of them had this saying: 'The secrets of the rose can teach you about life.'" Clear as a bell, she heard Grant's voice repeating the familiar phrase, his hands grimy with soil, face flushed from the sun, his grin radiant. He was so real in that moment, she could have believed he was standing there.

Then, like a mirage, the image dissipated, and she was alone. Again.

Shelby swallowed, stared at the bush nearest the doors, the last one Grant had planted. Deep Secret he'd named it.

"Anyway, that's my plan," she murmured. "Aimee and I don't need all this room." Not anymore. Not with just the two of them.

Or would there now be only one person living in her grandmother's home? She pushed away the ugly thought, concentrated on the detective. "Anything else you need to know?"

"You grew up in this house?" Natalie Brazier seemed surprised.

"With my grandmother, yes. My parents died when I was young. Gran took me in, cared for me, loved me. She helped erase—" Just in time Shelby stopped herself. There was no point in rehashing her childhood. "I was a researcher. This was home base. She told me it would always be mine. That was after I'd come back from Istanbul. I was hired to retrieve a painting for a museum. I met Grant in Istanbul."

Shelby watched the men moving methodically across her lawn, knew they were police, scouring the ground for any clue they might find.

"Look, none of that past history matters, does it? I just want to find my daughter." Her arms ached to hold that squirming little body, to feel those pudgy hands cup her face, kiss her cheek with a sticky sweetness that mere water couldn't wash away. Would she ever feel that again?

"We're trying, Shelby. Humor me, will you?"

As if she had a choice? Shelby let her glance slide around the room, felt a stab of anguish when it came upon the Christmas portrait they'd had taken the summer before, while the roses still bloomed. Aimee, beautiful beyond description in her white fairy-princess dress, as she called it. Grant, brown and fit from that trip to Greece, with his arms around "his girls." Herself, grinning, blissfully happy, totally unaware her world would soon shatter. In the weeks and months that followed, Aimee was the reason she'd hung on, kept it together. The Christmas cards with the picture sat in the basement yet, still boxed, never to be sent. But this one photo she kept up here. It helped ease the loss of Grant somehow, helped her remember to be grateful she had his child to love.

Aimee. Her baby. If Aimee didn't come home… Fear for her beloved girl clawed at her. She was so tiny, so innocent. Shelby's heart shuddered. She could no more stop her tears than the rush of love that welled up inside her.

"I'm sorry," she apologized over and over, "I can't seem to stop crying."

"You go ahead and cry if you want. Believe me, I understand." Obviously uncomfortable, Natalie got up, walked around the room. "This is an interesting old house. How many rooms are there?"

"H-how many rooms?" Shelby considered it a most dubious inquiry to make at this particular time and began to wonder about Natalie's experience in cases such as this. Shelby's patience was running short, she wanted action. "I don't know how many rooms there are. I never counted them."

"Did your husband mind living here?"

Shelby blinked. She'd always assumed Grant had loved the old place as much as she. But she realized now that she'd never outright asked him. Something else there hadn't been time to do.

"He always said he liked this room the most. We couldn't have bought anything like this house, not at first, certainly not until we got the business off the ground. But it was my grandmother's home and she didn't want to leave. It seemed easier to move in with her when she started to fail, give her those last few years in the place she loved, among her roses. Of course, when Aimee came, we were glad she was near, that she could watch her great-granddaughter grow up."

She knew she was babbling and grasped for control. Suddenly a new thought hit. Shelby felt her eyes widen, knew she was staring at Natalie. She should have expected this!

"What's wrong, Shelby?"

"I know how this works," she said, crossing her arms over her chest. "What's the percentage of parental involvement in cases of missing children—eighty per cent?" She glared at Natalie. "You suspect I may have had something to do with my daughter's disappearance. That's why you questioned me about the garden. You think I buried her?" She stopped, regained control, then continued. "Well, I didn't! Search every room, go through every yard of the grounds. Tear them up if you want to. I don't care. But you're wasting time and I don't know how much time Aimee has!"

"I didn't mean to imply anything." The hollowness of the words echoed around the room. "It's standard procedure."

"I don't care about procedure. Just find my daughter," she ordered through clenched teeth.

"Shelby, I wasn't trying—"

"Listen to me, Detective. I love my daughter more than my life. I'll give anything I possess to get Aimee back, do anything I need to. I don't care how much it costs, I don't care what extremes we have to go to. I just want her back—safe. Do you understand?"

Natalie didn't answer immediately. Instead she walked

across the room, sat down, leaned back against the sofa, her face inscrutable. Finally she broke the silence.

"All right. Let's find Aimee."

TWO

"I hope I'm not intruding. I saw you sitting out here, and wondered if there was something I could do."

Tim Austen's quiet voice roused Shelby from her contemplation of the hedge beyond. She blinked away the shadows, watched him shift from one foot to the other, hands thrust into his pants. In all the time she'd known him, her neighbor had always looked perfectly comfortable here. Now he seemed oddly fretful and that surprised her.

Of course, this wasn't any ordinary day. Tim's sandy-brown hair stood in bed-head tufts all over, as if he hadn't taken time to comb it. His rumpled beige corduroy pants bagged at the knees. The worn flannel shirt he favored now hung partially untucked, a clear sign of his distress. Normally Tim was fastidious about his clothing. Sympathy tugged at her. He was missing that effervescent five-year-old as much as she was.

He opened his mouth, shut it, opened it again, then finally spoke. "Are you all right?"

"No." She motioned to the chair opposite. The tears had stopped. Now she was drained of everything. The first few hours after an abduction were crucial. How long had it been since they'd taken her?

"Shelby?"

She glanced up, saw his concern. "I'm not all right, Tim. I want my daughter back."

"I know you do. But Aimee is fine, Shelby. We have to believe that." He stared at her, his eyes filled with shadows. "The writing said she was safe."

He must know how ridiculous that sounded. To believe a promise scribbled on a mirror? Frustration at his gullibility nipped at her heart and tumbled out in the tone of her words.

"I don't believe that. And neither do you. She was safe here with me, Tim. Happy and healthy and loved. How can she be safe away from the one who loves her most? That's ridiculous!" The angry words emerged harsh and bitter, but it felt good to finally unleash some of the violence that whirled inside her.

Tim jerked back as if he'd been stung, eyes wide with surprise.

Shelby knew she should apologize, but she couldn't. Not now, when she'd been waiting on tenterhooks all day and all night for something, some tiny ray of hope to cling to.

"You really want me to trust the scribblings of a kidnapper?" She shook her head, her freshly washed hair bouncing from shoulder to shoulder. "I don't think so."

"But Shelby, you have to have faith. You have to. You're the one who said God…" Clearly worried by her angry glare, he flopped into her white wicker chair, crossed one leg over his knee, then took it down. "I'm sorry," he mumbled. "I saw you sitting here and knew you couldn't sleep. I thought I'd keep you company but I'm making things worse. You look tired."

Tired? If only that's all it was.

The mirror hadn't been kind earlier. Shelby knew her hair was a mess, unstyled, frizzy, dangling around her face like a mop. Pushing it behind her ears only emphasized the lines under her eyes, the down-turning pull of frustration at the corners of her mouth, but she hadn't wanted to waste time on makeup or hairstyling. She'd made it in and out of the shower in four minutes, lest she miss the kidnapper's call for ransom.

Only there hadn't been any call.

"I heard them talking, you know, Tim, the police manning the phones." She didn't look at him, didn't want to see the pity on his face. "I went down around midnight to get a drink. They thought I was upstairs resting so they were talking openly. They're just as worried as I am that no demand has been made."

He frowned, glared over one shoulder at her house, as if he could transmit his thoughts through the walls.

"I don't imagine they know that much about kidnapping," he offered. "I don't think it happens all that often in a city as quiet as Victoria."

"It's not just the local police involved now. They've called in the RCMP, a missing persons unit, and I don't know who else. I don't really care who they call, as long as they find my daughter. But how can that happen when they have no leads, no suspects, nothing to go on? The neighbors weren't even awake." She lifted her head, caught a strange expression on his face. "You didn't see anything, did you?"

He was about to answer, but Shelby forestalled him, held up a hand. She already knew what he'd say.

"No, of course you didn't. You were asleep like the rest of the world." Bitter disappointment nipped at her. No chance of a lead here. "Anyway, I'd imagine the police have already asked you that question, haven't they?"

"Several times." Tim reached out, touched her arm. "But I'd answer it a hundred times if I thought it would help. I'd do anything to spare you this pain." He gulped, swallowed. "I love that little girl, too. You know that."

"Yes, I do." Shelby covered his hand with her own, moved by the tears in his eyes. "I'm sorry I sound so cross with you. I'm just…afraid."

His fingers squeezed hers but didn't let go. The warmth transmitting from his hand to hers eased the sense of loneliness she'd felt earlier. The hushed night sounds slowly died away. To the east, the horizon began to lighten with its first predawn glimmers. Shelby had always loved the early morning. It was as if God was saying, "Here, I'm giving you another chance. A new day, fresh and clean. Do something wonderful with it."

What was He saying this morning? Would today bring Aimee home?

"It's hard to keep hoping, Tim," she whispered. "All the terrible things you hear that happen to kids—they come back when the night is quiet and there's nothing to hold back the fear. They replay over and over." She caught her breath, fought to steady her voice. "In my mind I keep hearing those news reports about that little girl that was abducted last winter. What if Aimee—"

"No!" He jumped to his feet, his color high, eyes blazing. "Don't say it. Don't even think it! Until we know differently, Aimee is fine. Do you hear me? She's fine!"

Startled by his vehemence, Shelby stared as Tim paced across the patio. Then he seemed to regroup.

"I'm sorry," he murmured, his face drawn in a tight mask. "But I can't bear to think like that. Please, have some faith, Shelby. Just a little bit of faith."

She wondered if his reaction had something to do with his past. He'd never told her more than that an accident had caused the scars covering his face and hands. His words penetrated.

"Faith? What exactly does that mean, Tim? I've always wondered. Do you keep hoping when everything seems to be telling you there is no hope?"

He shook his head. "It's not what you hope. It's Who you hope in. Isn't that what Aimee's always singing about?"

The reminder resonated within her. If ever there was a child of hope, that child was Aimee. They'd waited so long for her—five long years when Shelby had secretly feared she and Grant would never have a child. And then Aimee arrived. From her very first day, she'd been a happy, contented baby. She's spoken earlier than usual, her voice a soft musical tone to her parents' ears.

By two she was repeating everything she heard, accompanying the words with a tune she composed inside her brain. Oh those songs! Songs of joy, of happiness, of wonder. Songs of hope. Shelby had to believe that precious voice would not be silenced.

She heard a sound behind her, twisted to see who was there. Natalie stood tall, silent, hands hanging at her side. She had an odd look on her face, as if something had surprised her.

"Is anything wrong?" Shelby asked the detective.

"I'm not sure. There's a man here, Daniel McCullough. I believe you told me he runs your company." Natalie's elegant demeanor appeared barely disturbed by her night on the sofa after she'd refused to accept one of the many spare bedrooms Esmeralda kept prepared. "He says he must see you."

"Daniel's here? At this hour?" Shelby rose. "Where is he?"

"I'm here, Shel." He'd trailed behind Natalie and now eased past her. "I know the police don't want me here, that you're expecting to hear something. Or maybe you already have?" One bushy eyebrow rose expectantly.

Shelby shook her head, swallowed the lump lodged halfway down her throat.

"Oh, I'm so sorry." One hand reached out to brush her

shoulder. His thin body sagged at the news, as if he, too, felt the loss of the small, bustling girl who'd called him "Unca Dan" from the first time she'd spoken.

Shelby cleared her throat. "You said you needed me. What is it, Daniel?"

"This." He thrust out a small, brown padded envelope toward her. "I don't know when it came in. I'll check as soon as the regular staff gets in, but I found it on your desk this morning when I arrived. I figured it might be important, maybe something about Aimee."

Daniel always arrived at work in the early hours—that was nothing new. But going into her office without calling to ask—that was unusual. Still, she'd called him last night, told him about Aimee. Maybe he'd had an idea to help. She glanced down.

"Who would send me something via Finders?" she murmured, turning the envelope over and over. There was no return address, no markings of any kind, other than the scribbled letters of her name. "I haven't been in my office in months."

"Which is why I don't think it came through the mail. There's no postage, for one thing. And Joanie knows to route all your stuff here."

Daniel often neglected to eat, so that his body had learned to run on adrenaline. Shelby recognized the telltale signs from his glittering eyes and knew adrenaline was pouring through his veins now. He shifted from one foot to the other, shoved his hands into his pockets, then reversed his action and dangled them at his sides. Finally he clasped them behind his back. His amber eyes, framed by the narrow black glasses he'd begun wearing lately, honed in on the envelope like a missile locked on target.

"Could it be important?"

Shelby shrugged, glanced at Natalie for direction. But the

stylishly competent officer seemed confused by her scrutiny of Tim.

"Natalie? Am I supposed to open it, or wait for fingerprints, or what?" Shelby prodded.

Natalie metamorphosed as she straightened her shoulders, the in-charge persona firmly back in place.

"I suspect Daniel's prints, and yours, have already obscured whatever was on it, and that whoever sent this was very careful not to leave a trace, but we'll try all the same." She drew two surgical gloves from her pocket. "Let me open it."

Shelby had to force herself to hand it over. She wanted to rip the envelope open and examine its contents. One part of her warned that they were probably nothing. The other part of her wanted desperately to believe that something inside that thick brown paper would lead them straight to her daughter.

Natalie examined the envelope in minute detail.

"Too thin to be a bomb," Tim told her, his voice quiet.

Natalie quirked an eyebrow at him. Shelby saw the flash of sparks, knew that neither completely trusted the other. It was odd, really. Tim was usually so easygoing.

"And you know this because…?"

"I've read up on it. I had to do some research." His chin thrust out in a belligerent jut meant to resist her attitude. "I do a lot of research. It's crucial to my work."

Shelby ignored the scowl. "You read about bombs to write children's books?" Now she was curious about her unusual neighbor.

"Can we just open it?" Daniel had obviously lost patience. He reached out as if to wrest the envelope from Natalie.

"Sure. But I'll do it out here." With one lithe twist, Natalie moved out of his reach, strode to a patch of grass, fifty feet from the house. "Ready?" She slit the package, turned it upside down.

Something small and gold slipped onto the grass. Something very familiar.

Shelby flopped onto the grass, reached out to gather Aimee's locket into her hands.

"Don't touch it!"

The warning came from two sets of lips. Tim looked chagrined, Natalie furious. He stood silent as the cop grabbed the radio from her belt and called headquarters to request a fingerprint technician. That done, she pulled off one glove, handed the locket to Shelby and told her to look inside.

She didn't have to look, of course. She knew that locket, had helped Grant choose it for their daughter's fourth birthday. The tiny scrolled lettering in the heart on the front read Aimee. Inside were two pictures, hers and Grant's. But there was also a slip of paper, much like the one found inside fortune cookies.

"There's something here," she mumbled, unnecessarily as it happened, for the others were already gathered around her, watching.

"Finders, Inc.?" Daniel scowled at the name on the paper. "Someone's playing a trick We didn't take her."

"*Finders, Inc.* That's the name of your business, right? And they took the trouble to print it and stick it inside the necklace." Natalie pinched the paper between two gloved fingers and turned it over. The same words appeared on the back. *Finders, Inc.*

"Yes." Shelby was just as puzzled as Daniel, but she picked up on the speculative tone of Natalie's voice. "Why, I wonder?"

"Look inside the envelope. Maybe there's something else." Tim squatted beside her, his face inscrutable as he watched the way Natalie carefully examined the interior. "There's a note."

"I can see that, Mr. Austen."

Everyone's attention focused on the envelope as a slip of paper fell out. Shelby stared at the sprawl of childish letters across notepaper with the Finders logo printed across the top.

Aimee is safe. Don't worry.

"Don't worry?" Shelby snorted. "As if!" She watched Natalie turn the paper over, scrutinize the back. "Why is this written on company stationery?"

"Exactly my question. This handwriting looks like a child's."

"It's not Aimee's. She always makes the *A* in her name very decorative."

Natalie's intense inspection seemed completed. She replaced the paper in the envelope and put both it and the locket in a plastic bag she had pulled from her pocket, then looked at Shelby. "I think we'd better begin investigating your company, Mrs. Kincaid."

"Us?" Daniel shook his head. "But why? What possible reason could one of our employees have for taking her child? We return things, we don't steal them."

"Can you tell me who else would have access to your letterhead, your company notepaper? The general public?"

Flustered, Daniel opened his mouth, closed it, then finally spoke. "N-no. But—"

"Actually, a number of people could have found a sheet of it." Shelby rose. "I have several pads of that very notepaper in the house. I know there's a pad on Grant's—that is, the desk in the study. And probably one by the phone in the kitchen, as well." She offered an apologetic smile. "I used to scribble notes to myself on them and I often carried a pad home with me. There must be a number of them around. Whoever took Aimee could have easily taken a single sheet, or a whole pad, for that matter—if they'd been in this house before. And they must have, to get in so easily. Don't you think?"

"This case is a puzzle within a puzzle." Natalie's epithet was terse and short, spat out in a whorl of frustration. "No apparent motive, no ransom note or call, no tracks. No fingerprints. No clues until today, and now this one is tainted."

Then, as if suddenly aware that she had an audience, she straightened, called over a waiting technician and handed him the evidence.

"So what do we do now?" Shelby asked when it became clear that Natalie wasn't going to volunteer any opinion on the state of her investigation.

"We wait. If your, er, manager?—will give me the names of your employees, I'll have someone check them out."

Daniel glanced at Shelby, and in one imperceptible movement of his head transmitted a *no*. That could only mean that right now he had someone conducting a sensitive search. Police investigations would mess that up.

"I'll go you one better. I'll check them out myself."

The idea had burst upon Shelby only a moment before when she'd seen the company logo on that slip of paper, but it was a good one. She was sick and tired of sitting around, waiting. She needed to do something, anything, to help find Aimee. Checking out employees who had already passed an extremely thorough investigation would be little more than busywork, but at least she could prove that her employees were trustworthy.

"You? But we need you here."

"Why?" She faced Natalie head-on, saw the confusion in her eyes and realized she had to soften her tone. Natalie was not the source of her frustration. "You and I both know there isn't going to be a ransom call, Detective. Not after this long. Anyway, I don't think taking Aimee was about money. It's about something else. Right now, I don't know what that could be, but maybe I'll uncover something at work."

She knew it sounded weak, as if she was running away. But she had to do something!

"I can't sit here, waiting for the phone to ring, asking myself a thousand times why I didn't rush in there and stop whoever did this, blaming myself for her disappearance. I have to act. Can't you understand that?"

"I can." Tim stepped forward, patted her on the shoulder. "And I think it's a good idea." He turned to Natalie. "Surely you and your *team* wouldn't turn down whatever help Shelby's company can offer? After all, Finders has a sophisticated system dedicated to finding people and recovering lost things. Maybe they could help your...er...department?"

The faintly challenging note in his voice puzzled Shelby. What was he implying?

"You don't think my office or the police department is handling this case properly?" Natalie's tone was icy.

"I never said that."

"You've hinted at it more than once." Natalie shrugged her elegant shoulders. "I don't really care what you think, Mr. Austen." She laid heavy emphasis on his last name. "I'm in charge here and I intend to find that little girl." She nodded at Shelby. "Go ahead. Do your checks. You've got files on everyone, I imagine?"

"We have." Daniel smiled.

"I'll want to see them."

"I can arrange for copies to be sent to your office, but you don't have to bother. If anyone can find out something that's not obvious, it's Shelby. Research is what she does best. No stone unturned." He held out his arms. "I know it's not the best of circumstances, but welcome back, Shel."

"Thanks. I think." She returned his hug. Already Shelby felt better, as if she could somehow come to grips with this by doing something to help Aimee.

Natalie watched them, her veiled glance hiding her true feelings.

"Anything, however small, that could connect your daughter to someone in your company is what we're looking for." She waited for Shelby's nod of understanding. "We're patched into your phone here in case something comes through, but I expect you to contact me immediately if you find anything. *Anything*," she repeated with emphasis.

"Of course. We have worked with the police before, you know, Natalie. We also have a very secure method of screening incoming calls to Finders, Inc. I'm not unfamiliar with the way things are done." Shelby frowned. "I certainly wouldn't dream of holding anything back that could jeopardize the safe return of my child."

The detective's cheeks flushed, but all she said was, "Right," before she turned and walked back inside.

"Bossy, overbearing, pushy…" Tim ran out of words.

"What's going on with you two?" Shelby was curious about his attitude. "You've been at loggerheads ever since you met."

"Something about her bugs me. I don't know what it could be, other than the aforementioned attribute of pure bossiness." Tim shook his head. "Forget about our personality differences, Shelby. Go and do what you have to do."

"I'll do it," she agreed. "But I hate it. We screen very carefully. Once our staff have been cleared, we do periodic updates and yearly investigations. It's all part of the very specialized work we do. I don't see how anyone in our offices could be implicated in this."

"Nor do I." Daniel walked along beside them, his forehead pleated in a frown. "But I'll be glad to have you there, Shelby. I'd like to keep this as low profile as we can."

"Is something wrong with the company, Daniel?"

He appeared to debate his answer. Finally he spoke, his voice soft, reflective. "Now's not the time to burden you with work, Shel. Let's just concentrate on Aimee. The rest can wait for a more appropriate time."

He wasn't telling her everything, and she knew it. But for now, Shelby wouldn't press him. Daniel might be holding his own counsel until they could speak freely. Or he might not yet be sure of his facts. One thing she knew—Daniel was as loyal as any of her employees. Grant had trusted him implicitly. So did she.

Daniel may not want to bother her now, but if something was seriously wrong at Finders, she intended to find out during her own probe. Finders, Inc. had gained its reputation because of its specialized capability to locate and recover without eliciting undue attention. One rotten apple could spoil the entire business; seriously threaten their ability to handle confidential work, especially those government contracts they periodically won. So she'd do whatever she could to ensure that Daniel's investigation would stay hush-hush. For now.

Shelby left home to the tune of Esmeralda's grumblings about the policemen who'd moved into the house she'd lovingly cared for these past twenty years, men who couldn't get enough of her double chocolate cookies, men who left footprints from the rose garden on her clean carpet. Shelby left, knowing the older woman was just as upset about losing Aimee as she was. Looking after the officers would keep Esmeralda busy.

But as Shelby drove through the security gates and onto the lot of the company that she and Grant had built, a shiver of trepidation crept up her spine—which was probably natural. After all, she hadn't returned to Finders since Grant's death. Perhaps that accounted for the foreboding she felt as she watched the security camera track her steps, punched in her pass code to transmit the secure sequence that sent the elevator to the top floor. The feeling didn't lessen when she unlocked her office door.

Everything was as she'd left it, though Joanie, her secretary, had already pulled the files and placed them on her desk. And apparently the cleaners had also been in for there wasn't a speck of dust on the clear glass surfaces. When she caught a glimpse of the photo on her desk, a snapshot of her and Grant laughing at each other on a catamaran off the Sicilian coast, her heart took over and she struggled to remain calm.

He'd died here, on these grounds.

The knowledge stabbed anew, but time had taught her how to handle the pain. Shelby drew in deep breaths, forced herself to turn away, focus on the names numbered on a list beside the files. She sank down in the comfortable chair and began an intense scrutiny of each. When Shelby glanced up two hours later she was not a whit closer to finding a betrayer.

Aimee's photo on the window ledge stared at her, the image so real she reached out to touch it before reality impinged.

Why had she thought she'd find an answer here?

Whoever had taken Aimee had gone to incredible lengths to leave no trace.

Her field staff were skilled at concealing themselves in any situation. She and Grant had trained them to be resourceful and as far as she could tell no one had stepped over the company line by even a feather. In fact, during the past ten months they'd honed their skills, adapted, changed; while she'd remained at home. Now she needed to be sharper than they. It was possible that Shelby had lost the edge that had once made her the best tracker in the world.

But she intended to get it back.

THREE

"I must see her now."

The strident voice from the hallway drew Shelby's attention from the information she'd found. She glanced at the door, blinked several times to refocus her eyes, bleary now from studying her computer screen. But when the noise outside didn't abate, she got up, walked over and pulled the heavy door open. So much for soundproofing.

"Joanie?" She looked for her secretary, saw her face-to-face with Russ Carson.

"I'm sorry, Shel. Apparently he doesn't understand English very well."

She knew Russ had taken Joanie's words as an implied slam against his foreign birth because two spots of angry red colored Russ's sharply chiseled cheekbones. If ever there were prototypical face and body features for a spy, Shelby had long ago decided that Russ had them. He didn't possess the suave debonair style of a spy from a movie, but with his gaunt body and sharply honed features, he certainly looked like someone who'd come in from the cold and never warmed up. Of course, Russ dressed specifically to enhance the tough-guy effect with lean-fitting jeans, a black turtleneck and always a black leather jacket.

"Have we got a problem here, Russ?" Shelby modulated her voice to its mildest tone. With the company since its inception, Russ would no doubt recognize she barely controlled her temper, but right now Shelby didn't care. She needed to make progress if Aimee was to be found and thanks to his interruption, she was getting nowhere fast.

Russ assessed her from between narrowed eyes. Finally he shook his head, his shoulders dropped their arrogant slant. But he didn't back down.

"There is no problem here. But I must speak to you, Shelby. It is very important." As usual when Russ was excited, his accent became more pronounced in spite of his attempts to cover it. Each word he spoke was precisely enunciated, but doing so slowed his sentences to a stilting structure that only emphasized his language difference.

"I'm busy right now, Russ. I'm sure Joanie told you that." She turned, moved toward her office. "We can reminisce later."

"Reminisce?" He shook his head. "I do not speak of the past. The present is what concerns me. You cannot find the little Aimee without help, Shelby. I am that help."

Something in the timbre of his voice stopped her. She turned, scrutinized him.

"You? What do you know about Aimee's disappearance?" she demanded, mentally running through his history with the company.

Russ Carson—Grant's partner in past covert operations that neither had ever openly discussed—knew exactly how to get in and out of a building without being detected and his means did not employ disguise. Perhaps Natalie was right to suspect Finders' staff. Russ certainly had the training and know-how to carry out an abduction. But it made no sense for him to take Aimee. He loved her, she'd seen that for herself a thousand times over.

Shelby told herself to get a grip. Suspecting every person who crossed her path wouldn't help. Answers, not speculations, she reminded herself.

"What do you know about my daughter, Russ?"

"Probably less than you, right now." He shrugged. "But I do know the police are not as efficient as we are in these matters."

"By we, I'm assuming you mean Finders?"

"But of course." He stepped closer, dropped his voice. "I have been doing this work for years. I know my record, and so do you. I get results." The proud arrogance was back. "I've found a hundred items, located people no one else could find through sources no one else can use." His voice dropped, his accent grew more pronounced. "I can find the little one, Shelby. Give me the chance. For Grant's sake."

She'd just spent four grueling hours sifting through a plethora of documents, and nothing, not one single clue had emerged. She was no closer to finding her daughter than the police were. There was no way to tell how much longer she had before the kidnappers did something drastic.

If they hadn't already.

Shelby made up her mind in that instant. "Come in here, Russ."

He followed her into her office, his kid leather boots making no sound on the hard tiled floor. Russ was like a panther, he could move faster, quieter, than anyone she'd ever met. His passport might say American, but thanks to his foreign birth and his father's diplomatic status, he also had more connections than any other agent they employed. Maybe, just maybe…

"I'm quite sure the police wouldn't appreciate the aspersions you just cast on them, Russ." She smiled. "But you've got a point, and right now I don't care about what the police think. I want my daughter back. This is where we are so far."

She laid out the sequence of events for him in crisp, concise points, knowing that even though he took no notes, his brain would absorb every detail. When it came to information, Russ's mind worked like a microcomputer.

"So the police think that because this note was written on our company paper, the abductor is one of us." He raised one eyebrow. "This is also what you think?"

"I can't afford to write anyone off. I want my child back. That's my primary goal here." She met his gaze, held it. "I won't lose her, Russ. I will not lose another member of my family. Do you understand me?"

His eyes flickered, lost their clear blue sheen and turned the gray of a Russian blizzard.

"I understand." His confident voice changed, the inflection soft, entreating. "The death of Grant changed all of us. But I am here to help, Shelby. I would never allow his child to be hurt. Never." He muttered something unintelligible, probably one of the foreign idioms he often used but seldom explained.

Shelby knew the decision was hers. She could authorize him to go ahead and conduct his search, or she could reject his help. Which probably meant he'd keep right on looking anyway. Russ didn't give a fig for authority figures. But his search might go faster if she approved it.

Shelby was reminded of Russ's visit to their home last Christmas, how he'd comforted Aimee with tales of his grandfather and the things he'd done to make Russ's childhood Christmases special.

He must have seen the decision in her eyes.

"All right. We begin now. You will tell me all, please, Shelby. The police, what have they done?"

She told him what she knew, which wasn't much.

"Imbeciles." He kissed his fingers into the wind. "I could get more from a stone. No prints, no tracks, no knowledge of how the security was breached? It is preposterous!" He turned, strode to the door and yanked it open.

"Where are you going? What about these files?" she demanded, frustrated by his whirlwind exit. But then Russ had always ignored the usual routes, had always forged his own way. In the past, Grant had sometimes chastised him for rushing in. But Russ got results. At the moment, Shelby wasn't about to question him on his methods. That could come later. If he found something.

Russ held the door open with the toe of his boot.

"I do not believe the answers lie in your files, Shelby. But before I know where to begin, I must have more information. I will get it. Now." He disappeared out the door.

"Well, thanks for the help." She sighed. Personally she, too, was less than convinced that the abductor was among her staff but she wouldn't quit until she'd ruled everyone out. It was boring, lonely work that she despised. These were her friends, her coworkers. Or they had been. It seemed disloyal, even hateful to suspect one of them of doing this.

Shelby flopped down in her chair, staring out the window at the fading sun. Her glance landed on the picture on her desk and she picked it up, stared into the cherubic face with its feathery-blond hair, button nose and Grant's wise eyes.

"Where are you, sweetheart?" she whispered. "Please help Mommy find you."

She longed to feel those chubby fingers tickle her neck, yearned to hear that high-pitched voice squeal with delight. It had taken so long to accept Grant's death as part of God's plan. Even now she still had questions. But taking Aimee, too—surely God didn't want that?

"I love her so much, God. I want her to come home so we can make our double fudge strawberry peach sundaes." The tears would not be stopped. "I want her to come home because

I don't think I can look after our butterfly garden without her help. I don't think I can go on if she's not there, God. Please send her home."

The silence in her office was exactly what she'd craved earlier. But now Shelby would have gladly exchanged it for just one of Aimee's giggles.

"God, you know what's happening. You know where she is. Please keep her safe. Please don't let anyone touch—" She gulped down the words, refused to say them. "You love her more than I ever could. Please bring my child back to me."

Shelby opened her eyes, stared at the beloved face once more. As she did, she felt the band of tension around her heart begin to ease. God knew what she was going through. He understood. In the depths of her mind, she comprehended that He was in complete control of everything that happened to her. But somehow she wished she understood why He'd allowed this.

She remembered Tim's words. *A little bit of faith.*

Right now, that's about all she had.

She replaced the photo and, with a sigh, turned back to the computer. God would do His part. Now it was time for her to do hers.

By the time Shelby had completed the last of the files, the clock on her computer read 10:45. She'd checked in twice with Natalie. No call had come in regarding Aimee's whereabouts, no ransom call had been made. No note had been delivered, no new evidence reported. Natalie sounded curt, as if she were holding back her temper when she said Russ had dropped by the house. So had Tim.

In an odd way, Shelby understood Natalie's frustration, knew exactly how she felt. They had all gone over and over the same things. If there had been some tiny clue to latch onto and ferret out, she could sink her teeth into it, bury herself in figuring it out. But there was nothing. Whoever had done this knew exactly what he was doing and had left no trace evidence, no witnesses to their silent departure, not even any footprints in the freshly turned soil below Aimee's window. Natalie must be as frustrated as she.

For Shelby there was no reason to go home. The house was empty without her daughter. But she did need to rest, shower, change clothes. Besides, if she hung on to that crumb of faith, maybe tonight the nightmare would end.

Reluctant to stop, but well aware that she'd made little progress, Shelby logged off, secured the file with her password and waited while the machine shut down. It seemed to take longer than usual and she made a mental note to have the company technician check for malfunctions. She locked the files in her desk, pocketed the key.

She was almost at the door, about to leave, when a knock halted her actions. Her nerves inched up a notch, though she knew the company's security system would be on, that no one who didn't have the correct security clearance would be able to get into the building. But …

"Come in," she called, fingers clenched around her purse.

"So you *are* still here." Daniel stuck his head in. "I'm not sure it's good for you to be working such long hours your first day back, but I am glad you're here. Have you got a moment for me?"

She wanted to go home, to see if her faith had worked, if someone somewhere had found out where Aimee was being held. But Daniel's serious expression stopped her.

"I was leaving, but I can spare a few minutes. Nothing to rush home to," she tried to joke, then bit her lip.

"We'll find her, Shel. Just keep hanging on." He moved toward her, patted her shoulder. "Actually, that's why I wanted to talk to you. I heard about the ruckus with our resident bad boy this afternoon. I'd have been here, but I only found out a couple of hours ago, too late to be of assistance."

"It's all right, Daniel. Russ just wants to help."

"And you're letting him?"

The tone of his voice bothered her.

"Why not? You two used to be best friends. Has something happened to change that?" Shelby watched the guarded look cloud his eyes. "Have you argued with Russ about something?"

"Not really. I just thought you and I agreed that I would head up things here. But now Russ has practically taken over, countermanding my orders—"

"Daniel." She stepped closer, laid her hand on his arm. "You know that I've depended on you, and will continue to depend on you to keep Finders going. You have my full support. But this is my child, and she's missing. I can't afford to turn down anyone's help."

"Ah, but why should she refuse my help, eh, Daniel?" Russ stood in the doorway, hands on his hips. "I am the only one who seems to get results."

His arrogance had once made Shelby laugh. But now, the word *results* took her breath away. "You found something."

"Ja. I found—something." He strode in, leaned one hip against her desk. "This Natalie, the oh-so-elegant police detective. You know her well?"

"I don't know her at all. Except that when I called the police, she came. Why?"

"Curious." He shrugged. "The lack of clues, that is surprising, yes?"

"I guess they were very careful." She nodded. "But yes, to answer your question. I would have thought there would be something they could use."

"Yes, I think that, also. But Miss Natalie—she says there is nothing. The security panel has only one code entered for that night, a code which the good Natalie says belongs to you. The fibers from a snip of cloth left in the window belong to material in men's pants sold by the thousands. It may have been there for months. These police find no fingerprints, though they have thrown their powder all over the house. Even the handwriting on the mirror is childish, like that of a thousand kindergarten children—and so virtually untraceable."

"Stop being melodramatic and tell us what you found." Daniel's eyes blazed with anger. "Can't you see how you're upsetting her?"

Russ glanced once at Daniel, his face hardened. He seemed about to say something, but after a glance at Shelby, changed his mind.

"I apologize, Shelby. I do not mean to act inadvisably. But before I say more, I must ask a question. When you stood at the window that night, you did not hear a car, did not see someone drive past? Perhaps you heard footsteps below, running away?"

She shook her head.

"No. Russ, you talked to the police. You've been to my home. You know Aimee's room is at the back, above the garden. Grandmother owned a huge section of land behind the house, which I've kept undeveloped. There's no road back there for a very long way."

"Exactly so." He straightened, crossed his arms over his chest. "Yet this thief, this abductor, he steals this child, not a tiny sleeping baby, you see, but a little girl who is liable to awaken when picked up by a stranger. And yet, there is no sound. Why? Does he drug her? *C'est possible.* But I do not think there is time before Mama Bear arrives. And he has no getaway car waiting for him at the back, therefore he must carry the child around to the front of the house." He shook his head. "Very strange."

Russ had been partly raised in France. Perhaps that's why

he fell into the language whenever he spoke of Aimee. Shelby said nothing, simply stood, waited. Russ was onto something, she could see it in the glint of his eyes.

"He is a wonder, this phantom of ours. In truth, our thief is so accomplished, he does not even leave footprints in the flower beds below. How is this possible? Is he a ghost? I do not believe in ghosts."

"The police said there was no evidence of footprints." She glanced at Daniel. Clearly he didn't understand what Russ was getting at, either.

"No, there is no evidence. This I checked for myself."

"And?"

"There is no evidence of footprints because someone has raked the area."

"Raked it? But how? When?" Shelby shook her head. "I was there, Russ. I hit the alarm as soon as I heard someone in the hall. I couldn't find Aimee. The police came almost immediately and they were all over the place. Surely they would have noticed if someone had worked in the garden."

"I am not so sure of that. You yourself were there but a few hours before, no? Your neighbor said he saw you raking the ground under some bushes near the house."

"Yes…" Tim. It would have been he who'd seen her. The old carriage house he rented was the only thing near enough their yard, since originally the two properties were one.

"And yet, on this freshly worked soil, there is no outline of a shoe, no markings whatever." Russ shook his head. "No."

"So someone came along behind and raked over his tracks? Is that what you're saying? But what does that tell us? That there was an accomplice?" Shelby couldn't wrap her mind around whatever he was intimating. The entire thing seemed like a nightmare, something that would happen to someone else. Not to her. Not to Aimee.

"Yes. I'd like an answer to that question myself. What exactly are you trying to say, Russ? You insinuated that you had something big to tell us. Well, let's hear it. Or is this another one of your hot air dances? Promise the world, deliver nada." Daniel's lips curled in a derisive smile.

"I always deliver. And you would do well to watch what you say, my friend." The words were spoken calmly enough, but it was the steel threading through them that made the impact. "I have nothing to apologize for. My record is clean. Can you say the same?"

"Why don't you come right out and accuse me of Grant's death?" Daniel demanded, his jaw locked so tightly it grew white with strain. "Why pretend to be a friend when all the time you blame me for not being here, for not backing him?"

Shelby gulped. The gloves were off now, and she had no idea how to stop this. They looked like two raging animals, each daring the other to step past an invisible line. But what was it all about? Daniel mentioned Grant. What had he to do with this feud? Did he feel guilty for his friend's death?

"Yes, you are right. I do blame you, Daniel. You should have been here. He was on a case that only you knew about. If you could not be there for him, you should have phoned me. I would not have left him here alone. To die."

"Stop it!" Shelby stepped between them. "No one knew the fire would start, Russ. Daniel wasn't here because Grant insisted he simply wanted to check out something. Who could have imagined he would get caught…." She stopped, drew a breath. "You have nothing to be guilty about, Daniel. The fire was an accident. Grant is gone. But I cannot, I will not lose Aimee. So say whatever you're getting at, Russ, and let's get busy trying to find her."

"Very well." Russ stepped back. "This is my opinion. The person who took Aimee knew exactly what he was doing. It was a professional job by someone who knew your routine, the house, the grounds, the security code, everything. Our 'ghost' left nothing to chance."

Shelby tamped down the questions.

"If you know, tell me!" she demanded. "Who did it?"

"I do not know that. Yet." He glanced up through his black lashes at Daniel. "But I believe it was someone close to you."

"You're hinting at me? This is ludicrous! Pure supposition with no facts on which to base it." Daniel turned his back and strode to the door. "I do need to speak to you, Shel. But I can wait until tomorrow." He twisted to look at Russ. "I suggest you wait till then also. In the meantime, find something solid on which to base your ideas."

He walked out, slamming the door behind him. Shelby turned on Russ.

"Daniel did not do this, Russ. I can't believe you would think he did. You, he and Grant were friends not very long ago."

"Yes." Russ held her gaze. "We were friends. Once. But things change. The person who stole your daughter had personal knowledge of things an ordinary thief wouldn't know. He left nothing to chance, not even his footprints in the garden. Either he or someone helping him knew the freshly worked ground would imprint and was prepared to cover those tracks."

"And you believe that person was Daniel?"

"I do not say exactly that. I say merely that you must be wary of whom you trust. I will keep digging, but you must be alert. These are people who wish you harm, Shelby. Be very careful."

While she stared after him, Russ walked out of the room, leaving her door ajar. A moment later she heard the elevator doors whoosh close.

She stood alone in her office, staring out the windows into the blackness while the sounds around her magnified a thousandfold.

The words of the Psalm she'd repeated over and over in the wee hours of the morning now echoed through her mind. She couldn't remember all of it, but one line sang through, sharper, more poignant than the rest.

"May He grant your heart's desire and fulfill all your plans."

Her heart's desire was known to Him. He alone could help Aimee now.

FOUR

Tim wandered through the house he'd rented for the past nine months, pausing beside the windows from time to time to see if Shelby was home yet. One hand absently rubbed the keloids forming on his face, an unpleasant reminder of the burns he'd suffered and of yet another operation the doctors had insisted he have—soon.

Like a looming cloak, the reminders of past operations hung suspended in the shadows of his mind—black timeless moments when he first came out of the anesthetic and the pain was too real, too piercing to be controlled. That space before the morphine kicked in, that was when the specters of what should have been threatened to tear his heart from his body.

No! He wouldn't go back there now, would never allow himself to dwell in that black pit of despair when he could stop it. They were gone, why think about what could have been? He thought of Aimee, sweet innocent Aimee, who had pushed against his self-imposed barriers, insisted he accept that life went on in spite of great tragedies. He missed her sweet giggle, her charming laugh and the tender way she touched his scars, as if they were somehow precious.

From the corner of his eye he saw Natalie, the police investigator, walk through Shelby's rose garden, pull out a cell phone and speak on it. Moments later she clipped it closed and returned to the house. Something about her had bothered him from the moment he'd laid eyes on her, but Tim had no justification for those feelings. In the past eighteen hours she hadn't left her post or handed over the assignment to another—which should have garnered her some Brownie points. Instead an irritating niggle at the back of his brain wouldn't be silenced. Something wasn't right.

Finally Shelby arrived. He watched her plain black car roll up the driveway. Even at this distance he could tell from the slump of her shoulders that she'd found nothing new, learned no more than she'd known when she left this morning. Inside he felt a flood of awareness when she stepped out of the car.

She was so beautiful. Her hair flowed out behind her like a golden burnished cape, tousled curls dancing in the freshening wind, tall and slim yet still elegant, even after her ordeal.

She might have been any other businesswoman returning from a day at the office except that three men protected her from the cameras and microphones shoved into her face. Looking for another headline, no doubt. He glanced down at the newspaper he'd tossed to the floor in a fit of anger. Rumor, speculation— they had no facts. Why did they need to hound her so?

Her protectors shuffled her inside the house, physically pushing aside those who would stop them. Tim already knew they were policemen, charged with protecting the scene from nosy newshounds until the police were ready to release what they knew. Knowing that didn't make him any less jealous. He wanted to be there, to help, to do something. Instead he was on the outside looking in, the neighbor nobody noticed.

Tim moved to the side window of the kitchen and waited. After a while Shelby emerged in a pair of jeans and a loose shirt and a bright red quilted jacket. She carried a cup which he knew would be brimming with mint tea. Shelby loved mint tea. She found a chair and sat down, her face pensive.

Tim grabbed his own mug of cold coffee. He might be an outsider, but he intended to be there if she needed him. He walked through the hedge that abutted her property, pausing at the corner of the house when he heard someone speaking.

"I could not say this at the office, Shelby, but I can be silent no longer. I must tell you to watch out for Daniel. He has been acting very strange."

"Strange?" Shelby's voice carried to Tim, clear and filled with puzzlement. "What do you mean strange, Russ?"

"I mean this—he hides things. He comes back late at night when everyone has gone home. The next day I hear something is missing from the warehouse. I ask Daniel but he will not explain. I do not like to say it, but I think Daniel is in trouble. What other reason can there be to keep so many secrets?"

"Secrets?" She stared at him, a frown marring her beauty. "What secrets does Daniel have?"

"I have no secrets from you, Shelby. You can ask me anything."

Tim peeked around the corner, saw the man he'd met this morning standing in the doorway, his lean body erect, his face glowering. Russ and Daniel glared at each other like tigers.

Though Tim thought it would probably be prudent for him to leave and return when Shelby's guests were gone, walking across the pebbled area would disturb them and reveal he'd been listening. Judging by the anger resonating through both men's voices, Tim also had a feeling that he might be called upon to intervene. He decided to wait.

"Why are you bothering Shelby again, Russ? If it's merely to blacken my name, can't it wait?" Daniel strode forward, his thin face tight with anger. "I have done nothing wrong and I have nothing to hide. I'm sorry I wasn't there when Grant needed me, but all I can do now is run the company the best way possible. I told you I knew about the warehouse thefts and that I had implemented special security measures to track the thief. What more do you want?"

"To know about these 'special' measures."

"I'm not prepared to discuss that with you, Russ. It's a matter of company security. As I told you before." Daniel glanced at Shelby, then back at Russ. "Perhaps I should come back another time."

Tim didn't like his tone. According to Shelby the two friends had previously enjoyed a good relationship. What Tim didn't understand was why they seemed enemies now.

"There's no reason in the world you should have to drive back out here to see me," Shelby murmured. "You look tired, Daniel. You should get some rest."

"I'll rest when Aimee is back at home with you," he murmured.

"So sincere," Russ sneered. "I wonder—can we know what lies behind such a voice?"

"I don't like your tone. Why don't you say what you really mean?" Daniel stood directly in front of Russ. The two glared at each other menacingly. The situation was descending from bad to worse and Shelby was paying the price.

"Good evening." Tim stepped around the corner, feeling tension land on him like a thick blanket. "Have I come at a bad time?" He scrutinized each man in turn then looked to Shelby for direction. "Perhaps I should go?"

"I don't know," she admitted, her lips pinched tightly together. "Russ and Daniel seem to have some personal differences which I was not aware of."

"But I'm sure neither of them would want to hamper the

investigation into Aimee's disappearance." He glared at both of them, saw the flush of shame wash over Daniel's face. Russ merely clenched his fists. "There are media everywhere, gentlemen. They're looking for something to splash all over tonight's news. Unless you both want to be tomorrow's front-page story, with an accompanying article describing how Shelby's friends make her life miserable, it might be prudent to present a united front. Otherwise Shelby's company is going to suffer."

He watched two quite different reactions to his chiding.

"He's right. Finders, Inc. has a lot of wealthy clients who don't want to be known. If they see us in the media, arguing, we're not going to look very professional. Forgive me, Shelby. I'm afraid I wasn't thinking clearly."

Daniel's swift apology relieved Tim. He had no right to preach to these two, but he was concerned about Shelby. He noted that Russ also covered his angry look, managed to seem chastened.

"I must also apologize. I do not wish to upset you. I will leave now, but I think not through the front. A woman waits there to talk to me and I do not like her questions. If I may use your hedge?" Russ inclined his head toward Tim, barely waited for his nod of approval.

"Of course. Go ahead." Tim stopped. Russ had already disappeared.

"I need to show you this, Shel. I have prepared a statement for the press. If you'd like to look over it first, I'd appreciate that. Then I'll go out and read it to them."

She scanned the sheet Daniel handed her, nodded and gave it back. "It's fine. What picture of Aimee will they use?"

"I gave them one I'd kept on the security file." His face softened. "Natalie is against our publicizing it, and I'm sure we will get some crank calls, but if one person remembers her, if just one lead comes of it, it will be worth it." Daniel held out a hand to Tim. "I understand you initiated the effort to have posters made and distributed all over town. Thank you."

"Tim!" Shelby rose, walked over to touch his arm. "I didn't know. That was kind. Thank you."

"A committee will hit the streets with them as soon as a public announcement is made. It's the least I can do. I want her back, too."

"I know." She smiled through unshed tears which made her eyes shiny and squeezed his heart. He covered her fingers, held them and stared into her lovely eyes.

Daniel cleared his throat.

"I'm on my way then." He leaned over, murmured quietly. "I'm sending you some documents, Shel. Please read them when you're alone." He cast a sideways glance at Tim, chewed his bottom lip. "I'd intended to talk to you about it earlier, but—"

"What is it?" she asked curiously.

"Just…some business stuff." He leaned down, brushed his lips against her cheek. "Hang on, Shelby. We'll find her."

"Yes," she agreed. But the conviction in her voice wasn't as strong as it had been.

Tim watched the other man leave, then turned his eyes on Shelby. She slumped in her chair, her gaze on the rose garden beyond. Her forehead pleated in a frown of concentration.

"Grant loved those two like brothers. They used to argue all the time, but it was good-natured squabbling. Not like what I heard tonight."

"Perhaps they're jealous of each other," he suggested, wondering why such a thing should happen now, after so many years. Was it because Shelby's return to Finders threatened each of them? "You've handed over the reins of the company to one, given the other permission to conduct his own investigation into Aimee's abduction," he murmured, studying her response.

Shelby shook her head.

"Russ doesn't have any illusions about his importance to the company. He knows he's the top recovery agent we have, probably the best there is. Daniel's speciality was always information gathering. He's a master at disguises, at slipping in and out without anyone knowing he was there. Even though he's management now, he still goes into the field occasionally if he thinks our information is suspect."

Tim waited, knowing she was thinking this through aloud.

"I think this feud goes beyond jealousy, but I can't figure out what triggered it." She relayed Russ's remarks about Daniel being responsible for Grant's death. "Do you think he seriously suspects that?"

"I think it's more important to know what you think."

She tapped one finger against her bottom lip, her gaze on something he couldn't see.

"Russ is hard to read. He's of Russian descent and though he's lived in North America for a long time, he's very close to his family and retains a lot of ties to the old country."

"You're thinking that might turn him against Daniel? But why? Daniel knew that, surely? And he hasn't changed, has he?"

"No, but I haven't followed things at Finders as closely as I could have. I didn't want to face going back and so I let Daniel take over for me. Russ is a bit of a wild card. Maybe Daniel had to rein him in. Or he may be nursing a grudge because Daniel ordered him on some mission he thought beneath him. Russ has a big ego. Maybe he's chafing at having Daniel as a superior—a job he now wants to handle." She raked a hand through her hair, disturbing the glossy strands of gold. "Maybe I was wrong to set one against the other."

"You haven't done that." He hated seeing her like this, second-guessing a decision she'd made months ago. "You're their boss, Shelby. You chose Daniel as leader. If Russ wants to be part of the team, he's obliged to work under the conditions you set. If he doesn't like it, he can always ask for a change. Same with Daniel. Don't let their temper tantrums change your mind. You made your decisions because you had a good reason. Stick to that, or change it if you feel it's necessary, but don't be swayed by what someone else wants."

"You're right, of course. It's just that I've been away from it, I suppose. Daniel's kept me posted on major developments, cases they were handling. But my primary focus has been on Aimee and the rose garden." She motioned to the bushes heavy with blooms not yet open. "Aimee and I don't need all this space. The house is too big, too empty. It has historical significance to the community so I thought if I donated it, the rose garden would be a memorial to Grant."

"You can still do that."

"Yes." She looked at him, her gaze troubled. "But I need to have Aimee safe before I move on." Her fingers gripped his. "Inside me a voice is screaming to know why we haven't had a ransom call, a threat, a demand—something. The only thing I can come up with is that somebody took her because—"

He watched her struggle and suddenly understood what she meant.

"No, Shelby. Aimee is alive. You have to keep clinging to your beliefs. You have to hang on to God's promise to help us when we need Him." He felt like a hypocrite saying that but this wasn't about him. It was about Shelby and her missing daughter, a little girl he couldn't believe God would take from her loving mother.

But then he hadn't believed—

"You're a fine one to talk about hope."

Shelby's voice broke through the nightmare that waited to creep into his brain. He stuffed it back, concentrated on the conversation.

"What do you mean?"

"Well, you haven't mailed that manuscript yet, have you? Aimee told me before—" She gulped, dashed a hand against her eyes, then continued in a slightly wobbly voice. "Aimee said you told her you have to do some more revisions. How many revisions will you do before you send the thing out to find out if it can be published, Tim?"

"It's not the same for me. I am a history specialist. Or I was. I can't afford to make a mistake. If some date doesn't jibe with my story, my name will be mud."

She tilted one eyebrow at him. "They're children's stories, my friend. Delightful tales set in your favorite milieu, which you know like the back of your hand—and you're trying to tell me you might make a mistake with a date?" She was openly scoffing. "You were a museum curator in London. I can hardly imagine you'd get the job if they worried about you making those kinds of *mistakes.*"

"The stories aren't ready yet." He refused to look at her, knew he'd see that stubborn chin jut out at his lie.

"You know those books could help children learn about the past in a fun, nonthreatening way, yet you refuse to send them to a publisher. It doesn't make any sense, Tim. I think you're stalling. The question is why."

He'd come here to help her through a rough time, to offer his shoulder, if she'd take it. But in true Shelby style, she'd turned the tables and put the focus on him.

"I'll get around to finishing my stories, Shelby," he hedged, "but we were talking about your problem and the reason your two friends are at each other's throats."

Esmeralda Peabody cleared her throat. Everyone who knew Esmeralda knew she was as soft as a marshmallow inside but she liked to project a gruff, tough facade. Except when it came to Shelby, and especially Aimee. Esmeralda never spoke more gently than when she was addressing the little girl. Now that she was missing, the older woman's face seemed like a mask of fury.

"The mail came," she mumbled, handing Shelby a sheaf of papers. "Police checked it all. Nosy parkers. Probably nothing but junk anyway." But she waited, hands hanging by her sides while Shelby sorted through it.

Shelby set the flyers to one side, and checked the envelopes.

"Daniel sent something," she murmured as she slid out a file from the long white envelope. It landed in her lap.

Tim glanced up, surprised when she allowed the file to slide to the ground. Her fingers clenched around a sheet of paper.

"Oh, no," she whimpered.

Tim jumped up, moved beside her. Shelby clutched a picture of Aimee holding a copy of that day's newspaper, a huge grin stretched across her gamine face.

He turned his head and yelled for the detective. Natalie came at a run. Her skin blanched to ashen as she stared at the picture. It seemed an unusual reaction to Tim, who nudged her.

"Aren't you going to do something?"

"Yes, of course." Natalie snapped out of her stupor, ordered Shelby to freeze, then carefully lifted the sheet out of her hands with a tissue. "Where did this come from?"

Esmeralda showed her. Tim's attention remained totally on Shelby.

"Are you all right?"

After a moment she nodded. "How could he do it? I thought he loved her. Aimee's always called him Uncle Dan."

Tim said nothing, merely bent, picked up the folder she'd dropped.

"What is that?" she demanded, her shoulders straightening, eyes blazing with temper. "A ransom demand? To think he was here, pretending to be so concerned." She opened the manila file, scanned it. "I don't understand this," she muttered after several moments.

"What's wrong?"

"Why would he do this?" Shelby's attention was locked on the documents she perused. "This can't be," she whispered.

Natalie was standing off to one corner, issuing orders into her cell phone like a drill sergeant.

Tim grabbed the opportunity, leaned close and asked, "What is it, Shelby? Tell me quickly before Natalie takes it away. I'll help if I can."

She looked up, blinked, focused.

"It's about Russ," she whispered. "These documents show he's been detained by customs officials several times. Twice they've warned him about items he's brought over the border. Apparently he's been identified as a possible security threat by several governments."

"Would this be natural, something to do with his job?"

"Finders, Inc. does not engage in illegal activities." She glanced at the file once more, shook her head. "I can't tell you more. Don't have enough information. But I can't understand why Daniel included it with the picture."

"A mistake," he suggested.

"Daniel doesn't make those kinds of mistakes, Tim. Not ever in as long as I've known him. He holds everything close to his chest until he's ready to reveal it." Her words were automatic, her mind obviously on the picture Natalie still held.

"He said he was sending me something but I never imagined, never even dreamed…" She drooped in her chair, her eyelids closed as she groaned. "Oh, Daniel, how could you?"

Esmeralda's attention was so centered on the picture of Aimee that she barely responded when Tim poked her arm, motioned to Shelby and mouthed the word *coffee*. But being the devoted employee she was, she took one look and acted.

"That's enough with you now, Shelby Kincaid. The good Lord didn't bring us this far to dump us and you'd best not be doubting His ways or the friends He sent you. Into the library with you," she ordered. "This fellow can light the fire. The evening's chilly. I'll bring some coffee." She disappeared before Shelby could counter.

Since Natalie was still knee-deep in her phone call, Tim grasped Shelby's arm and led her toward the library, fully aware that her fingers still clutched the file, evidence that Natalie would insist on seeing.

"Sit down. Breathe deeply. Let's try to think this through."

She seemed in a daze, confused yet angry. "None of it makes sense to me. First Russ hints that Daniel is hiding something, then Daniel sends over this file. He had to know I'd see the picture, that I'd be upset. So why—I thought he cared about us, but to do this…." The more she spoke, the more angry she became. "I want him arrested right now. I want him to tell me where he has my daughter and why. I want answers. Natalie!"

The police detective hurried into the room, no doubt at Shelby's raised voice. Tim was prepared for her entrance. What shocked him was the appearance of the man behind her.

"What's wrong?" Daniel demanded, scanning the room in a quick glance.

"You are wrong." Shelby's sense of betrayal leached through her voice. "If you think you can get away with this, you're dead wrong. I want my daughter back, Daniel, and I want her now."

"I know that." He frowned, stared at her. "I'm trying to help, believe me."

"Trying?" Shelby jumped up, ripped the paper from Natalie and shoved it under his nose. "Is that why you sent this to me? Because you're trying? Detective, I want this man arrested for kidnapping."

Tim had never seen Natalie move so quickly. She had Daniel in handcuffs before he could do more than sputter.

"Shelby, there might be some other explanation for that picture," Tim offered, unable to believe a man who ran a company like Finders would be so foolish as to let himself be caught that easily.

"You think I sent that picture?" Daniel looked from Natalie to Shelby to Tim. "I didn't. I've never seen it before. So will someone please tell me what is going on here?"

"Like you don't know." Shelby stared at the floor where the picture of Aimee had fallen, tears rolling down her cheeks.

"Believe me, I don't know."

Tim took pity on him. "You sent a file to Shelby today, didn't you?"

"Yes." Daniel frowned. "What's wrong with that? I wanted to keep her abreast of what I'm doing, especially now."

"That picture was in the file." Tim watched the other man's thin face whiten.

"Why keep Mrs. Kincaid abreast now—especially?" Natalie's eyes had narrowed to mere slits. She kept her focus on Daniel.

"We've had some items…disappear from our stock."

"You lost things?" The slits widened. "I thought you had all this high-tech security to prevent that kind of thing from happening."

"We do," he muttered, his mouth tight. "Somehow, someone has either avoided it or found a way to break through. At the moment, I'm not sure which is true."

"So we *are* looking at one of your employees," she stated triumphantly. One finger pointed to Shelby. "I knew it. If you hadn't gotten in the way, Mrs. Kincaid, I could have arrested this man much earlier and perhaps already have found your daughter."

"Wait a minute! That's not true. Why would I take Aimee? I have no desire to harm her and I'd be stupid to think I could get away with it. Stupider still to throw suspicion on myself."

"That's what you want us to think, perhaps." Natalie studied him.

"Then what's my motive?" Daniel demanded, voice grim with barely suppressed anger.

"Money."

Tim didn't understand the odd look Daniel sent Shelby, nor her slight nod.

"Undo his handcuffs." She shook her head at the detective. "Daniel didn't take Aimee. I know that. I guess I just lost it for a minute, grabbed for an easy answer. It wasn't him, Natalie. Let him go."

"He's the best suspect we have." Natalie held her position.

"Then you need to find another reason for him to have kidnapped my child. Daniel did not do it, certainly not for money."

"You know this because…" Natalie tilted one arched brow in a question.

"Because Daniel has more money than I'll ever have. He doesn't need to kidnap Aimee for money."

"Wait a minute!" Natalie squinted. "Howard McCullough." She snapped her fingers.

"Was my father."

"Oh, boy." She lifted her keys and undid the cuffs. "Sorry about that. I had no idea. You were an only child, weren't you?"

He nodded. "And yes, I inherited his wealth. But if you don't mind we'll keep that to ourselves. I like my privacy." He waited until she'd nodded before he turned to Shelby. "May I see the file?"

"It's here." Tim handed it over, watched Daniel open it, scour the pages.

"Everything I sent is here. Perhaps the envelope was tampered with. Where is it?"

Natalie hurried away to fetch it, her attitude toward him almost subservient.

Shelby touched her friend's arm in apology. "I'm truly sorry, Daniel. I know better than to suspect my friends but—"

"But with Russ intimating that I'm going behind your back and the added tension of this thing with Aimee and then that paper, you needed a scapegoat. I know that, Shel. Forget it." He waited a minute, but when Natalie didn't return he sat down across from Shelby and Tim. "Did you sign for the file?"

"I never signed for anything. Esmeralda brought the envelope in with the mail."

"Maybe she signed."

Shelby shook her head. "The police are checking everything. If a signature was required, they'd have given it."

"A signature was required. I heard my secretary give my specific orders to the courier—the package was not to be turned over unless you signed for it."

"Here's the envelope." Natalie held it out.

Daniel took the plastic-wrapped envelope, immediately handed it back. "That's not it."

"Yes, it is. I should know, I opened it." Shelby's eyes widened. "You said courier," she whispered.

"Yes, I did." Daniel turned to Natalie. "Please ask your men which one of them signed for a courier-delivered envelope." He named the courier, then pulled out his cell phone and conferred with his secretary. Moments later he snapped the phone closed, met Shelby's stare. "She has confirmation that the envelope was delivered to and signed by Shelby Kincaid."

"But I didn't sign anything! This is crazy." A noise made her turn. Esmeralda entered the room laden with a big tray and a pot she always used for her luscious hot chocolate, Aimee's favorite.

Tim rose, lifted the tray from her and placed it on a side table. A minute later Esmeralda began to pour out the sweet confection, dropping a few marshmallows in each cup. He handed them round, then sat down with his own.

"Tim, you were there when Esmeralda brought in the mail."

The question roused him from his thoughts about the little girl who was missing. He nodded. "Yes, I was."

"Do you remember—it was just lying there, buried under all the rest."

His answer was smothered by Esmeralda's.

"'Deed it was. I picked the whole mess off the hall table where one of those goons had tossed it like it didn't matter who read it. Mostly flyers, not much of interest. 'Cept for that envelope."

"This envelope?" Daniel held it up. "You're sure?"

Esmeralda nodded.

Natalie walked back in. "None of my men signed for anything. No envelope, no package. Nothing."

"Then how did this file get here?" Shelby asked,

No one had the answer. Tim glanced from face to face as they digested the only possible conclusion. Someone had been in the house long enough to pose as Shelby, sign for the package and tamper with it.

That someone had to be the one who had Aimee and it had to be someone who knew the house and the people in it very well. They were all thinking the same thing—who?

FIVE

A rush of relief swamped Shelby when Esmeralda announced a phone call for Natalie. Shortly after, the detective left. Something at the office, she said.

Esmeralda called them to eat in the kitchen, insisted Daniel and Tim stay to share the simmering stew she'd placed in bread bowls and accompanied with a fresh green salad. Shelby was fairly certain Tim and Daniel were as confused as she by the latest turn of events, but there wasn't much any of them could do as long as Natalie insisted on handling everything. Before Daniel left she'd tell him she intended to initiate another search on Finders, Inc. employees the following morning. It was unlikely she'd find anything and she knew it but she had to do something to keep from thinking about Aimee.

When they carried their coffee into the library, Shelby picked up the file Daniel had sent. She was glad Tim joined them. Maybe he could help.

"I'm not sure what you want me to do with this information about Russ, Daniel." She sat down in the big armchair, smiled as Tim sat across from her. It was embarrassing to realize how much she'd come to depend on seeing him around here. For now she'd pretend it had to do with Aimee.

She and Daniel needed another viewpoint. That's where Tim came in.

"I don't know that you can do anything with it, Shel," Daniel murmured. "I just wanted you to be aware of the irregularities that have been going on at the company."

She frowned at him. "You never *just* do anything, Daniel."

"Maybe not."

She studied him, her feeling there was a lot the other man wasn't saying increasing exponentially. What she couldn't discern was whether it had to do with Tim's presence in the room, or the uncertainty she glimpsed on Daniel's face.

"Are you connecting the disappearances in our warehouse with Russ?" she asked quietly, needing to get it said.

He looked shocked. "No. Nothing like that." His amber eyes grew dark. "Do you think that?"

"I'm not sure I'm the right person to ask tonight. My emotions are all over the place. For a few minutes I actually believed you might have taken Aimee."

"I didn't."

"I know." She paused, regrouped. "Let's go back to the items that are missing. What are they?"

"A diamond brooch, a gold coin, a lamp and a book. Here are some photos we took when the first three came into our possession." He snapped open his briefcase, pulled out a manila file and laid four photos on the table.

She caught Tim staring at the one of the brooch. A fleeting look passed across his face, as if he recognized it or had seen it before. But then it was gone. He glanced at the coin, the lamp. Nothing there. But that brooch…

"Do these four have anything in common?" Shelby asked.

"Not so far as I can find." Daniel sat silent, thinking.

"What happens when the items come to Finders, Inc.?"

The question burst into the silence abruptly. Tim turned a dark red, as if he hadn't meant to say it out loud.

Shelby didn't mind. He wanted to understand, to help. To take some kind of action. Her own need to do something, to free herself from this nightmare, felt exactly the same. She nodded at Daniel, letting him answer.

"First the article must be authenticated. If it has historical significance to the client, we try to track the item's passage through the years. Our appraisers take their turn judging whether the item is an artifact or valuable. Then we look for a record of provenance so we know the item can come into our possession legally. We have a legal department to make sure we incur no criminal liability for being in possession of stolen goods and if we find something irregular, we return the item to the rightful owner." Daniel glanced at him. "Of course the claim has to be legitimate, as well, but that work is usually done before we even agree to begin the search."

"I see."

"Oh, he's not finished, Tim. That's just the first stage." Shelby grinned. "Go on, Daniel."

"Each case we handle has a specific identification number which we use to track expenses, locations—a number of things. If it's a physical object, once we acquire it, it is allotted a place in its own individual vault. No one without proper clearance and the secure access code to that particular vault space will be able to get inside. When all the specifications have been met and we're satisfied that we've done all we can to ensure that the item belongs to the client, we call them in and hand it over." Daniel rubbed his foot against the hardwood as if to erase an invisible mark. "The client signs a waiver and the item is released from our custody. We do not handle anything illegal and we do not give up our search until we have results that force us to cease."

"Oh." Tim rubbed one knuckle against the knee of his corduroy jeans. Shelby wondered if the scar tissue was bothering him. Though she thought she knew him well, she now realized that Tim had never really told her how he'd incurred his injuries. She knew he'd been burned, of course, but nothing more than that. Suddenly she wanted to know more about the quiet gentle man who lived next door.

"So you see why having something disappear is a cause for serious concern."

"Yes." Tim nodded. "It means that someone can get in there anytime and take whatever he wants. But you don't think that person is Russ."

"Russ doesn't have clearance on all the vaults. No one does." Daniel frowned. "Well, Shelby *could* because she has the highest security level but her codes are changed randomly on a daily basis. No one is good enough to figure that out. Besides, her codes were not used on the vaults containing the missing items."

"Whose were?"

She was surprised when Daniel didn't answer immediately. He was hesitating. Why?

A flicker of worry inched up her neck and wrapped itself tightly around the nerve. "Daniel?"

"They used Grant's codes," he muttered, then held up a hand at her sputter of protest. "I know it sounds impossible, but it's the truth. Somehow we never got round to erasing his codes. Since he died and no one expected them to be used, they've never been altered, either. Somebody knew that, or they found out. They used them to gain entry and take those items."

"Video surveillance?" Tim asked.

Shelby stared at him, surprised to hear the question.

"None." Daniel shook his head.

"What does that mean? Finders, Inc. doesn't have it? That's hard to believe in such a high-tech business."

"We have it." Daniel's mouth tightened. "There is no video of anyone opening those vaults."

"But…how can that be?" Confusion flooded Tim's face. "Remote control opening?"

Daniel shook his head. Shelby knew he hated this, that he felt he'd somehow let her down, failed to do the job she'd given him. But how could he know—how could anyone have guessed?

"Grant's codes were never public knowledge," she murmured. "So who would have had access to them?"

"Me." Daniel looked defeated, weary and most of all depressed. "I didn't take Aimee, but I might as well have. This is all my fault. I should have erased them long ago. I just never even considered—"

"This is not your fault." She refused to let him be ground down. There was no time to dwell on what-ifs. "Think, Daniel. How could someone have found those codes?"

"Wait a minute!" Tim clapped a hand to the side of his head. "I just remembered something. The night Aimee was taken Natalie said there was only one code entered for the house security—Shelby's."

"Yes. I would have punched it in before going to bed. I always do that."

"Yes, but don't you see?" His eyes came alive. "The kidnapper must have that code, too. He used it to disable the security system. That's how he got inside without setting anything off. When the police come, voila! There's nothing to find but your number. No clues."

Shelby felt the blood drain from her face.

"What you're saying is that someone inside our organization, someone with a lot of knowledge and the ability to learn whatever he or she wants is behind Aimee's disappearance." Shelby gulped. "I think I'm more terrified than I was before."

"I'm sorry, but…I can't think of anything else."

Tim's warm fingers clasping hers eased some of the betrayal she felt and she summoned a smile. "At least you're trying to help. Thank you."

"I'd make it go away if I could." His soft murmured reassurance wasn't meant for Daniel's ear.

Somewhat surprised, she tilted her head to look at him more closely, found herself captivated by the expression in his brown eyes.

"I'm sorry I can't do more," he whispered. "I'm sorry this is happening at all. If you want me to go, just say the word."

"I'd like you to stay," she whispered back. "It…helps."

"Then I'll stay." He squeezed her hand again, then returned to his seat.

Shelby looked to see if Daniel had noticed them and was stunned by his haggard stare. "What's wrong?"

"Russ," he hissed. "I've just realized that Russ would know about the codes—how to get them, at least. He's been at Finders as long as I have, he knows the ropes."

And he'd been stopped by customs officials—several times. Shelby felt the shadow of doubt come creeping in again. How she hated this—suspecting everyone, including Grant's closest friends.

"Why?" she asked, speaking past the lump in her throat. "Why would Russ do this?"

"Do what?" Russ lounged in the doorway of the library, one black boot resting on its toe, ever the bad boy. "I am glad I have interrupted. What is it I have done this time?"

"He was at the door when I passed." Esmeralda poked her head around the corner. "He needed to see you, Shel."

"We're discussing the missing items, Russ," Daniel explained stiffly. "Someone who knew the codes, or knew how to get them, and had access to the computers had to be in on the theft."

"And so naturally my name it bubbles to the top?" His sneer hurt Shelby, but not as much as the sad look he turned on her. "Is this what you are also thinking?"

In that moment her brain recalled that photograph of Aimee and Shelby felt strong again.

"My daughter is missing, Russ. I have to at least consider every single possibility out there."

"Yes, please. Let us consider *everything*." His face tightened. "The times those items were taken, tell me the dates." Russ's blue eyes directed their steely intent on Daniel. He listened as the other man repeated the dates, then smiled, an enigmatic uptilt of his lips that held no humor. "Such an investigator as this is the head of Finders, Inc.?" he sneered. His face grew hard. "In such a powerful position, one must always be certain one knows the truth. You would do well to check your facts, my friend. On two of these terrible occasions, I was not in this country, nor even on this continent. That is recorded in my logbook, if you care to check."

"I'm sorry, Russ," Shelby offered when it seemed that Daniel would say nothing. "I know you don't like this, but I have to work through every detail, answer every question. If that makes it difficult for you, I apologize. But my daughter comes first."

"Of course she does, little Aimee. And about her I have news." He turned, beckoned to someone behind him.

Shelby's jaw dropped as one of her operatives stepped into the room.

"Hello, Callie. It's good to see you again." Though relatively young, Callie Merton had studied Daniel's disguises and learned to develop a unique ability that transformed her face and demeanor into that of an ingenue from the wealthiest home, a grandmother on the wrong side of eighty, or a teenybopper high on drugs. At the moment she resembled a weary bag lady.

"Hi, Shelby. I'm really sorry to hear about your trouble. We all love Aimee."

"Thank you." She glanced at Russ who nodded at Callie.

"Show her," he ordered.

Callie bent down, picked up a paper bag and slid her hand inside. "I was tracking a target downtown. I followed him inside a pawnshop and found this." She lifted away the bag. "It's awfully like the doll Grant brought back from Japan for Aimee, isn't it?"

Shelby's breath snagged in her throat. She tried to remember the last time she'd seen the doll but couldn't. The similarities were strong but there was only one way to be sure if this doll was Aimee's.

"May I see it, please, Callie?" She took the doll. Grant had a thing about marking his property. No doubt it was a result of the work he'd done, but he always distinguished his belongings with a special symbol. If the doll was Aimee's, the symbol should be on it.

"What are you doing?"

She ignored their curious stares and the questions and began probing under the clothing of the tiny porcelain doll. She found what she sought at the back of the neck, just under the ties that held the doll's traditional clothes in place.

"It's Aimee's," she whispered, her forefinger sliding over the soft pink petals of a rose carefully inscribed to look like a tiny tattoo.

Russ's garbled expletive broke the silence. "Now at last we make some progress." He looked at Callie. "Return to the store in a different disguise. More than once if necessary. Ask questions. There may be a video camera with a picture of the one who sold this doll. We must learn more."

"I'll do my best. Hang on, Shelby. We'll find her." Callie disappeared.

"So now we may get an answer."

"Yes, we may." She felt like a traitor suspecting him. "Thank you, Russ."

"It is my pleasure to be of assistance. I have just one request."

"Go ahead." What now, she wondered, feeling the tension in the room accelerate. She glanced at Tim, felt heartened by his quiet presence and gentle smile of encouragement. "What is your request, Russ?"

"Since we are looking at those who have access to codes and security, I have a suggestion." He faced Daniel. "Perhaps you would be so good as to tell us what *business* it is that has taken you to Tokyo twice this month, and to Singapore three times before that. The very dates, I might mention, on which three of these items vanished."

Shelby couldn't suppress the gasp that rose from her chest and echoed around the room. She stared at Daniel as the questions rose and swirled around her brain.

Whom could she trust?

Admiration for Shelby grew as Tim wondered how long she could remain stoically calm before the stress took over. Face impassive, her gaze remained on Daniel as he explained that his trips had been made in regard to a new client, a well-known businessman who wanted to keep his anonymity but had been scouting the company in hopes of employing Finders, Inc. to discover the whereabouts of a family heirloom.

"If you'll come in tomorrow, Shelby, I'll show you all the particulars. I'm sorry, Tim, but I'm not at liberty to release his name. I made a promise."

"There is no reason I would need to know." But Russ wanted to. Tim could see it written all over his face before the other man saw him and hid his expression.

"Thank you. So since we've cleared that up, I have to leave. I've got work to do." Daniel rose, studied Shelby for a moment, then said good-night.

Russ waited several moments, then he, too, rose. "I am sorry if I upset you. It would seem important to examine all questionable areas. I did not want to put Daniel in the bad light but I am concerned for your safety."

"My safety?" She stared at him in disbelief. "Why?"

"Daniel has too many secrets. This man he speaks of, when did he so suddenly appear? Why now? And why does Daniel need also to visit Sweden and Australia if the client is Japanese? Something is not right, Shelby. I do not want to accuse, but I must find out. Daniel's quiet ways are not mine, I admit this."

"What are you saying—or not saying?"

"Me? I do not say that which I cannot prove." Russ's voice remained soft but there was a hint of something sinister buried in his words. "The system you and Grant employed is a good one. We all have checks and balances on us at Finders, Inc. But I have a wondering—who checks Daniel?" He waited a moment, raised a hand in farewell, then disappeared.

Shelby rose. "I need to get outside, to breathe some fresh air. Will you come with me?"

"Of course." Tim lifted her jacket from where it was draped across the sofa back and held it for her to slide her arms in. Together they walked through the house, across the patio and onto the path that led them to the rose arbor.

"I noticed Russ always speaks with an accent."

"Yes?"

"But you said he'd been in North America for years. Wouldn't he have picked up some idioms, become more conversant? His speech is so stilted."

"On purpose, I think." Shelby offered a faint smile. "Our

Russ likes to appear mysterious. The clients eat it up and so do the women. He's very popular among the ladies, you know."

"So you think it's affected?"

"No. I think he uses what he has in the same way that Daniel uses a disguise to find out information he needs. They are very different, but they are both very capable men."

"I see." He didn't want to bother her, so Tim kept walking. "It's a beautiful evening," he murmured, thankful that the land at the back of her grandmother's house had remained undeveloped. Whoever tried to approach from there would traverse brambles, deadfall and an underbrush so thick that anyone pushing through would leave marks. And that was assuming they managed to first overcome the barbed-wire fence.

"Soon the roses will bloom." Her voice was soft, gentle as she paused beside a bud-covered bush. "This was Grant's happiest time of the year—the time of promise, he called it. He never knew exactly what his hybrids would produce but he said the secrets of the rose were worth waiting for. He was right."

"You still love him," he murmured, then wished he'd kept silent.

"I think I'll always love Grant. But I'm getting better at dwelling in the present. Aimee helped me through the hardest parts simply because she needed me to be there, body, soul, mind and spirit. She always asks so many questions." Shelby smiled as she reached out to brush a finger over the new green leaves of a rosebush.

Tim noted the little plaque stuck into the ground beneath—Deep Secret. A man who went on covert missions but also grew roses. He had a hunch Grant Kincaid had been just as unusual as his two friends.

"I had to sort out my own feelings pretty quickly to be able to give Aimee the answers she needed."

"I remember those Aimee questions!" He made a face that soon had Shelby giggling. "Why, why, why. One answer always led to another question with her. She just couldn't be satisfied."

"You're so good with her you must have had a lot of practice." She turned her head, a question in her eyes. "I've realized just how little I know about you, Tim. Do you have a family somewhere, a child?"

"No." It was rude not to elaborate but he simply couldn't make himself say more. Not yet. Not now. Besides, he didn't want to depress her. "Aimee would be offended if she heard you call her a child."

"I know. Sometimes I think she's older than I am." Shelby sank onto a wrought iron bench, tilted her head back to study the stars. "I have so many questions. The answers are all up there. It's too bad I couldn't reach up and pluck them down. Then I'd know what to do next. I feel like I'm being torn in seven different directions at the same time."

He sat down beside her, not knowing how to help. "If there's anything I can do…"

"Actually," she muttered, looking directly into his eyes, "there is. I don't know who to trust anymore, Tim. Everybody around me seems suspect. I know it's not true, but I'm afraid I'm missing things." She paused. "Would you come with me into the office tomorrow?"

"Me? Go into Finders, Inc.?" Another glimpse into her world. He wanted to go. But why would she ask him? "What for?"

"To be my eyes and ears. I want to go over the personnel files again."

"I wouldn't be any help with that. I don't know anything about researching people's backgrounds."

"Maybe not, but you would be able to look at the files of the missing items, wouldn't you?"

"I could do that." He wanted to help her through this. "What are you hoping to find, Shelby?"

"A connection, however faint, to Aimee's kidnapping. A clue to who is betraying me. Something."

She looked so forlorn in that moment that he would gladly have agreed to do anything she asked if it would have made her smile. But one thing held him back.

"You wouldn't have to introduce me around or anything, would you?"

She shook her head. "Not if you don't want me to."

"I don't." He gulped, forced himself to explain. "I know it's vain and silly, but people always stare at my face. Sometimes they even ask questions. I don't want to answer any questions about the marks on my body."

She reached out, gathered his damaged hand into her smaller one. "You don't have to. But maybe talking would help."

Talking about that day had never helped. Neither had three years of seclusion and condemnation let him forget. Nothing had. But she didn't know that.

"There is a private entrance Grant had installed when we built the place. He wanted to be able to get in without the whole staff knowing he was in the building, and to leave just as easily. Before he…died, he used that entrance constantly."

That sounded like the actions of a man who suspected someone in his organization wasn't on the up-and-up. Tim sat up straight, determined to pay more attention to what she said.

"When he was on a case, his mind was always working. Sometimes he'd get up in the middle of the night and go to the office, just to conduct a search or pull up a file. That's what happened the night he died. He'd been fussing for days about something but all he would tell me was that he'd explain when he had it figured out."

"And he never got a chance to explain?"

"No." She shook her head. "He was home for dinner. We both put Aimee to bed. I was tired and I thought we'd have a quiet night but Grant said he had to go out, then he wanted to play in his rose garden for a while. I didn't mind. In fact, I fell asleep in the den. About ten o'clock he came rushing into the den, grabbed his briefcase and said he had to check something at the office. He kissed me, told me not to wait up. That's the last time I saw him."

"I'm sorry."

"I know." She sighed. "He was in the warehouse when it happened. There was never a satisfactory answer to why he died. We have state-of-the-art fire suppression and sprinkler systems that had been tested and approved not one week before. For some reason, neither cut in until it was too late. All the police could tell me was that he must have been trying to find a way out through the smoke, hit his head and fell. He never got up."

They sat together in the night as the stars twinkled above. Not a whisper of wind moved the trembling aspens at the end of the garden. Any sound that reached them was muted, barely discernible.

"Losing Aimee—it brings it all back. It can't happen again, Tim. You probably won't understand this but Aimee is the only piece of my family that I have left and losing her would be as if my life had never happened. I can't accept that. We have a history together, we love each other and we need each other for the future."

"I understand perfectly." The squeal of burning rubber, the burst of shattering glass and the soft almost silent 'Oh!' he remembered every night grabbed his insides and twisted them into a knot. He shoved his hands into his jacket pockets, felt the tiny square of a book, Aimee's book.

"I almost forgot." He pulled out the tiny hardcover story about a giraffe who had no neck. "I was going to give this to you. It was at my house."

Shelby stared at his hand, at the cardboard square resting on his palm. She didn't speak for a very long time, but when her eyes finally dragged to his face, he saw unbelievable pain in them—and something else. Distrust.

"What's wrong? Why are you looking at me like that?"

"You, too," she whispered. "I thought…I was positive I could trust you."

"You can." He glanced from the book to her face. Something was very wrong. "Why are you staring at me?"

"That book was in her room the night she was taken," Shelby whispered, rising from the bench and stepping backward toward the house. "She couldn't have left it at your place unless she was there after someone kidnapped her. After you kidnapped her."

"Shelby, I—"

"It was you!" Tears poured down her face. "Give me back my daughter!"

SIX

Twenty four hours in a day seemed so long now. Empty stretches of time with no sweet giggle to brighten the mornings, no endless round of questions to keep dark memories away.

Now she didn't even have Tim to count on.

Shelby wandered aimlessly through the house. Everything looked exactly the same, and yet it wasn't. It would never be the same again. She'd been certain he was on her side, honest, forthright. And yet she couldn't shake the feeling that once more she'd been duped, cheated. Three of them: Daniel, Russ, and now Tim, each keeping some secret that filled her with doubts.

She glanced at the library door again, wondered for the hundredth time when they'd be finished.

It was odd that Tim hadn't protested when she'd insisted on calling Natalie last night. He'd simply nodded and waited quietly outside. Even now the police were going through his home, tearing apart everything, hoping to find one tiny clue to Aimee's whereabouts.

Sheer tiredness forced her to sit down. Shelby chose the living room because the morning sun poured in its many windows and because she could look out onto Grant's precious rose garden and wait for some sense of peace to fill her heart. It was a long time coming.

"You were always so good at seeing through people, Grant," she whispered. "I wish you were here now to tell me what to do about Tim." She'd trusted the man with the most precious gift she'd ever been given. Had she been wrong? Aimee had Grant's intuitive sense about people. Surely she would have picked up on anything unusual.

Then Shelby remembered.

"Mr. Tim has a secret," Aimee had said one night. "A big sad secret that makes him hurt right here." She'd laid a hand over her heart. "I try to help him. He likes to tell stories so I let him tell me stories."

Shelby had always thought the sadness or perhaps pain disguised as sadness she'd glimpsed in Tim's eyes came from his burns. But maybe there was something else, something she'd missed. Something horrible. She didn't want to think it of him, but that book…She grabbed the phone, dialed Finders, Inc.

"Daniel? I want you to run a full-scale search. On my neighbor."

"Tim Austen?" he asked after several moments' pause.

"Yes."

"I'll order it right away." No questions. Good.

"Can you keep it top secret? I don't want it to get around that I'm checking him out."

"Certainly."

She could hear the curiosity in his voice, but Daniel didn't ask any questions. Dear Daniel. "I'm bringing him with me today, but I want that on the q.t., too."

"Here—to Finders, Inc.? Why?"

"He ran museums, Daniel. He's a history brain. I'm going to get him to look over the files of those missing items, see if anything occurs to him." She pinched her lips together, then admitted the truth. "Anyway, I want him where I can see him. It can't hurt, can it?"

"I'll get a pass made up. Which door?"

"Grant's. Anything new on your end?"

"I've discovered that the video from the nights the items were taken has been spliced. There are pieces missing."

"Nobody noticed this before?"

"No. It was a very professional job."

"What about the guards?"

"Three different ones. One case of food poisoning occasioning many restroom trips, a false alarm that took everyone's attention for about forty minutes, and a faulty camera."

"So it's definitely someone on the inside."

"Looks like it. I'm running down possibles now."

She hated that, hated the thought that someone she trusted could have stolen from them. But then deceit seemed to hover all around her.

"Shelby?"

"I'm here, just thinking. I'll be in later, when the police are finished with Tim." As she hung up her fingers brushed the journal lying on the top of the sofa table. She touched the leather cover. Esmeralda's work, no doubt. She had a habit of using things to express what she would never say out loud. Apparently Esmeralda thought she needed to read Grant's journal.

Shelby picked it up, opened it and experienced a rush of mixed feelings as the precise black lettering took shape in her misty eyes.

Deep Secret: signifies that hidden place inside of us that we don't want others to see. Black-red buds: sin disguised as something else. The roots of evil must be exposed to the light in order for true healing to occur.

For Grant, even life lessons had been connected to roses. Shelby folded the book closed, thought back to those last few hours of his life. After dinner, before he'd taken off, he'd been sitting here with her and Aimee, discussing their next vacation.

"I can't go anywhere until I get this case sorted out. Something's not quite right."

She'd been too self-involved to ask more. If only she knew what had sent him back to the warehouse.

The door opened, she heard a murmur of voices and rose, moving quickly into the hall. Tim stood there, his face impassive, his eyes sad as they rested on her.

"There's nothing in his house to suggest he took Aimee," Natalie told her. "And his story checks out. The book we found in Aimee's room was water-stained. He claims he bought her this one to replace it and that she forgot it at his house."

Shelby jerked her head up to stare at him. "Why didn't you tell me?" she whispered.

"I tried, Shelby. But then the book didn't seem important in light of everything that's happened. Anyway, I kept forgetting to bring it over." He stepped forward, stopped. "I swear I didn't take her, Shelby. I had nothing to do with Aimee's disappearance."

She wanted, needed to trust him.

"Please believe me. I would never have taken that little girl from you. I know how hard it is to lose someone you love."

The words struck a chord in her heart, maybe because of the anguish she could see etched in his eyes. Her grandmother's words echoed inside her head.

"Sometimes, Shelby, you just have to take people on faith."

"But what if they hurt you?"

"That's the risk you take for living. Most of the time people are as honest with you as you are with them."

"Can you trust me? Can you believe me? Because if not, it's better if I don't come back over here again." He shoved his hands in his pants pockets. "There's no way I want to add to your worries. You have enough with Aimee. So you decide, Shelby. I'll do whatever you want."

She took a deep breath. "I believe you."

"I've got to get back to the office," Natalie murmured. "My report is due. I'll see you later."

She left quickly, as if there was something she had to get done.

"She's certainly in a rush." Shelby glanced down as Tim's fingers circled her wrist, then she met his gaze.

"Thank you for trusting me. I won't let you down. I haven't lied to you and I'm not going to start."

"I hope that's true." She studied him. "I want to ask a favor."

"Anything."

"Will you come to Finders with me now?"

"You still want me to go?" He looked surprised.

Shelby nodded. "I want to follow every single lead we have. I don't know if there's any connection with Aimee, but I intend to find out."

"Good. I'm ready whenever you are. There's just one thing."

"Oh." She paused in her walk to the garage door to glance at him curiously. "What is it?"

"Do you mind if I hide in the backseat?"

She frowned at the strange request, then noticed one hand rubbing at the scar tissue next to his left eye. Realization hit her at the same time as a wave of sympathy. He didn't want the reporters outside to photograph his burns. He wanted to help her, but he also wanted to keep his anonymity.

Were these the actions of a man who would steal her daughter?

"I don't mind at all," she murmured, and led the way.

The crowd of newshounds parked outside her home had not diminished, but given her dark glasses and the speed with which she left the driveway, Shelby didn't think any of them had the chance to take a very good picture. Fortunately the gates of Finders, Inc., were controlled by security and Daniel had added a guard. Once they were inside the compound, she pulled into the underground area and into the spot Grant had used to access the building privately.

"You can come out," she told Tim, holding open the rear door for him to escape.

He pushed away the dark blue blanket and emerged rather tousled but with a grin. "I'll add that to my list of new experiences," he chuckled, brushed down his clothes. "Not the most comfortable way to ride, but rather interesting. What's next?"

"We go inside. I hope Daniel has—" She caught sight of the security guard standing by the door and grinned. "I should have known Daniel would be as efficient as always. I hope you won't mind letting him scan your hand?"

"Whatever it takes." Tim didn't seem bothered when the man held out a small machine that scanned his palm and fingers. "It's a good thing it's not the other side," he mumbled.

Because of the burns. She was going to have to ask him about that. Soon.

Once he had the approval he sought, the guard handed Tim a security pass, nodded at Shelby, then hurried away. She pulled out her own pass and ran it through the mechanism beside the elevator door. The elevator doors opened soundlessly.

"You have to run your card through, also," she explained. "Or else when you get in the elevator, the system will detect you and sound the alarm."

"Pretty high-tech." But he did as she asked.

A few seconds later the doors opened on the fourth floor and Shelby motioned him to follow.

"Where is this?" he asked, glancing around curiously at all the closed doors. "It reminds me of some movie, but I can't think of the name."

"Don't worry, no one will jump out and attack you," she told him. "Each of these rooms is an appraisal room. It has to be a secure area to handle the work we do." She kept walking to the end of the hall until she reached a glass door where a woman sat behind a clear glass desk, framed by a clear glass wall. Behind that were rows of file cabinets filled with what he assumed was some kind of documentation. "Hello, Anika."

"Shelby!" The woman rose, reached out and hugged her as if she'd truly missed her. "How are you? No one told me you'd be in today."

"It was a last-minute decision. I'm fine, thanks. I need to see the appraisal files on several items." She turned. "This is Tim Austen."

"Hi, Tim." Anika rose. "Come on in," she invited, opening the door to the room behind her. "Do you have file numbers?"

Shelby held out her list, waited while Anika removed the files from four different areas. "Here we are."

"Thank you. I'd like to sign them out, please."

"Certainly." Anika led them back to her desk, typed something in on her computer, passed each file over a scanner, then pointed to the electronic pad sitting on one corner. "If you'll sign, please."

Shelby scrawled her name across the pad, waited for the green light that signaled it had been accepted, then took the files. "I'm not sure when I'll get them back to you. Thanks, Anika."

"You're welcome. Nice to meet you, Tim."

As they walked back down the hall, Shelby noticed Tim's curious study of the unusual walls. She smiled but said nothing. Some things explained themselves...eventually.

"We'll go to my office now," she told him, sliding her pass through the security box. He followed suit without saying a word. Only as they stepped out of the elevator in front of her office and beside the one Grant had used did Tim finally speak.

"This is quite a place. Rather like a maze."

She left him staring through the glass wall that gave a view of each floor beneath it.

"Daniel's waiting to speak to you," Joanie told her.

"Send him in, please." She cast a glance at Tim, who seemed entranced by something below.

"I'll look after him, don't worry, Shelby."

"Thanks." She tossed her purse on a side table, sank into her chair and logged on to her computer. She expected to find a file on Tim in her mail but there was nothing. A knock on the door signaled Daniel.

"Come on in."

He slipped inside, closed the door behind him, then held out a manila folder. "This is what you asked for. He checks out."

She scanned the information and stored it for future reference. Timothy James Austen, 34, last know address Boston, Massachusetts. He trained at some of the best Ivy League schools, traveled overseas for practical work at Egyptian, Turkish, and French museums. She read it all, not even pausing until she hit on the words at the bottom.

Widower.

He'd been married? Never once in all these months had he mentioned his wife. But then why would he? He'd probably been too busy mopping up her tears about Grant.

"So that's what he meant," she murmured.

"Pardon?"

"Nothing." But Shelby remembered what he'd said and her heart ached for him. *I know how hard it is to lose someone you love.* "I gather you did the usual checks. Nothing's off."

"Not a thing. Doesn't owe anyone, has two credit cards with no balance. Hasn't left the country in three years. Hospital bills and treatment are all covered by his insurance from his last known employer. He's on medical leave until further notice. He could go back whenever he wants."

"But he hasn't." She mulled that over. "Because of the burns? Or because he doesn't want to?"

"I guess you'd have to ask him." Daniel reviewed the rest of what he'd found. "You asked me to keep it quiet, so I didn't even put it on the computer. I'm feeling a little uneasy about all our security after those thefts. I have three separate sources running checks. Wherever there's a hole, they'll find it."

"I hope it's soon." Shelby thanked him for his work. As soon as he left she called in Tim. "So let's take a look at these files on the missing items. Since we don't have the actual pieces for you to examine, I've ordered the lab to send us some prints of the pictures they took."

"Okay." He sat down in the chair she indicated and picked up the first file. "I don't know that much about jewelry, Shelby."

"I don't need to know value. I want to know if you see any historical significance." He nodded, leaned over the table once more. Shelby wondered at the funny sense of relief she felt at having him here. Not very many minutes ago she'd believed him guilty of kidnapping. What had changed?

She had. She'd been trying to handle this alone, struggling with her doubts and fears because she was so desperate to know about Aimee. But Daniel hadn't kidnapped her and neither had Tim. She knew that now.

Tim could have taken her daughter any one of the hundred times she'd run to his house for a visit. There was no reason for him to wait until the middle of the night and sneak into her house to take Aimee. Besides, he'd have no idea of her security codes. Aimee hadn't even known them.

Shelby had to trust someone, needed to feel that she wasn't alone in this miasma of horror. That someone would be Tim.

"I don't see anything unusual about the pin, Shelby. The lamp is an old colonial one. Your appraiser's description agrees with my thoughts—eighteenth-century English, probably used by a courtier. Not terribly valuable unless you know which court. There may have been some markings, but nothing is noted here. Without seeing it, feeling the metal…" He shrugged apologetically. "That's the best I can do."

"The coin?"

"Spanish." He nodded. "Probably recovered from some galleon buried at sea. The picture doesn't tell a lot, but your appraiser noted Queen Isabella in the inscription. If he was correct, the coin would be fairly rare and quite valuable. Not earthshaking, but to a private collector it's a nice piece to have."

"The book?"

"Yes, the book." He paused, glanced over his shoulder at her. "I don't know what I can tell you. It's puzzling. It's a history book in story form, dealing with European aristocracy. From what I see here, it might be valuable to someone who thought they had a family member included in one of the stories, but otherwise it's just an old book written by someone I've never heard of. The English is stilted, judging from the passage your people copied, so I'm guessing it was either translated or written by someone whose primary language was not English. Beyond that, I don't know."

"I see." Frustration waited to envelop her. Shelby thrust it away, refusing to give up.

"Perhaps if you could tell me something about the client—not who it is," he rushed to explain. "Just the reason they wanted it."

"It isn't there?" She picked up the file that should have had the agent's number and initial on it and frowned. "That's odd." She walked into the hall, called her secretary and asked her to find out who'd initiated the appraisal. Then Shelby returned to Tim.

"I guess I'm not much help. I'm sorry."

"Don't be. You can't be expected to know everything." The words slipped out. It took a moment before she realized what they'd sounded like. "I'm sorry," she murmured. "I didn't mean—"

"Shelby?" Her secretary's voice broke into the silence. "The case was Grant's. He opened it last April."

Shelby sat down behind her desk to think. Grant's? A book?

She punched in Daniel's number, asked him if he'd known.

"I noted it but I never thought much about it. You know how he hated anyone to know what he was doing. It was a point of honor with him that he always kept his client info private."

"There is no client info, Daniel. Nothing. I have the reports. There's nothing here but Grant's name."

There was a long silence, then Daniel's low grave voice returned. "I'll be there in a minute. I need to talk to you. Something else has come up."

What now? Dread washed over her and she sagged against the back of the chair.

Where's Aimee, God? Why don't You help me?

"Shelby? Are you all right?" Tim stood in front of the desk, his face displaying his concern. "What did he say?"

"Something else is wrong." She sighed. "Grant often repeated a quote—if you can't handle the thorns, you shouldn't touch the rose. Something like that. Anyway, I feel like I'm in the middle of a thornbush and can't get out."

"That must have been what Aimee was trying to tell me." Tim's eyes flared wide with surprise. "I was once talking about taking out a sliver and she told me she'd helped her dad plant a rosebush once and gotten poked by a thorn. He'd bandaged it up and then told her that pain was part of their beauty, that you couldn't feel the velvety petals if you wore gloves."

"That was Grant." Tears threatened to rush down her cheeks at the memories. "He bought her this pair of tiny white gloves so Aimee wouldn't get poked but she was just like him, she wouldn't ever wear them. She loved to brush her cheek against the petals. I can't help wondering if she'll ever do that again."

"Oh, Shelby." Tim was around the desk in a moment. He pulled her into his arms, cradled her against his chest and brushed his hand over her hair. "I'm sorry I reminded you."

"Don't be. I want to remember everything, to think about it over and over. I have to. It's the only way I keep facing tomorrow, by keeping her fresh in my mind."

"She'll be back, Shelby. God will bring her home." He pulled back a little, used the backs of his damaged fingers to wipe away her tears.

"But when?" she whispered, mesmerized by the tenderness she found in his arms. "When?"

"Only God knows that," he whispered, then his lips brushed against hers.

The door flew open. Tim stepped back quickly, cold air filling his arms where he had sheltered her.

"I'm sorry to interrupt." Russ stood in the doorway. "I need to speak to you."

Shelby sighed, sank down into her chair. "Go ahead."

Russ's gaze swung to Tim, rested there for a moment.

"Is it about a case?" He shook his head. "Then Tim can hear it. What is so important, Russ?"

"Someone has accessed my computer."

"Who?"

"That is what I am saying—I do not know. I have told no

one my passwords." His blue-gray eyes turned to steel. "There is a traitor in this building and I believe I know who it is. Daniel will stop at nothing to discredit me and now he has stolen my work."

"That's ridiculous!" Daniel stood in the open door, his black glasses balanced on the top of his head.

"Is it? You were in my office last night."

"Of course I was. I left you some memos on infrastructure changes I've made." He squinted. "How do you know I was there?"

"I have ways."

The two began hurling insults at each other, comments about past operations Shelby neither understood nor followed. The diatribe got louder until she thought she would scream. Was no one above suspicion?

A piercing whistle cut across the angry voices. They paused, turned to stare at Tim.

"You two are unbelievable. Have you forgotten what the agenda is here? We're supposed to help find Aimee. Not make things worse for Shelby. Can we please focus on that—"

The wail of the fire alarm cut off the rest of his sentence.

SEVEN

An hour later Tim surveyed Shelby's troubled face and wondered if he dared ask the question uppermost in his mind.

"Was it a ruse?"

She sank down in her office chair, her blond hair strawberry-toned in the wash of late-afternoon sun. "I don't know. We have security checks running now. The appraisal rooms, the vaults, the files, everything locks automatically when the fire alarm goes off so the opportunity to take anything isn't there—if that was the point. We'll just have to wait for Daniel's report."

She hung her head forward, rubbed one hand over her pale neck.

"You're tired," he murmured, wishing he could hold her again and thereby ease some of the pain from her. But she'd drawn that mantle around herself again, the one that pretended she was in control, that everything was all right. How he wished he'd given her that stupid book days before, as he'd meant to.

"I feel like one of those rat animals—gerbils," she corrected. "They race round and round on a wheel that goes nowhere. Exactly like I'm doing." Her bluish-green eyes studied him. "You never told me you were married."

"No, I didn't." He stepped behind her, placed his fingers on her shoulders and began to massage the tight cords of tension. At first her muscles tightened, but after a tiny groan Shelby gathered her hair into a mass of tumbling curls and pinned it to the top of her head with a plastic clasp.

"That feels wonderful. You could probably give up the museum business and take up massage therapy without any change in income," she told him, her voice whisper soft as she bent forward. "You certainly have the touch."

"My wife used to get migraines. Sometimes a neck rub could help, if it was in the early stages. If not, nothing but utter silence in a dark room would ease her pain." He hadn't meant to say that, hadn't wanted to talk about the past at all. But somehow, here in her office the connectedness he'd felt earlier had grown stronger.

"Grant never had headaches, in fact he never seemed to suffer from any illness at all. He was always so busy, always on the go." She tilted her head to one side, allowing him access to the knot between neck and shoulder. "I sometimes felt weak and useless next to him."

"You're not weak, Shelby. You're one of the strongest women I've ever seen. You said Aimee is like Grant, but she's like you, too. She has that same inner core of determination and grit that doesn't recognize the word *no*." He cut himself off, embarrassed that he'd verbalized what was in his heart. Now he sounded like the leader of her fan club.

Maybe she thought so too, because after a moment, Shelby drew away, rose from her chair and faced him.

"Thank you for saying that, Tim. And for the massage. My neck feels so much better."

"But you'd like me to go now?" he asked, understanding the uncertainty that feathered through her eyes. "Yes, I should get back. I'm expecting a phone call."

"Oh." She was too polite to ask.

"My eye," he explained. "The scar tissue is getting too thick. They want to do another surgery to remove it. And I'm losing some mobility in my hand, so I suppose that will have to be rectified soon, as well."

"Oh, Tim, I'm sorry."

"It's okay. I'm used to them. Best just to get it over with." Liar. Every time he went under the anesthesia his last thought was that no one would notice if he never came out. "I'll let you get back to work."

"I'll show you out. You'll need a ride, won't you?" Shelby ushered him down the hall and into the elevator.

They emerged in a semicircular entrance that gave him a better view of the curved glass-walled floors above. He could see through all but the top one. That remained an impenetrable black. Some kind of shield perhaps.

"Callie! Did you learn anything new about the doll?"

He turned, barely recognized the operative he'd met at Shelby's. She stalked toward them, long legs encased in denim, a denim shirt tucked in at the waist. Her whole attitude sang, 'Nashville, here I come.' The change was remarkable.

"Hi, Shelby. No news yet. I'm going back shortly for a meet. I'll talk to you after that if I find something."

"Great. In the meantime, could you do me a favor? Tim needs a ride home."

"Sure."

He noticed how everyone skated away from asking her about Aimee. Clearly they were concerned but he suspected no one wanted to hear that she'd learned nothing new.

"Will I see you after dinner?" he asked sotto voce.

"Why not come for dinner. Esmeralda always makes enough for an army and I don't have much of an appetite these days. Around seven?"

"If you're sure?"

"I'm positive. And thank you for helping out here. I wish I could find a copy of that book, but according to Daniel, it seems to be a one only." Shelby clammed up as a group of Japanese men in expensive-looking business suits left the elevator with Daniel.

Tim could see her mind was on work. Good. She needed a break from imagining worst-case scenarios about Aimee.

"Would you mind providing me with copies of whatever you have from the book, Shelby. I have a friend who might be able to help."

"Certainly." She chose several papers from the file she still held and handed them to a woman who disappeared for several moments, then returned with copies. Shelby held them out to him. "Will that be enough?"

"Yes, to start with. Thanks." He shifted uncomfortably, realized she was waiting for him to go. "I'll see you later, then."

"Yes. For dinner."

But as he rode home with Callie one word that reappeared on the copied pages bothered him. *Revolution.* The word appeared darker than the rest. He had a hunch it meant something, though what, he didn't know.

Though Tim had not returned to work, he had kept in touch via the cyberworld, retaining contacts in the business. Maybe he could learn more from them. After phoning to make a consultation appointment with his plastic surgeon he straightened the mess the police had made of his office. The rest of the house could wait until after he'd put out some feelers.

Tim posted his question on several international bulletin boards, then contacted the three men he knew who were the most knowledgeable on European history. It was a long shot, of course, but maybe, just maybe…

* * *

Ten past six. Less than an hour to finish and get home.

Shelby leaned back in her chair to stare at the computer screen. Before her lay the system for tracking codes used within the building. Using the information she'd been given, she finished typing in the special orders that would identify and forward to her computer a record of every person who used the facilities and equipment at Finders, Inc., the length of time they were on and which machines were employed.

When she was finished, she sat staring at the screen, her mind replaying what she knew. Someone had broken in to the building and stolen those items. Only three people were supposed to have access to most of the systems—Russ, Daniel and herself. Since each of the men claimed innocence, she had to look elsewhere for a suspect and to find the reason behind the thefts.

Today's experience only added to her wariness. There had not been a fire in the building. Someone had deliberately set off the alarm. Shelby was determined to make it impossible for that to happen again without the guilty party being tracked. If they tried to bypass the measures she'd put in place, the alarm system would be immediately activated.

Satisfied that she'd done everything she could, Shelby logged off, noting again the sluggish response of her machine. Well it was almost two years old and the technology had leaped ahead. Perhaps it was time to update, except she hated that, worried that some bit of information would be left on the machine, perhaps to be found by someone else.

Finders, Inc. couldn't allow that—especially not with their newest contract. Daniel's connection to Tokyo had paid off. The Japanese men she'd seen in the lobby had contracted Finders to locate an artifact that had disappeared during the Second World War. It wasn't going to be easy but it was going to be interesting. And it proved Finders was still the best in the business. The Japanese had been extremely impressed with their operation.

Shelby almost switched the machine off, then decided to reboot and change her password. Since she hadn't been in since Grant's death, it hadn't been altered and that was against her own policy. Once that was done she left the building and drove home.

With spring's arrival, the evenings lengthened. The air that rushed in through her window was soft and sweet with the newness of life. Blossoming cherry trees, nodding daffodils, and colorful tulips proclaimed a fresh start. Shelby used her driving time to enjoy the views while her mind sent unspoken petitions to Heaven on Aimee's behalf.

She had to roll up her window quickly when she arrived in front of the house. The usual swarm of media waited to attack and she only breathed a sigh of relief when the garage door finally slid shut blocking them all out.

"Esmeralda?"

The house was quiet. With nothing new happening in Aimee's case, Natalie had left one man on duty inside as a courtesy. Shelby preferred it that way. Whoever else was available needed to be looking for Aimee.

"Anything new?" she asked the guard who looked as though he was about to nod off.

"Sorry. Nothing yet." His eyes held only sympathy.

"Thanks." Her heart squeezed tight and she had to force herself to breathe evenly before she could move. Shelby dropped her jacket and briefcase onto a nearby chair and padded into the kitchen. Esmeralda sat in one corner, eyes closed. A light touch on her shoulder and the other woman jolted awake, eyes wide.

"Don't you be doing that to me, young lady! You scared

me out of two years and at my age I need every second on this earth I can muster." She surged to her feet and began to rattle the pots and pans simmering on the stove.

It was a cover and Shelby knew it from the sparkle of a tear that hadn't quite disappeared from the corner of Esmeralda's brown eyes.

"I miss her, too, Esmeralda," she whispered as a hush descended on the kitchen reinforcing the lack of a chirping little voice asking for another taste.

"Of course you do, baby. Mamas always miss their chicks, no matter how old they are." Esmeralda scurried around the island to envelope her in a cinnamon-scented hug. "But we're not going to go fussing and fuming about why, are we? No, sir, we aren't. This horrible thing happened, but all things are sifted through God's hands and He's got a reason. Don't know what that is right now, but Esmeralda doesn't have to know."

Shelby remained on her stool and leaned against the comforting breast of the woman who'd been like her second mother.

"Your grandmother went through an awful lot, honey. I watched her handle losing her husband, your mom and dad, and then her health. Through all that she taught me that the most important thing about any testing is to hang on. Just because we go gettin' a little trouble doesn't mean we start telling God how to do His job." Her strong fingers soothed a pattern of ease as they moved over Shelby's head. Her voice was like a river of strength pouring over her sore and weary heart.

"But she's been gone so long."

"The Lord's had this whole wide world in His hands for longer than you and I been around. He's not about to let it drop now. 'I will not be afraid' the Good Book says and I don't aim to tell God I'm too sorry a soldier in His army to hang on to that promise and wait for Him to work it out."

How blessed she was to have this God-loving woman in her home. Esmeralda had seen her grandmother through thick and thin and now she was here for Shelby and Aimee. However bad things got, Shelby was never alone because God had given her Esmeralda.

"Thank you," she murmured, wrapping her hands around the ample waist and hugging Esmeralda fiercely. "I don't know how I'd handle this without you here."

"Well I don't aim to be leaving soon so you'd better get used to it." The starch returned to Esmeralda's voice. "Skinny as a rail," she muttered, her hands sliding down Shelby's back. "Probably low blood sugar that's making you weepy." One last pat and she moved away to busy herself with something in the fridge, hiding her own feelings.

Shelby let her go because she knew Esmeralda wanted it that way. She didn't believe in weeping over what she couldn't change. She was strong and independent. Always had been.

"You want to start with some soup? I made a nice chowder."

"I guess." Shelby remembered. "But it will have to wait a bit. I invited Tim over. Is that all right?"

"And why wouldn't it be? The poor waif's been wandering around that backyard of his as if he lost his best friend. Keeps looking over here. Checking to see if you're home, I suspect."

"You think he's checking on me?" Shelby frowned at the knowledge that Tim had been watching her that closely. "Why do you say that, Esmeralda?"

"'Cause he does the same thing every day. Watches out that window or sits outside until you come home. Next thing I know he's over here. And it's not just to see Aimee," she added, one eyebrow lifted in that broad hinting manner she used to emphasize her point. "He likes you."

So this strange connection she felt to him wasn't all one-sided. Still…

"Esmeralda, Grant hasn't been dead a year."

"What's that got to do with anything?"

"Well, to suggest that there might be something romantic between Tim and me—there can't be."

"Who are you trying to convince?" Those beady brown eyes pinned her down. "I know you loved Grant. But he's gone now and you're a beautiful young woman. You've tried to devote yourself to Aimee and the garden but it's not enough and you know it."

"Well, now I've got Finders, Inc. to worry about, too."

"Fiddle." Esmeralda smacked a salad onto the breakfast bar. "Finders has been doing just fine without you. You're using it because you're running away."

"I am not!" Shelby picked out a radish and chewed it as she thought that over. "From what?" she asked softly.

"From life, from moving on, from the future and what it might hold. Running like a scared little rabbit."

"I'm not running away." She glared at the other woman's broad back. As if she felt that glower, Esmeralda turned around. It was clear to Shelby that she was not backing down.

"Sure you are," she insisted, her fingers plucking freshly baked buns from a sheet and setting them into a napkin-lined basket. "After you sell the house, when Aimee's gone to school and Daniel has Finders under control—what will you do then, Shel?"

"I don't know what you mean. I've always kept busy," she insisted.

"Busy, yes. But will busywork make you happy?" Esmeralda shook her head. "You're a good mother, honey. That little girl loves you dearly. But someday she's going to step out into the world and leave you behind. One of these days you'll find yourself alone. What will you do then?"

"I have friends. I do things."

"Honey, you've shut everyone out." Esmeralda set down the butter dish and reached across the black granite to enfold Shelby's hands in hers. "Haven't you noticed? Those girls you used to giggle and laugh with don't come around anymore. The shopping trips, the lunches together, the pool parties— they've all stopped while you locked yourself into this tight little world where only Aimee and those rosebushes matter."

Had she done that? Shelby wanted to deny it but the truth was she couldn't remember when she'd last gone out for lunch or sat in the hot tub sharing secrets with the friends she'd always known. Shopping? Well, she did that mostly online now, not that she needed much.

"Look in the mirror, Shel. You're a beautiful woman, but you haven't been taking care of yourself. You stay up until all hours, get up at the crack of dawn. You don't eat unless I push you and you haven't done your laps in that pool since— I don't know when. Might as well drain the thing and fill it with rose bushes," she grumbled in disgust.

Shelby glanced over one shoulder and caught a glimpse of herself in the mirror. She'd worn her hair long because Grant liked it like that, but now it was dry and flyaway, without the glossy sheen. Hardly beautiful. She reached up to press the ends down and saw her unkept fingernails. Quickly she snatched her hand down, turned away.

"I can't concentrate on me while my daughter is gone," she told Esmeralda. "Who cares what I look like?"

"Aimee will. She'll want her Mama strong and ready to help her." Esmeralda drew in a deep breath, then continued. "We don't know what she's going through, sweetie. God has it under control and we can count on that, but when she comes home, that little girl is going to need you. You've got to be ready for anything, Shel. You've got to be strong and prepared and you can't be that if you won't look after yourself. You've—" She stopped.

Shelby rose in a huff of fury as the anger raged inside. "You weren't finished. Say it and get it over with."

"Very well, I will. Nobody is an island, Shelby. No matter how strong we want to be, we need other people to depend on, to lean on, to enrich our lives. You can't keep closing yourself off just because Grant is no longer here. He died, but you didn't. You have your whole life ahead of you."

Shelby thought about it long and hard, trying to sift through the pain and shadows. Esmeralda was speaking the truth. But all Shelby could see in her future was emptiness, aloneness and a heart that felt ripped and torn. The future was for thinking about when Aimee came back, not now.

She pushed it away, looked up into Esmeralda's dark gaze and knew the older woman would not let her get away with it.

"All right. I promise I'll try to get back to normal. But that doesn't mean Tim will be part of it. He's a friend, but that's all I want."

"Ask yourself why," Esmeralda suggested. "I'll go let him in."

Shelby hadn't even realized Tim had walked across the back, though the kitchen windows gave a perfect view. As she watched him scrape his feet on the doormat, she couldn't help noticing the rich maroon of his silk shirt, how well it fit his broad shoulders and wide chest. He wore a dark tweed jacket that brought out the golden glints in his hair.

Tim was taller than Grant had been. But where Grant had been lean and lanky, Tim projected substance, strength and not only in his muscles. She could see it in his face as he walked in the door, searched the room and found her. A smile tipped the corners of his mouth, pushing it up into the puckered marks on his cheeks.

He was strong, reliable, dependable. But she couldn't love him. She'd only ever loved Grant. They'd been a unit, a family, a couple. To even consider letting someone inside that circle, to imagine that someone else could take Grant's place—she jumped to her feet.

"Come on in. I think Esmeralda has everything ready. Would you like to eat in here?" Her voice was too loud, too fast. Shelby took a breath and told herself to calm down as Tim's stare turned curious.

He was just a friend, she reminded herself. That's all she wanted.

"Sorry I'm late," he murmured, taking the bar stool she indicated. "I was in a chat room with a friend of mine who had some ideas about that book of yours."

Relieved with the change of topic, Shelby leaned toward him. "Did you learn anything valuable?"

"It depends on your idea of value. My friend thinks the book is sort of like a diary. I scanned those copies of the sheets you gave me and sent them to him. He says he's seen this type of thing before, a personal historical record. Someone has it printed into a book and it's handed down from father to son. Your client must have been trying to track his roots."

"Since Grant didn't include that information, there's no way to know." An idea flickered to life. "Except that Daniel didn't mention that anyone has come forward to ask about it. You'd think that if they hired Grant to find it, they'd want to know what has happened to the investigation. And why would someone steal a history of someone else?"

"Enough business." Esmeralda set a bowl of steaming chowder before each of them. "I'll say grace," she declared, plopping herself down at the breakfast bar. She closed her eyes, sighed and began.

"God, this is me, Esmeralda. You know I'm real tired today. I want my little girl back here with her mama. I want whoever took her to be put in jail. But you're God so I'm going to wait for You to work this out. Please bless this food, thank You for loving us. Amen."

Shelby forced herself to pick up the spoon and taste the soup, though her throat felt blocked with tears. Esmeralda and Tim gamely kept the conversation moving until she was able to join in again.

Later as she and Tim sat on the patio with their coffee, Shelby realized that most of the tension in her shoulders and neck had slipped away, thanks to Tim's silly jokes and funny stories.

"This patio really offers everything, doesn't it?" he murmured, staring across the yard. "You almost wouldn't know the pool is there, tucked behind the garden the way it is. When you're swimming, the scent of the roses must be heavenly."

"In mid-June they'll start blooming. You'll be able to tell for yourself." She leaned back in her chair and let the light breeze caress her face.

"I'm not sure I'll be here in June."

Shelby sat up, deeply shocked. "You're going away?" A sense of loss washed over her. "Why?"

"I have to have more surgery. The doctor is tentatively scheduling it for June, but I hope they can do it sooner." He rubbed one corner of his eye. "The scar tissue is beginning to affect my vision. I want it corrected."

"Oh." She didn't know what to say. She knew from Aimee's explanations that Tim didn't like to talk about the operations and assumed that was because they were painful. But surely not life threatening?

"It's not a big deal, Shelby. I've been through many before." He grimaced. "And more to come."

"I'm sorry. It must be very hard for you."

"Do you want the truth?" He leaned forward, met her stare with his own. "I try not to think about it. I know it has to happen, I know it's going to be painful, but until I actually have to face it, I prefer to think on better things."

"'Whatsoever things are true, whatsoever things are honest,'" she murmured, tilting her chin into the wash of dying sunlight.

"Pardon?"

"It's a Scripture verse. Philippians, I think," she murmured, recalling those quiet evenings from so long ago. "My grandmother loved the Bible, the beauty of the language. We often sat out here memorizing portions together. That was one of them." She took a deep breath, tried to recall the exact phrasing.

"Finally brethren, whatsoever things are true, whatsoever things are honest, whatsoever things are just, whatsoever things are pure, whatsoever things are lovely, whatsoever things are of good report; if there be any virtue, and if there be any praise, think on these things."

"It's a good verse to remember," he agreed. "Elevates your thoughts from the mundane, the horrible and the what-ifs. I need to remember that. It's too easy to get bogged down by the horrible things that happen."

Like Aimee's disappearance, she thought.

"It's so hard to stop wondering if she's warm enough at night, if she's had enough to eat, if someone brushed her hair. If she's hurt—" Shelby bit her lip to stop the flow that only made her worst nightmare feel more real.

Tim reached out, clasped her hand in his and squeezed.

"She's all right, Shelby. God will keep her safe till we find her."

A high-pitched scream effectively choked anything Shelby would have said.

"My computer alarm." She jumped to her feet and rushed into the den where her laptop sat on Grant's desk.

"What's wrong with it?" Tim shouted from behind her.

"Nothing. It's doing it's job." She sat down and began punching in sequences. "Somebody is breaking through the security at Finders." She moved toward the door. "I intend to find out who."

EIGHT

Tim stood on the sidelines, watching as Shelby frantically punched in access numbers and codes on her computer at Finders, Inc., while Daniel waited beside her.

"Where was the breach?" he asked when she finally leaned back in her chair.

Shelby didn't say anything, simply rose and faced him. But he saw dread in her eyes.

"What's wrong?" Daniel glanced from her to the computer on her desk.

"It was a download to a remote location. From your computer, Daniel."

"Mine?" Clearly stunned by the revelation, Daniel stared at her for a few minutes, then headed for the door. "That's impossible. Come on, I'll show you."

Since no one told him to stay behind Tim followed them, studied the CEO's office while Daniel hunched over his own workstation. Like Shelby's, this office had a wall of glass that looked out over the entire operation. Tim knew from his visit to the lobby that though he could see out, no one could see in. The tinted window made it more secure. He didn't know why, but he was certain the office had once belonged to Grant Kincaid, Shelby's husband.

"Our firewall is inpenetrable," Daniel muttered as he hunched over the computer. "I've had the security boys check and recheck. They assured me it's hackerproof."

"Not so much now," Shelby muttered. She bent over and unplugged the cable connection. "Let's take you off-line until we can get an idea of what's going on." She waited for him to discern what had been taken.

"I've got it. They copied an old file," he muttered, fingers stabbing at the keyboard. "But that can't be right."

Tim watched as Daniel repeated a command over and over. Each time the computer gave the same response. Finally Daniel leaned back, his face tight with frustration.

"Show me." Shelby leaned forward, stared at the spot where his finger pointed, then recoiled as if she'd been burned.

"What?" Tim demanded, needing to know what was going on. Both Shelby and Daniel gazed at him as if he'd asked them to get the moon. "What did they take?"

"The files on Grant's last case," Daniel finally told him. "I'm getting Igor in here. I want to know exactly how they got in."

They waited, each immersed in their own thoughts until a big burly man buzzed to notify them that he needed access to the floor. There were no introductions. Daniel simply told him what he wanted and Igor began to work.

Tim moved closer to Shelby. "Are you all right?" he murmured, worried by her ashen face and the tiny tremor in her hand as she gripped the back of a chair for support.

"I don't know. Why would anyone want to know about Grant's last case? It doesn't make sense."

"Come on, sit down." He helped her onto the sofa, then sat down beside her.

"I should have paid more attention. Maybe he said something I didn't catch. He was so consumed by business all the time." Tears trembled on the ends of her lashes. "I used to nag him about whether business came before Aimee and I. I knew it didn't but sometimes it was hard to see him leave us to come back here night after night."

Tim remained silent. He'd never imagined the couple's marriage had been anything less than idyllic. Of course this didn't mean anything. Sara had often accused him of being a workaholic when he'd stayed late too many nights, especially when a new piece came in to the museum and he wanted to make sure he knew everything there was to know about it.

In the hospital he'd realized his mistake. Those precious hours they could have spent together were lost now, irretrievable.

"He got to you through Shelby's computer," Igor rumbled, his voice breaking the silence of the room.

"Mine?" She frowned. "How?"

"Best guess? Your security isn't up-to-date. He found a back door in your system and used it to send something to Daniel. After that it was a simple jump to open your files, Daniel."

"I was going to talk to you about that. My computer has been very slow. Takes forever to log on and off. But until a day or two ago it wasn't even turned on." Shelby tapped a finger against her lips, her gaze speculative. "At least by me. Can you tell where the information was downloaded to?"

"I have a special little tracker that I've used in our programs that should help." Igor's fingers flew across the keyboard. Something that could have been a smile twisted his lips. "Ah, not so clever, are you?" He spoke over one shoulder. "Downloaded at an Internet site downtown. Probably one of those cafés. He would have had to have everything worked out ahead of time to get in and out so fast. I doubt if he's there still."

"How soon to fix this?" Daniel demanded, his face drawn in gray lines that made him look older.

"I've taken everyone off-line for now. Nobody can get in or out. I see Shelby's got a little tracking bug set up to catch whoever logs on and catalogs their entries. Not a bad idea." He grinned at her surprise. "Didn't think you'd slip that past me, did you?"

"I never really thought about fooling you. I just wanted to find out who's been bypassing our security."

"Me, too." Igor nodded. "He's not a novice. He knew exactly what he wanted, didn't waste time looking around. I'd guess nobody on the junior level. They'd have to know how we access job files by operative code, how they're arranged, that Daniel has all of them. I'm guessing level four or above."

"Okay, we'll start with that." Shelby's eyes hardened to blue flint chips. "I want this fixed, Igor. Once is a mistake. Twice is—"

"Not going to happen." He rose. "I'll take out all the remote access for now. If you two want something, you'll have to work in-house until I can tear our firewall apart. If we can route all the computer files so they release through just one person as we do the paper files, that would help."

"Done." Shelby looked at Daniel. "That's your department. I want Igor to start with your computer, then mine. We'll take this one and replace it with a new machine until we're sure nothing else has been compromised." She stopped because Daniel's beeper went off.

"Excuse me." He dialed a number, listened. "I have to go. I've got a lead on that missing brooch that I can't ignore."

"Go. I'll lock up here."

"Okay. But tomorrow I want to talk to you about that tracking bug of yours and who you were trying to catch." He met her stare unflinchingly. "I haven't done anything wrong, Shelby."

She nodded. He left in a rush, his long legs eating up the distance to the elevator.

"You want me to take this machine with me now?" Igor asked.

"No. You scrounge up a new one for Daniel first. Leave this one here for now. I want to check something else out."

"I'm sorry I let you down, Shelby. I don't know how he got in. I've disabled the route from your computer to Daniel's so it won't happen again, but I think you both should get something completely clean to work on until I find out what else is on there to be taken."

"Do that." She nodded. "Tomorrow morning."

"Got it." Igor left. Tim watched his descent in the glass-fronted elevator.

"Is he always here, on call?" Tim asked when it seemed as if Shelby had grown rooted to the floor.

"Quite a lot of the time. Or his assistant."

"So what happens now?"

"Now I conduct a little check of my own." She pulled up a file and printed off everything in it. Then she used a disk to copy the information and then erased her source from the computer.

The phone on Daniel's desk rang. Shelby picked it up. Even from six feet away Tim could hear Igor's voice.

"Found something interesting at the beginning of that log-in session. Our thief used your codes to get into the main system, Shelby. There was no try and fail. He knew exactly what you use."

"He used *my* passwords to steal from me?"

"That's about the gist of it. Somebody used your private way into your own security system to hoist what they needed. You need new numbers."

"But I changed them today."

"Just the log-ins. You forgot the others."

"Yeah." She sighed. "Okay. I'll pick new ones up tomorrow morning, too. Thanks, Igor." She hung up.

"Is that really his name?" Tim couldn't imagine anyone naming a child Igor.

"It's longer and more complicated, but that's what we call him." She walked over to the wall, keyed in a sequence. A door slid open revealing filing cabinets. Shelby picked her way through many of them.

"What are you looking for?"

"A file. A very specific file. Ah." She lifted out a dark blue folder, closed the drawer, then reset the security device. "I think I'm finished in here. Let's go."

Tim took a second look at her face and decided to hold his tongue. Something was going on and he didn't understand what it was. Better to wait and see.

Once they were back inside Shelby's office, she locked the door.

"Is that necessary?"

"I don't know. Lately I'm not sure who's on my side and who's stabbing me in the back." She blinked at him, her blue-green eyes narrowed in thought. "But I don't want to be interrupted and this way I won't be. Come and look at this." She slid the disk she'd made in Daniel's office into her computer. "This is a copy of Grant's last case. I pulled the paper file to compare."

He scanned the screen which listed the particulars Grant had noted, read them out loud.

"Marta Krakow was his client's name. She hired him to find…" He paused. "A chicken?"

"Grant loved to play games with his files." Shelby smiled. "It was his way of making it more difficult for someone to track what he was doing. The one thing I'm certain of is that he wasn't tracking a chicken."

"Finders, Inc. has had trouble like tonight before?" Tim

was somehow surprised by this, though he knew little about company operations.

"No. We've had glitches here and there, of course, but nothing major. The game-playing started years ago when Grant, Daniel and Russ belonged to a special task force that was assigned to covert operations. In case I didn't mention it, they're all highly competitive. Sometimes Grant would learn something and want to follow it up before he shared it with the others so he'd embed little phrases or words in his files." She scanned the rest of the contents of the disk, then opened the paper file. "Now we're getting somewhere."

"Chicken—egg! A Fabergé egg," Tim whispered as he followed her finger over the information. "Which, according to this, he found." He stopped, turned his head and met her steady scrutiny.

Shelby leaned over to peer at the file.

"That doesn't make sense." She stared at the documents, her glossy head moving from side to side in disbelief. "These notes indicate that Grant brought it here. Therefore, it should be in the warehouse."

"And it's not?"

"I've never seen a mention of it. I can find out." She called up a file on the inventory list using the code number Grant had recorded. "No such file."

Tim barely heard her, his mind busy assimilating what information he could glean from the picture Grant had taken of the object. About this he knew quite a lot. Maybe he could finally help her.

"Fabergé eggs are extremely valuable, Shelby. And highly collectible. We had one on exhibit in London when I was there. I was offered a lot of money if I'd just let the security lapse—let it disappear." He glanced down at the papers. "Why would Grant's client be after this one?"

"He doesn't say." Shelby leafed through the papers, paused and bent over, studying something he couldn't see.

Tim knew that someone in Grant's position would have known the value of the egg, and if he didn't, he'd have had it appraised. But as far as he could tell there was no appraisal in the records Shelby held. Surely he would have told his wife if he'd located such a wonderful thing?

He heard her quick intake of breath, saw her eyes widen, her color disappear.

"What's wrong?"

"Look." She pointed to a number scribbled on a corner inside the file.

"Yes?" Numbers. So what?

"This is the security code for my house. Daniel has the security code for my house, Tim." She blinked, stared at him with something like despair seeping into her eyes.

"But what—"

"He could have disabled the system and walked in at any time. He could have stolen Aimee," she whispered.

"You don't believe that, Shelby," he protested, watching as the doubt and fear ravaged her beautiful face and left her defenseless.

"I don't know what to believe anymore. I've tried to stifle the doubts, to tell myself it's just circumstantial, but I keep coming back to Daniel. I'm—I'm afraid," she whispered.

It hurt to see this strong capable woman so bowed over, longing to hold her child. Tim reached down and drew her up, into his arms where he sheltered her against his chest. She poured out her pain in a river of tears and soft muffled sobs that only made her more precious in his eyes.

"It's okay, Shelby," he whispered, drawing his hand down her silky hair. "It will be okay. Remember what Esmeralda said about God being in control. You and Grant taught Aimee about God being her best friend, how He's always near, always watching. Don't you think He's doing the same for you?"

"I—I don't know anymore. I feel so alone. I want to believe she's okay, but it's hard. You know?" She lifted her head and peered at him through the wash of tears. "Aimee is my only child. She's a part of me."

"I know." He snuggled her head against his chest, brushed his lips against her forehead and debated whether or not to tell her. "Daniel knows that, too."

"But what if—"

He shushed her by placing his fingers across her lips.

"Listen to me. After the—after I was burned, I told God I didn't want to have anything to do with Him ever again."

Those nightmarish days stung in the recalling. He'd coded the pain by color. Red was intense, unbearable. Orange meant stabs of sharper anguish interspersed the steady hurt. Yellow was that constant, unyielding suffering that would not go away. Agonizing days, minutes, hours, weeks—they all ran together like an artist's palette run amok in orange.

"I couldn't understand why it had happened, kept asking that over and over. When no answer came, I thought it meant He didn't care. That I'd been abandoned." He sighed, focused on the present. "That made me ask more. But no matter how many times I asked, no matter how hard I demanded an answer, there was no explanation. All I knew was that it had happened. I was badly burned. I could either give in and let the infection finish what life I had left, or I could take control, fight and find out what was next."

It sounded so easy. But he didn't want her—didn't want anyone—to know how much that decision had cost him.

"I began to look around the hospital and I realized that I wasn't the only one who was suffering. There were children who'd been unfairly treated by people who should have loved them. There were old people who'd suffered through years and years of hardship but valued life so much they fought to live one more day." He tightened his arms around her just a fraction, knowing what he said next would be hard to hear. "Bad things happen all over, Shelby. That doesn't mean God isn't there with us. I'd been skating away from that truth but Aimee's been hammering it home ever since I met her."

"What do you mean?"

"Aimee talked to me about losing her father," he murmured. "She talked a lot."

"What did she say?"

"She said she missed him, that she wished she still had a father to play with and tell secrets to, but that she wasn't alone." Shelby was openly staring at him now. Tim cleared his throat, continued. "She said her father had taught her that there was another daddy who always watched over her, would always listen to anything she wanted to say and most of all, one who would always love her, even when she did bad things."

"She and Grant often talked about God when they were working in the garden." Shelby's smile wobbled but held.

"Those must have been precious times." He cleared his throat. "Aimee has his words and the basis of his faith tucked deeply into her heart, Shelby. She knows who to call on, and she knows that He'll be there to listen and understand. Wherever she is, Aimee knows that she is not alone. You have to know that, too."

"Yes, I did. Do. Thank you for reminding me."

He straightened his arms, held her away so he could see her eyes.

"The thing is, bad things happen…to everybody. Rain falls on the just and the unjust, the Bible says. It doesn't matter why it happened, it's enough that it did and now we have to deal with it." Big talk, Austen. It was time he dealt with it himself.

"You're saying I should ignore my doubts and get on with my work," she whispered, glancing around the office.

"I'm saying you are stronger if you look at this realistically. Even if Daniel took Aimee, and I do not believe he did, what can you do about it?" His hand strayed to her cheek, his gnarled fingers relishing its smoothness. "You can't force him to tell you where she is, assuming he knows. All you can do is keep searching, keep praying and wait for God to show you the next step."

She was silent for a long time. But when Shelby looked at him again there was a glint of spirit shining in her face.

"You're right. But why don't you think Daniel is involved?"

"He's worked here all these months, running Finders as best he can. He's tried to give you space, but the moment you come in, he's prepared to take second chair. That doesn't sound like someone who's out to hurt you. Yes, things have gone missing, but he's not writing them off, he's got somebody actively working on it." He paused, reconsidered. "I've seen his face when he comes to the house, Shelby. It's hard for him to go there. I think he misses Grant and that he feels he's somehow failed him by not being able to find Aimee."

"Daniel has never been able to talk much about Grant since he died. They'd been tight for a long time. Grant helped him deal with his father's expectations."

"Maybe watching over Finders is Daniel's way of paying Grant back."

"Maybe." She slipped out of his arms with an apologetic look. "I'm sorry I bawled all over your shirt. I seem to keep dumping my woes on you."

"I don't mind, Shelby. I'm glad if I could help you a little bit. Aimee has helped me so many times that it's only fair I should be here for her mother." It was more than that and he knew it, but this was not the time. "Shall we take a second look at that file and see if we can learn anything new?"

She nodded, swiped a hand across her cheeks then sank down into the chair again, her shoulders a little straighter.

Tim stood behind her, his eyes on the pages but his mind a thousand miles away in a time before this.

He'd been preaching to her about trust, about knowing that all things came from God. But in his heart a nugget of stubborn grief would not be melted. Why had God wanted him to lose everything? To be a spectator as his world dissolved in a fiery crash that stole his future and left him with years of pain seemed the cruelest of punishments for whatever he'd done wrong.

He couldn't make himself accept it, couldn't quite believe that the God of the universe couldn't have done something, anything, to prevent what had happened.

"Tim! Look!" Shelby's hand grabbed his, clung to it as her other hand smacked on a small bit of paper stuck to the last page of the file.

"It's Greek to me," he murmured, suddenly aware that though he could see her slim white fingers squeezing tightly around his, he could not return her grasp.

"Greek. Very funny," she said drolly, her gaze intent on the words. "Of course it's Greek. Daniel and Grant used to send notes to each other in it all the time. Something they learned in the boarding school they attended, I think. Anyway, that's what this is. And it's not Grant's handwriting."

"Daniel's," he guessed, his mind still on his useless hand. He'd have to have the operation soon. The doctor had said that once lost, his range of motion would be difficult to recover. And Tim wanted to recover it, he wanted to heal so badly.

Shelby Kincaid was a beautiful woman who'd been married to a man resembling a statue Michelangelo might have chiseled. Tim looked nothing like a male model. But if Shelby ever saw him as more than a good friend, if she ever gave the slightest sign that she was interested in him, he wanted to be there for her—body, mind, soul and spirit. Not some maimed, useless has-been.

The past was buried, dead and gone. He regretted it, but there was nothing he could do. But the future—perhaps the future was in front of him, waiting for the right moment. She wouldn't want a scarred, weak cripple.

And he wasn't going to be one.

"I can't believe this." Her strangled whisper drew him back to the present and he peered down at the words she'd translated onto a pad.

"I don't quite—"

"Daniel not only thinks that Grant's accident wasn't an accident," she told him haltingly, her eyes growing stormy. "He thinks Grant was deliberately targeted to stop him from completing his case."

"Wow." He didn't know what to say. Was it pure speculation or did Daniel have some reason for his thoughts?

"But that's not the worst of it, Tim." She silently reviewed what she'd written, then leaned back in her chair, her face whiter than he'd ever seen it.

"Just tell me what it says."

Shelby took a deep breath. Her gaze fastened on him like a laser beam.

"These latest entries are dated last night. Daniel believes the warehouse fire that killed Grant was deliberately set to stop his investigations."

"But who—"

"Wait. If I'm translating this properly, Daniel actually

thinks that Grant's death and Aimee's abduction are linked, that Aimee was taken because of something Grant did." She stared at him, her heart in her eyes. "I could lose my daughter forever, Tim, just like I lost Grant. All because of something that happened over ten months ago, something I don't know anything about!"

Cold hard anger formed in the pit of his stomach.

Lose a child?

Not again. Surely God wouldn't let it happen again.

NINE

"Listen to me, Shelby."

She'd never seen Tim Austen so serious. He crouched in front of her, his hands pressing her shoulders back against the chair as he spoke. The scar tissue around his eye puckered tightly, accentuating the damage to his face.

"Aimee is going to come home, and she's going to be fine. You have to hang on to that and focus your energies on stopping whoever is trying to hurt this company." He paused, his frown hardened. "Your husband died here at Finders, Inc., trying to find out the truth. You have to finish the job he started no matter where it leads—because it might just lead us to Aimee. That child is the most precious gift you'll ever be given and you can't let her slip through your fingers."

"I don't want to, but—" He was so vehement. What was going on behind those brown eyes? Shelby wondered.

"Then don't let it happen." His hands chafed hers as he spoke. Shelby wondered if he even realized he still clung to her. "Over the past three years I've had a number of...discussions with God. I don't understand His ways or why He chooses to do things as He does, but right now I'm certain of one thing."

"What's that?"

"That if we take the first step, He'll be there to lead us to the second."

A tension lay in the room, thick and oppressive, weaving across her shoulders in a net that suddenly seemed too heavy to lift. Shelby shook her head.

"It sounds good, but I'm just me, Tim. I'm not some movie secret agent. I can't magically pull Aimee from the arms of whoever has her. I don't have an ever-flowing battery of intelligence that will lead me to her. There are no leads!"

She surged to her feet, paced across the room and back again, the frustration of it eating at her.

"You have better than that."

She whirled around to glare at him. "What?"

"Think about it for a moment, Shelby. Would you have come back to Finders if it hadn't been for Aimee?"

She shook her head. She hadn't wanted to be reminded of what she'd lost.

"Then you would never have known, never have suspected that Grant's death might not have been an accident."

"You think that's a good thing?" she asked, incredulously.

"I think that if Grant died because of something someone did, that if his death wasn't an accident—I think you want to know that, don't you?" His brown stare didn't let up. "I know you, Shelby. You want to know the truth. That's why you and your husband started this company, why you help people recover what they've lost. Now it's time to make Finders, Inc. work for you. Maybe this is the only way you'll find out what happened. Maybe you're the only one who can."

She stared at him, her mind working overtime as she thought about what he'd said. Her conclusion scared her.

"You think Daniel's right," she whispered, stunned by the knowledge. "You think Grant's death and Aimee's disappearance are connected. Why?"

"Because Aimee's disappearance doesn't make sense." Tim stared at the floor, at his brown leather loafers, his voice a notch above a whisper. "All along it's puzzled me. No ransom, no clues, no reason for them to take her. Unless—"

"Yes? Unless what?"

He hesitated, didn't meet her stare. Fear rose up, threatened to steal her composure. Shelby swallowed.

"Tell me what you're thinking?"

Finally Tim looked up. "Unless she's going to play a part later."

"I don't know what that means, Tim." Shelby felt as if her brain was racing a hundred miles an hour. Mentally, she grasped what he was saying, but inside she didn't want to believe it.

"You mean my daughter is a pawn, held in case her abductor's need her later? For what?"

"I don't know. I'm not sure pawn is the right word. Maybe they needed her gone to get you back here." He threw up his hands. "It's all just guesswork. I have no proof of anything. I'm really only postulating theories."

"But that makes sense, I think." Her mind shifted the puzzle pieces so they began to fit a pattern. "Grant found this egg he was looking for, according to his notes. But we can't find it. Maybe someone else couldn't find it, either. We've already had four thefts, maybe they were just a ruse, things the thief took when what he really wanted was the egg."

"It's possible, I guess."

"But who? Who is this person and why would he have done that?" She stared at him, hating that familiar sense of suspicion that loomed in the back of her mind and popped out whenever she talked to anyone who had known Aimee.

He stared at her for a long time before he spoke.

"I told you I can't make sense of how God works in my

own life. But maybe that's why you're here, in the position you are. Maybe only you can solve this. You knew Grant, knew how he worked, how his mind worked. You care more about Aimee than anyone. Maybe you have to be the one who unravels the mystery."

"I don't know where to start."

"Start here. These are Daniel's notes. He also knew Grant very well. The two of you should be able to come up with some theories as to his last case."

"Yes, we should." The decision was made. Shelby shut off her computer, rose, tucked the file under her arm and motioned toward the door. "You're right, Tim. Finding my daughter, getting the answers I need—it is up to me. Beginning tomorrow morning, I'm going to be making some changes at Finders, Inc. I'm going to ask Daniel to help me probe deeper into Grant's case."

"Good." He smiled, took her hand and squeezed it.

"I'm sick of living under a shadow. I'm going to pray and with God's help, I'll find out the truth, the whole truth. Maybe then I'll get my daughter back."

She tugged her hand from his, moved toward the door, holding it open until he'd walked past. Then she locked it, swiped her security card through. As they rode down the elevator together, the first tiny flickering of hope flared inside her heart. Maybe…

"You've been really great to help me out like this, Tim. Will you come in with me tomorrow, too?" Her heart sank as she saw his negative response.

"I can't, Shelby. I'm really sorry. I talked to the doctor today. He wants me in tomorrow for an assessment to prepare for my next surgery." He held up one damaged hand. "I'm losing my mobility in this hand too fast to wait much longer. I can probably put them off on this one," he pointed to his eye.

"But the doctors will insist on doing the hand surgery as soon as it can be scheduled. I knew that months ago. I just didn't want to face it." He paused. "If you really needed me, though, maybe I could cancel for another time."

"Don't be silly." She was ashamed of even asking him. He'd already done so much. "Of course you have to take care of yourself. Anyway, you can come over after and I'll tell you all about what we've learned."

"I'd like that. I care very much about Aimee. I want to see her home safe and sound."

"Yes." She unlocked her car, watched him climb into the back and sprawl across the backseat to hide from the reporters as the questions built inside her brain. Suddenly she wanted to know what had caused those scars, why he never spoke of that time. She drove toward home debating on whether or not to ask him. Once safely past the reporters and inside the garage, she twisted to look behind her.

"Will you come in for a cup of tea?"

"It's late. I think I'd better go home. You need to get some rest so you can prepare for tomorrow." He climbed out, held her door. "But thanks anyway."

She walked beside him into the house and through it toward the back patio. Once they were outside in the night air he paused to look down into her face, the moonlight pooling shadows around them.

"Thank you for letting me help, Shelby. If you need me again, remember I'll be right next door."

She nodded. Waited. After a moment he leaned down, brushed his lips against hers.

"Good night." He turned, began walking away.

"Tim?"

"Yes?"

There was no easy way to broach the subject so she blurted

it out. "Will you tell me what happened?" He looked puzzled and she rushed on. "To you, I mean. How you got the scars?"

A hundred expressions flitted across his damaged face, none of them giving her any clue to what he was remembering. Silence stretched between them, only the crickets and a few night birds daring to speak.

Tim half turned away from her so that his face was in shadow. When he spoke his voice was so quiet Shelby had to lean nearer.

"I'll tell you sometime, I promise. But not tonight."

Then he was gone, a shadow among shadows, crunching over the gravel, silent over the grass; only the rustle of the hedge announced his departure.

Shelby sank onto a chair and breathed in the scent of Grant's roses as she tried to puzzle out the odd note in Tim's response. Reluctance? Yes, certainly. But something darker lay beneath his hesitation.

No doubt the pain he must have sustained made him wary of talking about his injuries, but something other than that kept him silent. Something that made her wonder if she should have left the past alone.

Early the next morning Shelby had it all laid out in front of her—the file with the handwritten notes, the Greek and translation, everything that she wanted to discuss with Daniel. He was in the office, she'd seen him earlier on the surveillance camera, talking with Russ in the warehouse.

Igor had been in. Her computer was a brand-new model. She called him in and he explained what he'd done to safeguard it.

"I haven't got the whole place secure yet, but I will," he promised. "Get your new security codes on that machine right away."

"I will. Thanks for doing this so quickly."

"Matter of honor, Shelby. Nobody breaches my system without me tracking him down." He left, his jaw jutting out angrily.

Shelby's hand hovered over the intercom, intending to call Daniel, until a knock sounded at her door.

"There's a deliveryman here. He will not hand over whatever he has to me," Joanie explained, her eyes flashing with anger. "He insists that only you can sign for this."

"Send him in." Another mystery.

"Mrs. Shelby Kincaid?" A man she didn't know walked forward and handed her a very small box. "I was told to give this to you personally." He turned and walked away.

"Wait a minute! Who are you? Who is this from?"

"I don't know." He shrugged. "A woman gave me a hundred bucks to deliver it to you. I should have charged her more. This place is like Fort Knox."

"A woman. Can you describe her?"

"Medium build, brown hair, middle age. Jeans and a T-shirt. Sneakers."

She questioned him for several minutes but could gain little more information.

"Lady, I didn't pay that much attention to her. She wasn't much to look at but when somebody offers me that much money to carry a little box three blocks, I don't ask questions."

"Three blocks. Thank you, sir. Get his name and number with some ID to confirm it," she told Joanie quietly, then watched them both leave.

Shelby knew it would be smart to have the box go through an X-ray before opening it, but she made no move to call the police department. There was something very small inside, it rattled just a little.

HOW TO VALIDATE YOUR
EDITOR'S FREE GIFT!
"THANK YOU"

1 Peel off the FREE GIFTS SEAL from front cover. Place it in the space provided at right. This automatically entitles you to receive two free books and an exciting surprise gift.

2 Send back this card and you'll get 2 Love Inspired® Suspense books. These books have a combined cover price of $9.98 in the U.S. and $11.98 in Canada, but they are yours to keep absolutely FREE!

3 There's no catch. You're under no obligation to buy anything. We charge nothing—ZERO—for your first shipment. And you don't have to make any minimum number of purchases—not even one!

4 We call this line Love Inspired® Suspense because every other month you'll receive books that are filled with riveting inspirational suspense. These tales of intrigue and romance feature Christian characters facing challenges to their faith and to their lives! You'll like the convenience of getting them delivered to your home well before they are in stores. And you'll love our discount prices, too!

5 We hope that after receiving your free books you'll want to remain a subscriber. But the choice is yours—to continue or cancel, anytime at all! So why not take us up on our invitation, with no risk of any kind. You'll be glad you did!

6 And remember. . . just for validating your Editor's Free Gift Offer, we'll send you 2 books and a gift, *ABSOLUTELY FREE!*

YOURS FREE!

*We'll send you a fabulous surprise gift
absolutely FREE, simply for accepting
our no-risk offer!*

YES!

PLACE
FREE GIFTS
SEAL
HERE

I have placed my Editor's "thank you" Free Gifts seal in the space provided above. Please send me the 2 FREE books and gift for which I qualify. I understand that I am under no obligation to purchase anything further, as explained on the opposite page.

323 IDL EE42   **123 IDL EE52**

FIRST NAME	LAST NAME

ADDRESS

APT.#	CITY

STATE/PROV.   ZIP/POSTAL CODE

Thank You!

► DETACH AND MAIL CARD TODAY!! ►

© 1997 STEEPLE HILL BOOKS

(LISUS-EC-06)

Steeple Hill Reader Service™ – Here's How It Works:

Accepting your 2 free books and gift places you under no obligation to buy anything. You may keep the books and gift and return the shipping statement marked "cancel." If you do not cancel, about a month later we will send you 4 additional books and bill you just $3.99 each in the U.S., or $4.74 each in Canada, plus 25¢ shipping & handling per book and applicable taxes if any.* That's the complete price, and — compared to cover prices of $4.99 each in the U.S. and $5.99 each in Canada — it's quite a bargain! You may cancel at any time, but if you choose to continue, every other month we'll send you 4 more books, which you may either purchase at the discount price...or return to us and cancel your subscription.

*Terms and prices subject to change without notice. Sales tax applicable in N.Y.
Canadian residents will be charged applicable provincial taxes and GST.

Tossing away her inhibitions, she used her fingernail to slit open the tape then lifted the lid. She stared at the small microcassette lying inside. A strange woman had sent her a tape recording.

Using a tissue she lifted out the cassette and put it into the small Dictaphone she sometimes used. Taking a deep breath, she hit the play button.

Daniel's voice, whisper soft, emerged.

"I have to do this. You know that. There have been enough questions, enough problems with customs. I don't want to alert them that anything funny's going on with this shipment. Just act as if it's the usual Finders, Inc. merchandise and we should be okay."

Nothing more.

Shelby replayed the tape several times and each time the knife plunged a little deeper into her heart. So Daniel had taken the items? It had to be him. But had he also taken Aimee?

She grabbed the phone and found herself dialing Tim's number. On the sixth ring she hung up, remembering he'd told her he wasn't going to be there. She stared at the small cassette for several minutes before she reached a decision. This had to stop. Her doubts were running rampant, mostly because she was so afraid for Aimee. Maybe she was wrong again. Maybe there was a rational reason for the words on this tape.

Tim's words echoed inside her brain. He'd reminded her that if she believed in God, she had to trust Him. But trust Him to do what? Maybe God had sent her this tape so she would know who to investigate first. But Daniel—her heart protested at the betrayal.

Her thoughts flew to the man who'd helped her through the past horrible hours. If he were here, Tim would know what to do. Tim would press on, dig out whatever information there was and make his decision based on the truth.

So would she. That decision made, Shelby pulled up every bit of research she could find on Daniel McCullough. There was nothing new. Russ had been right, he'd been to Tokyo several times, but that was because of business. Maybe it was time to let Russ vent and really listen to what he said. She hit her intercom button, asked Joanie to find Russ and send him in.

He ambled in several minutes later. Shelby wasn't fooled by his nonchalance. She could read wary suspicion in the back of his eyes.

"Good morning, Russ. Have a seat."

He sat, but not one sinew of his body relaxed. "Good morning, Shelby. I am happy to see you back behind that desk. I wish it was for another reason."

"Me, too." There was no easy way to voice her suspicions, so Shelby got right to the point. "Several times you've made insinuations about Daniel. I'd like to know why, Russ."

His eyes widened fractionally before he glanced down at his boots, hiding his expression from her. "You have found something?" he murmured.

"I've found nothing. I just wondered why you'd turn on someone you once called friend."

"I do not turn on him." That brought his head up. His gray eyes snapped sparks of blue lightning. "Daniel is my friend. But I am concerned about him, about what is happening here, with the company. Perhaps I should not have said what I did about Grant's death. I know too well that Grant liked his little secrets, that he answered to no one. Daniel could not have stopped him from coming back that night if Grant had wished otherwise. I know this and yet…"

Shelby knew that infinitesimal little pause was planned. "Go on."

"Always Daniel prefers the silent way. When we used to go on missions he would always favor the sneak attack." He tapped his forefinger against his leg. "Me, I prefer the full frontal assault. Grant was our mediator. He could blend logic and emotion and come up with a plan. I miss him."

Shelby swallowed around the lump in her throat. "Has Callie found anything new?" she asked. She would not be distracted from what she needed to know.

"I do not believe we have a solid lead. The pawnshop owner remembered only that a woman brought in the doll."

A woman. The hair on Shelby's arms rose. A woman had sent the tape recording also.

"Callie questioned him many times but always he remembers an average woman of average age, height and weight, in average clothes. That is of no help."

His look of sheer disgust almost made her laugh. As if anyone would dare to keep their identity hidden from Russ.

"You said Daniel had gone to Tokyo. How did you come to know that?"

Russ made a face. "I had him followed."

"What?"

"I know this is not the accepted way, Shelby, but I felt in my heart that something was wrong. Daniel was most secretive whenever I asked him anything. I wanted to start an investigation on the missing warehouse items but he forbade it, said he would handle it in his own way." Russ stretched out his hands. "You know how he works. Every *I* it must be dotted, every *T* perfectly crossed. He is like the Galapagos turtle, poking along but making no progress. Eventually I began to suspect he was not always telling me the truth." He paused, frowned at her. "This will hurt you, but I must speak my doubts. I do not think that Grant's death was accidental. I have checked the records—before Daniel sealed them. The fire could never have gotten so large unless the suppression system was not working properly."

He waited, as if he expected her to burst into tears. Shelby cataloged every nuance while keeping her own face impassive. "Yes, I'd heard that."

"Then you think he was murdered, also." Russ muttered something she couldn't understand. His face contorted into an ugly mask. "Why is it that I am not told of these things? Always I am kept on the outside."

"I'm not keeping you out of anything. I've only been back a couple of days. I will not condemn Daniel without knowing more. At the moment I'm interested in your thoughts on him."

"You do not care how Grant died?" He shook his head. "This I do not believe."

"I can't do anything about that, Russ. But I can and will find my daughter. Can you help me with that?"

"But of course! I do anything. Only tell me what." His eyes widened. "Ah, I see. You suspect Daniel. So I will tell you what I know." He tented his fingers together, then began. "He has many secrets. No one knows where he disappears to. Sometimes a call comes…he leaves. When he returns he has no answers. He pokes through the warehouse at odd times, after hours. He orders up many case files to be taken to his office but will not talk about what he is looking for."

Russ didn't know anything. He was merely voicing suspicions and Shelby had enough of her own.

"Do you know anything about Grant's last case?" she asked.

Russ blinked, but otherwise she could not read his expression.

"He never spoke to me about it, Shelby. I do not know specifics."

Was that the truth?

"He was searching for a Fabergé egg." She watched his face.

Russ whistled. "Ah! A well-heeled client then."

"I don't know that. I do know that Grant made a notation that he'd found the egg and therefore I assume he put it in the warehouse. Unfortunately, we can't seem to find it."

"Do you want me to look?"

She shook her head, frustrated by the lack of answers she'd found.

"No, thanks. I've already done that. I'd prefer it if you concentrated your efforts on finding Aimee. There has got to be a lead somewhere."

"Yes, I think this, also." He stared at her for a moment, then his eyes widened. "You think there is a connection between this egg and the little Aimee," he whispered.

Shock, surprise, something else—his eyes narrowed and Shelby could read no more.

"I don't know," she repeated. "It's just a theory and I'm trying not to discount anything. I want my daughter back."

"Of course." He leaned forward. "I have encountered one discrepancy in the policewoman—Natalie? —in her report."

"Yes?" Perhaps Tim was right. Maybe Natalie hadn't done her job as well as she ought.

"There was one neighbor who said that the night of the little Aimee's kidnapping he saw a car come up the street and park. It was there until he went to bed."

"No one mentioned this! Maybe it was the kidnapper."

"I am checking. I have already told the police what I think of their sloppy work."

Shelby scanned the desk, the file, the tape player, noted Russ's curious stare. Everything was a muddle. She didn't know which way to look, where to center her attention most. She needed to talk this out with someone, but not Russ. He couldn't be impartial about Daniel and that's what she needed most right now, someone to tell her whether her instincts were on target or way out.

Tim.

"Keep checking, Russ." She rose as a hint, wanting him to leave. "Maybe you'll find the clue the police didn't."

"I will." He rose, also, glanced at the file she'd only half covered. "You have work to do. I will leave."

"Thank you for coming."

"I will help however I can, Shelby. I want the little girl back where she belongs—with you." He half bowed, then left.

Shelby stared at the door for a few minutes, then returned her gaze to the papers in front of her struggling to mentally organize what she knew into some kind of pattern. But nothing made sense.

Daniel, Russ—she now found herself suspicious about everyone at Finders. Even Joanie, who brought in the day's mail with a message that Tim was on the phone, seemed to be hiding something. And that was crazy. Shelby picked up the phone.

"You're back already?" she asked. One glance at the clock told her more time had passed than she realized.

"Yes. You sound…odd. Is something wrong?"

She needed a sounding board, someone to help her put everything she'd learned into perspective. Tim would have no strong feelings about either man. Maybe he could help.

"Shelby?"

"I'm just leaving, Tim. But I wondered if you'd mind coming over to the house. I want to talk to you about something."

"Sure. In fact, I'll wander around the rose garden while I wait for you. My specialist asked me the names of some of your roses and I think I must have gotten the names wrong because he sure didn't recognize them and he's big into roses." He paused, waited a moment. "Is that okay?"

"Of course. Look as much as you like. I'll be home

shortly." Once Tim had hung up, Shelby began stuffing the files into her briefcase. At the last minute she tucked in the tape recording. She programmed her new codes into the computer. When her office was secure, she left, anxious to spread everything out on Grant's battered old desk and try to make some sense of it.

The officer wasn't at her door when she arrived, but came ambling around the corner from the kitchen as she shrugged out of her jacket.

"Nothing yet, ma'am," he told her around a mouthful of Esmeralda's apple crumb cake. "Sorry."

She nodded, checked the mail. Nothing significant. But there was a video case sitting beside it. "What's this?" she asked the guard.

"Beats me."

Since he didn't seem overly concerned, Shelby picked it up and carried it through to the den. Maybe it was one of the many she'd taken of Aimee, though she was certain she'd labeled all of them. And put them in the armoire.

A wash of yearning swept over her to see Aimee's sweet face, to hear her treble voice once more. Shelby tossed her briefcase into a chair and opened the armoire. She slid the tape inside the player, sat down on the cozy sofa she and Grant had often shared and hit the play button.

It was a video of Aimee all right. But Shelby hadn't taken it.

The kidnapper had.

TEN

The scream shook him to his core.

Tim raced inside, followed the cop through the house to the den. Shelby stood in front of a white sofa, her face drained of all color as she stared at a black television screen.

"Shelby?" He waved the cop back, crouched beside her, folding her hands in his. They were icy-cold. "What's wrong?"

"The tape. Look at the tape," she whispered.

She'd been watching something. He glanced around, saw the remote lying at her feet and picked it up. He hit Play. A picture of Aimee sitting on a park bench appeared. She was grinning as if having the time of her life. Her spun-gold hair shone in the sunlight, her blue eyes worry-free. She pointed to a newspaper lying at her feet. He froze the video, read the date. Today's.

Behind him the cop cursed. A moment later he was outside the door, rattling orders into his radio.

Tim took another look at Shelby, pressed the play button once more, upping the sound.

"Hi, Mommy. Isn't this fun?" Aimee flickered her fingers in a wave. "I love you, Mommy. Bye."

The screen grew snowy. The presentation was over.

Tears streamed down Shelby's face. She stared at him. Finally two words slipped out.

"She's alive."

"Yes, she is. Now we have to figure out how to get her back."

Moments later the house was teeming with police. Several hours passed before things quieted. Natalie finally took possession of the video, but not before Shelby asked to speak to her. Since her hand remained in Tim's, since she stood beside him and didn't ask him to leave, he remained in place while the distraught mother posed her question.

"Why didn't you tell me there was a witness, Natalie?" she demanded.

He wasn't certain he'd heard correctly. Witness? What witness? Tim glanced at Shelby, watched her eyes narrow. He followed her gaze, focused on the other woman who suddenly seemed very uncomfortable.

"He wasn't a witness. He simply saw a car."

"A car that sat by the curb for a long time."

"That isn't a witness." Natalie's thin lips set in a tight line. "Besides, this is a police investigation. I'm not obliged to inform you of any details."

"Oh, come on!" Tim stared at her in disbelief. "This woman's child is missing. I'm sure that your police chief and the media would both be surprised to hear that you don't think you have a duty to keep the child's mother 'informed.'"

Natalie flushed, changed tactics. "I'm sorry, of course I want you to know what we're working on, Shelby. Forgive me. I'm just at my wit's end with this case. I haven't slept very well."

She hadn't slept well? Tim could hardly believe what he was hearing.

"Is there a witness or not?" he asked, glaring at her while his arm moved to shelter Shelby. Where did she find the strength to go on?

"A man saw a car sitting by the curb the night of Aimee's abduction. He didn't see a person, he doesn't know when the car left and he didn't get a license plate. He thinks the car was black. Or blue. Or it might have been brown." Natalie lifted one eyebrow as if to ask what he thought of that.

He wanted to yell at her, demand answers, demand she get a grip on herself and act like a professional. But Shelby was tired. He felt her sag against him and knew she needed some peace.

"Is there anything else you need to know, Shel?"

She shook her head, but her eyes held Natalie's like a tractor beam. "In the future, please do *keep me informed* of any and all leads you may find. Otherwise I'm going to ask for someone else to be assigned."

"Of course I will. Please, accept my apology again."

"I'll see you to the door." With one glance at Shelby, he removed his arm and escorted the policewoman to the front door, lips pressed tight to stem the diatribe he suppressed with difficulty.

"I wasn't trying to be unkind," she murmured, one hand on the side of the door holding it open. "I am busy and it's easy to overlook things."

Tim held his tongue.

"It's not an easy case," she defended.

"For her, especially. Good night." He waited until she'd walked out the front door, shut it behind her. The on-duty cop who'd been left offered a half smile of understanding.

"The ice princess isn't easy to relate to, is she? She's only been here a couple of weeks but most of the guys have already given up trying to be friendly to her. She just shuts everybody down with that glacial glare."

"Natalie has only been here a couple of weeks?" Tim didn't know why but he'd assumed Natalie had been in her position for ages.

"She transferred in. Don't remember from where, but the department is always short of staff. From what I heard she asked to be assigned to this case."

"Why?" Might as well learn all he could.

"Beats me. Don't think she knows anyone here, so maybe it's to keep her busy."

"Yeah. Maybe. Thanks."

"No problem. I hope we hear something soon. I hate missing kids cases."

"Me, too." Tim walked back into the den, his mind processing what he'd learned.

"Is she gone?"

He nodded.

"I want to show you something." Shelby rose, picked up her briefcase and in a matter of moments a voice filled the room.

"Isn't that—"

"Daniel. Yes." She told him everything that had happened.

Tim listened without speaking, hoping he could somehow help.

"Russ has made his doubts about Daniel known to me many times. I've always discounted them as jealousy." Shelby gnawed at the tip of her oval nail. "But maybe he has a reason to be suspicious. Maybe I've missed something important, Tim."

"Like what?"

"I don't know. I feel like I'm in a maze, like there's something I'm supposed to learn or figure out and I can't quite grasp it."

He knew exactly what she was talking about. "Looking for the lesson, I call it."

Shelby frowned in confusion. He smiled. She looked exactly as he must have when he first saw the article.

"I was reading something today that gave me a new and

different perspective on how God works. Remember in the New Testament where it talks about the fruit of the Spirit?"

"Yes, though I must say I've never felt like I've been blessed with any of it. Love, joy, peace, patience—they're wonderful descriptions of Jesus but they seem to come and go on a fleeting basis in my life."

"Because you're learning and that takes time. The article I was reading said that God helps us develop the fruits in our lives by allowing us to go through things in which our natural nature is to do exactly the opposite." She was looking at him oddly so Tim hurried to elaborate. "Think of it this way. How did you teach Aimee patience?"

"By making her wait for things, though she didn't like it much."

"Who does? But getting angry about waiting doesn't help get her what she wants. Same thing with peace—how would we even know what it is if we hadn't gone through chaotic and confusing times and learned how to trust God to get us through. Exactly the opposite of situations that we want, but in them we learn what we most need—how to become more like Him."

"So you think God is trying to teach me something by letting Aimee be kidnapped?"

"I think He's using her kidnapping to perfect a work He's already begun. Remember, God works all things together for good. He can take this horrible thing and rework it into something we can't imagine, but we won't learn the lesson unless we keep our focus on Him, see what He's showing us."

"I've never heard you talk like this before," she murmured.

"I've never thought like this before. I always had this voice in the back of my head telling me that God was punishing me, that bad things happened because He didn't care for me or because I'd done something wrong." He felt a surge of hope within him, just as he had this afternoon. If only he could explain it properly. If only he could help her grasp what he'd barely glimpsed.

"Go on."

"Aimee was taken. We can get angry, we can fuss and fume, we can fret and worry—but it's a waste of time. God knew aeons ago that someone would take Aimee so He made a plan. After all, He loves her more than we do. He has something in mind, a way to make this horrible event fit into His plan because that plan is bigger than anything we feel and experience."

"So what is the purpose in this?" she demanded.

"I don't know that yet. Maybe I never will. But the thing is, there's a reason. It's not a random act or some isolated incident, but it is part of God's plan or He would have stopped it."

Silence reigned in the room for several minutes during which Shelby mulled over what he'd said. Finally she looked up.

"I'm getting it," she murmured, and lifted a leather-bound book off the sofa table behind her. "Listen, Grant wrote this. I couldn't figure it out and maybe I still haven't but I'm beginning to understand." She read:

> I think the beauty of the roses comes because of me—
> I feed and water them regularly. I trim the shoots, I protect
> them. But I fool only myself because the roses that grow
> strong and vigorous—the best blooms, come from those
> plants that withstand the elements, the drought, the bugs.
> My newest one, Deep Secret, will be like that. I've dug
> it out from its native soil, planted it too near the house
> where the hot sun of the day will scorch it. But it will
> survive. It is strong and hardy, it will adapt.

"Adapt." He nodded. "Yes. He knew that bush would do all right because he'd prepared the soil for it, just as God filters everything that happens to us."

"So what's my next step?" Shelby glanced down at the documents. "I don't know where to turn."

"Then we pray." He dragged a chair near the desk, grasped her hand in his and bowed his head. Though embarrassed by his pitiful prayer, he offered it with a needy heart, desperate to know the next step in this journey of trust. "For we ask it in Your name," he whispered.

"Amen." Shelby smiled at him, her fingers squeezed his, sharing the peace of that moment. "Thank you," she whispered.

"My pleasure." The ache to hold her, to soothe away the lines that had formed around her eyes; the need to make her world right again assailed him. But he was not God and this was not the right time. Which made it seem strange when she reached out and lifted a long blond hair from his shoulder.

"I take it the receptionist at your doctor's is a blonde," Shelby teased, holding the long curling strand in front of his face. Then she dropped it into the garbage brimming with papers.

"I didn't notice," he told her, wishing he had the courage to explain that only one particular blonde interested him and she was right there beside him.

"Of course you didn't." She lifted the handset of the ringing phone, her lips tilted in a quirky smile which soon drained away. "Hello, Daniel. Of course. Come right away. Actually, I have something I want to talk with you about, also. See you then."

Tim waited, wondering what had happened now.

"Daniel's on his way here. He says he needs to speak to me immediately." She lifted her troubled gaze to meet his. "I'm going to ask him about this file, the tape, everything."

"I think that's a good idea." He stepped back so she could pass him. "There's no point in killing yourself with doubts. You need to ask him and see his reaction." He wanted to say more, to tell her he would be right by her side to hear the explanations, that he wouldn't go until she told him to. But Esmeralda rapped on the door before he could figure out the right way to say it.

"Daniel's here. Says it's important."

Daniel strode in, dropped his briefcase on the floor and grabbed Shelby's hands in one motion. He wrapped her in a hug. "I've found something," he told her, his face more alive than Tim had ever seen it.

"Daniel, I—" Shelby withdrew herself, her face troubled.

"Let me explain." He sank down on a sofa, but his eyes danced with excitement. "I never told you, never wanted to tell you, but from shortly after Grant's death I've had my suspicions that the fire at our warehouse was no accident. I think it was set deliberately and I think it was meant to stop Grant's investigations."

"I see." Shelby sat down across from him, glanced at Tim, motioned him to join them. "Have you taken your suspicions to the police?"

"I tried early on. They wouldn't listen. So I've been doing some investigations on my own. I thought Grant's last client was a woman named Marta Krakow, who emigrated here from Austria many years ago. I now believe the client was this woman's niece." He paused, stared at her.

"A month before he died Grant was in Austria," Shelby murmured.

"Yes. And not only Austria but he also visited several Eastern European countries. He has notes about finding a Fabergé egg. I think he brought it back here."

"Then where is it? In the warehouse?"

Daniel shook his head. "I've been looking for ages. It's not there. I've personally investigated every case the company was handling around that time. Everyone thinks it was an overhaul of company procedures for the new man, and I let them think it."

"Why?"

"Because we have a mole, a leak or a thief."

"Do you know who it is?"

He shook his head, the frustration evident. "No."

"I want you to listen to something." Shelby rose, played the tape recorder. "What is this about?"

"It's part of a cover I used to find out if certain employees who had access to the warehouse were prepared to bypass our regulations. Where did you get it?"

She explained the tape's delivery, then showed him the file she'd taken from his office.

"You thought I was up to something illegal? That I would betray you? I would never do that. I'm sorry you don't know that by now." He shook his head and the sad look disappeared. "I haven't got time to deal with this right now. I've got a lead, Shelby. An actual lead!"

"Maybe you should tell us." Tim saw the surprise cover Daniel's face and knew he'd forgotten his presence.

"Yes, of course." Daniel resumed his seat, Shelby followed. He leaned toward her. "Listen. Last night I figured out that Grant had a second file—one that had information about Marta's niece. She told him her aunt was once part of the European aristocracy. It's not clear why Grant went looking for this Fabergé egg—maybe it was a family heirloom the niece wanted from her long-lost aunt. We've done that before."

"At least a hundred times." Shelby smiled at him.

"Yes. But the thing is, I ran a check with immigration. Marta Krakow listed no relatives on her forms."

"So the story is a fake? The niece is an imposter."

"Can't tell yet." He grinned. "But I found Marta Krakow. She's in a nursing home where she is being kept sedated, supposedly because of her dementia."

"Why supposedly?" Tim asked, intrigued in spite of his determination to remain an observer.

"Because the niece has disappeared."

"So we'll go talk to this Marta woman."

"It's not as easy as that, Shelby."

Tim felt the other man's scrutiny, saw the way he glanced at Shelby, one eyebrow tilted as if to ask a question.

"You can say anything in front of Tim."

"Very well." Daniel hunched forward, his expressive face in shadow. "I'm being followed."

Tim chanced a look at Shelby, saw a flicker of surprise in her eyes.

"I want to talk to this Marta, find out if she knows why Grant was tracking the egg, learn anything she can tell me about this so-called niece. But I'm afraid that if I do, I'll endanger her. That's the last thing I want."

"Your specialty has always been disguises, Daniel. Couldn't you do something in that line—pretend to be someone else?"

"I could." His forehead creased as he thought it over. "The thing is, I can't figure out who's tracking me. They've been through my place, gone over my car. With the problems at Finders, I'm not sure I want to risk endangering someone else. Maybe Marta really does have dementia."

Shelby was thinking about something else, Tim could see it in the way she stared at the floor, one finger tapping a rhythm against her knee.

"Daniel, the file I took indicates that you think Grant's death wasn't an accident, that his death was deliberate and planned. Why?"

"Because of the sabotage on our suppression system," he answered. "That wasn't a last-minute thing. Someone knew enough about Finders to set an incendiary device in another area." He nodded at her gasp of surprise. "I found a trip wire hidden behind some crates on the sixth floor. According to our records that fire is what tripped the alarm. But Grant was in the warehouse, the fire that supposedly killed him was in the warehouse. Yet that alarm never went off until four minutes after the other one. Why?"

"How long have you known this?"

"Several months." Daniel's eyes begged her to understand. "I tried to talk to you so many times, but you didn't want to hear, Shel. I didn't blame you for that, but neither could I just let Grant's death go. I have to know the truth. He was my best friend. I owe him that."

Tim saw the tears trembling on the ends of her lashes and felt a stab straight to his heart. Shelby had loved her husband, since he'd known her it had been Grant this and Grant that. He was fooling himself to think she had any feelings for him. She just needed a friend.

"But why kill him, Daniel?"

"My theory? The arsonists knew Grant had found the egg and they didn't want it returned to its rightful owner. They still don't. I have a hunch taking Aimee was supposed to draw me off my investigations. Sending you the tape would have made you suspicious of me, maybe they hoped you'd fire me. Then my investigation would have to end."

"I came to that conclusion myself."

Silence echoed around the room. Tim watched Daniel for a few minutes, but as usual his gaze returned to Shelby. She was arguing with herself over something. Her blue-green eyes swirled with her thoughts. Suddenly she took a deep breath and rose.

"Your investigations aren't going to stop, Daniel. They're going full speed ahead. I intend to talk to this Marta and learn whatever it is she knows."

"How?"

"I haven't figured that out yet. I need to think on it for a while."

If it was a hint, it was a good one. Daniel rose immediately. So did Tim.

"It's late. We all need some sleep. We can talk about this tomorrow. In the meantime, Shelby, you can ask me anything. If you want to fire me or suspend me, that's fine. I don't care about me. But I have to know what happened to Grant, I have to figure out why he was killed and how it ties in to Aimee."

"You're sure it ties together?" Her eyes bored into him.

"I'm sure. This morning I remembered that when I first started asking questions after the fire a message was left on my desk. It said to forget Grant's death or the same thing would happen to me. Things got hectic, then Aimee went missing—I forgot about it. But they have to be tied together. Otherwise nothing makes sense." He moved toward the door, pausing only when Shelby asked him to wait.

In as few words as possible she told him about the video that had been left.

"I'm no expert in kidnapping but it seems to me that someone wants you to know that she's alive, that she's fine. They didn't ask for ransom, but they took a chance getting that tape here. The question is who?" Daniel shook his head. "It's so strange."

"You're going to find something even stranger," Shelby told him. "I'm the one who's been tailing you. I had so many questions, Daniel, and I couldn't make sense of what I was learning. So for the last two days I've had you followed by Samantha Enderson."

"Oh." His pupils behind the black glasses grew huge.

"I know you and she were dating once, that you shut her down when she asked for that transfer." Shelby held up a hand. "You don't have to explain why. But I figured she'd be able to spot any irregularities in your behavior. Needless to say, she didn't."

"I couldn't put it through. She wasn't ready for a promotion, Shel. She's one of our top recovery agents, but she hasn't got enough experience yet."

"Are you sure that's all it was?"

"I'm sure." He nodded. "Sam's made it pretty clear what she thinks of me. If she didn't find anything to incriminate me that's saying something."

"I authorized no one to go into your home, Daniel. I don't think Sam would do that without specific orders." She paused, waited for his nod of understanding. "As soon as I make a call, you won't be followed any longer. I'm sorry I doubted you again, Daniel."

"It doesn't matter, Shel. If it would help, you can have me followed all the time. But since you didn't send them into my place, I have to assume I have someone else tracking me. That makes it just as difficult to get to Marta."

"We'll think of something." She smiled, patted his arm. "Let's all pray about it tonight."

"Yes." He kissed her cheek, then left, his step lighter than it had been for days.

Tim couldn't make up his mind whether he should follow, or remain in case Shelby needed him.

"I'm so weary of these stupid suspicions," she mumbled, leading the way to the back patio. They'd barely seated themselves when Esmeralda came to bid them good-night.

"Rest well, sweetie," the older woman murmured as she hugged Shelby tightly.

"You, too." Shelby held her away, studied her tired face. "Do you need a break, some time off? There's not much to do here without—" She gulped, tried to smile. "Why don't you relax tomorrow?"

"I'll do nothing of the kind. This is my place, Shelby Kincaid, right here waiting for Aimee. I don't aim to be *resting* when she comes home for some of my chocolate tower cake." Esmeralda stomped back inside the house. A few moments later the front door slammed closed.

"Whoops." Shelby laid back in the lounger, stared out over the rose garden. "I used to be quite tactful, you know."

"She understands." Tim walked over to the edge of the patio, stared at the rosebush sitting beside it. Deep Secret. The one Grant had transplanted. "This one's going to flower soon. Look at the color of the buds. Rich burgundy red. I've never seen such a color." He leaned over, smelled the fragrance that rose upward from the tight buds.

"Yes." She sounded tentative, as if she wanted to say something and couldn't quite force herself. "It was the last one Grant planted."

Grant again. It was hard not to be jealous of him. Tim took his seat.

"I should be getting home. It's late and you're tired."

"Don't go yet." She turned her head, met his stare. "You promised that sometime you'd tell me how you got your burns," she murmured. "How about now?"

The past. For both of them the past kept intruding on the present. For her they were pleasant happy memories, but his were dimmed by anger and pain.

"Please tell me, Tim," she murmured and he heard the tears lurking at the back of her voice. "I need to think about something else tonight."

He couldn't deny her, no matter how much it hurt to go through it again.

"It happened three years ago," he began as the familiar vine of pain inched around his heart. "My wife and I—her name was Sara—were coming home from a gala evening I'd arranged to garner support for the museum. It was raining, a steady grey drizzle with a kind of clinging mist that wouldn't abate. She hadn't been feeling well and we'd left early."

"Oh." She sounded surprised.

"To tell the truth I was mad about that—there were some very important people there and I wanted to touch base with them. But Sara begged me to go with her and I could never say no to Sara, so we left."

He paused, leaned back and closed his eyes. The memories enveloped him like a smothering blanket and he heard himself speaking fast, trying to get it all out.

"It was a stupid needless accident caused by a drunk driver. He'd hit a truck loaded with petrol—gas, and he was trying to flee the scene when he hit us. I was thrown out, but Sara— she was caught in the wreckage. Then there was fire, burning hot, racing across the pavement. I tried to get her out, I pulled the door as hard as I could, but it was no use. It wouldn't open. I crawled inside, thinking I'd free her from the other side. It was hot, so terribly hot. Then there was a bang." He gulped, squeezed his eyes tight to stop the pain. It didn't work. He touched his cheek with his fingertips, felt the wetness.

"I must have passed out. When I came to I was in a hospital and the pain was excruciating. I kept asking about Sara, but I guess I made no sense. A week later I learned she'd died, our baby with her. We had only a month left till she was to be born." He squeezed the words out, his throat tight and hot. "Sara had been healthy all through the pregnancy, except for that one night. We'd decided to name our daughter Felicity."

He couldn't go on. He closed his eyes, drew deep cleansing breaths, the way he'd helped Sara breathe in Lamaze class. Then he stared at Shelby.

"I've asked myself the same question for three years. Why did she have to get sick that night? Why did we have to be on the road at that particular time? Why did I have to have my daughter ripped away before I could even hold her."

"I'm sorry."

He jerked to his feet, strode to the edge of the deck, his hands fisted at his sides. He barely heard her as the anger and the loss burst free of the place he'd always locked them away. "Why did God do that to me?"

"Oh, Tim." She moved behind him, wrapped her arms around him and held him. "I'm so sorry."

When at last he had himself under control, Tim turned around, felt her arms drop away. "It's not your fault, Shelby."

Her fingers grasped his, clung. He needed to finish it, get rid of the anger. Maybe then he could understand why.

"I never even got to go to the funerals because I was out for most of the first month. Either drugged up or in so much pain that I couldn't deal with reality. When I did know, I just wanted to crawl into the grave with them. I'd been so worried about my career, about getting a chance at a bigger, better museum. As if that mattered one whit."

"You can't blame yourself. Bad things happen, remember?"

"Yes." Summoning all his strength he shoved the memories away. "I couldn't go back there, not even if I could have returned to work. I knew I'd see her there, keep dreaming of the face I'd never get to see. Eventually I was sent here to a skin specialist—the best there is, they said. I met you and Aimee after the first consultation." He smiled, touched her cheek.

"I'd never been able to be around kids before but Aimee wasn't like any child I'd ever known. She had this…intuition, I guess you'd say. She didn't ask about my burns or the bandages. She asked about my books, dull musty old books a kid of her age couldn't possibly be interested in."

"So you started making up stories to keep her interested."

"Yes." He felt a grin itching at his lips as he recalled that fair-haired sprite perched on his sofa. "Aimee always wants answers. Her questions kept me digging for ways to help her understand the history behind the pictures she saw in the books. One day she said she wanted to make a book. I got on the computer, started writing down one of the stories I'd told her. Aimee corrected my mistakes then decided to do the illustrations. It was our game."

And now Aimee was gone, too.

"You probably think I'm an idiot for blaming God." He stared straight into her eyes, saw only compassion. "It didn't start that way. At first I just couldn't believe He'd allowed it to happen. He's God! Omnipotent, omniscient—I knew all that. But loving? I couldn't reconcile a loving God letting my child and my wife die that way. It was as if He had everything but He'd stolen the little I had."

"And now?" she whispered.

"I don't know anymore," he admitted, brushing the back of his hand against her hair. "If it hadn't happened, if I hadn't come here, I would never have met you or Aimee. I can't imagine life without either of you now."

Her beautiful eyes stared into his. Tim bent his head, touched his lips to hers. To his utter shock, she kissed him back as if she meant it. Her fingers crept around his neck as she moved closer. He wrapped his own arms around her and held her as he'd hold a precious jewel. Around them the spicy fragrance of almost-blooming roses filled the night air. He caught a whiff of the sweet flower fragrance Shelby wore, felt the silken brush of her curls against his face, the wonderful weight of her in his arms.

"No!" She pulled away, stepped backward. "I'm sorry Tim, but—"

Her hand had been against his cheek. Suddenly he understood.

"It's the scars, isn't it?" He knew how ugly they were, how terrible they felt. He might have a thousand surgeries but the damaged skin would never be completely erased. He'd never be handsome.

"No! It's not that at all. You're a wonderful man, Tim. A good friend for both me and Aimee. It's just—"

"Grant." Every fibre of his being groaned at the truth he'd known would always come between them. "It's Grant, isn't it?"

"Yes," she whispered, her voice broken. "I know he's dead. I know he won't ever come back. But I just can't…let him go. I loved him. He's my husband."

"I understand." He stepped away from her, moved into the shadows. He didn't look at her, didn't want to see the anguish on her face. He spoke softly, gently. "It's been over three years for me. I still miss Sara and our daughter, but I've had to move on without them. You aren't there yet."

She didn't say anything. And that was what hurt. He wanted her to protest, to deny what he'd said, to offer some other explanation. But Shelby didn't do that. All she did was repeat what she'd said before.

"I'm sorry."

"So am I." He turned, walked across the space to his own place. Just before he closed the gate he whispered, "Good night."

When he turned around, Shelby was gone.

ELEVEN

Shelby stood on the balcony of her bedroom, staring at the house next door. The lights had long since gone out. Tim was asleep.

Traitor! She felt the stab of those words as keenly as she had on the patio short hours before. How could she have truly loved her husband and yet allow herself to be attracted to another man? Not even a year had passed since Grant's death. What did that say? That she hadn't really loved him?

No. She knew that wasn't true. She'd loved Grant with every part of her heart. So why had she begun to feel things for another man, a man she barely knew and certainly didn't understand? A man who'd taken it upon himself to be there for her, to listen when she needed someone to talk to? A man who wasn't intimidated by her work?

But he wasn't Grant.

She veered away from that, thought about her daughter with Tim. How many times had Aimee run over to his house and interrupted a sad moment, or reminded him of what he'd lost? Yet Tim had never complained, never made her child feel unwanted. Instead he'd devised special stories for her, dreamed up innovative ways to teach her what he loved.

Tim Austen was an unusual man. Shelby had never thought

of him as remotely uncomfortable in his life, in spite of the ugly burns he bore. Until tonight.

Shelby sat on the balcony, her mind winging back to his face when she'd lifted away that blond hair. What had she surprised—guilt? Embarrassment? It almost seemed as if he wanted to hide something, but what was so secretive about a blond hair. It hadn't been her color. More of an ashen tone—like Aimee's.

The idea was working its way through her subconscious before she recognized it. *Tim must have recently been with Aimee.* But surely that was preposterous. The police had searched his home, found nothing. He wasn't the one who'd taken her.

Was he?

Oh, God, why do I always have these doubts? What is wrong with me that I'd suspect a man like him of stealing my child?

He'd lost his own daughter, been deprived of knowing the child whose birth he looked forward to. But that didn't mean he'd latch onto someone else, another child.

"He wouldn't do it. Not Tim."

The doorbell broke up the battle waging in her brain. The token police officer who'd been left at the front door had been removed late this afternoon. She was alone in the house.

Shelby wrapped herself in a thick terry housecoat and padded downstairs. She peeked through the security hole, saw Russ leaning against the door. Quickly she punched in her security code to disable the system, then unlocked the door.

"Russ? What are you doing here? It's very late."

"I know this." He glanced past her. "Are you alone?"

"Of course." She saw him shove his hands farther into his pockets. "Come into the den."

He followed her without saying a word. Once there he

couldn't seem to settle but went from one surface to the next, his fingers trailing along in an absentminded manner.

"Russ, I'm tired," she told him when several minutes had passed. "Please tell me why you're here."

"Yes, of course I shall do that. I am just…assembling my thoughts." He flopped down on the sofa, thrust his booted feet out in front. "This man who lives next door—how well do you know him?"

"Tim? Well enough to know he didn't take Aimee. Besides, I had Daniel run a check on him. He's clear."

"Is he?" Russ rose to his feet. "Then I should be leaving."

"Wait a minute! You can't come in here and ask about him, then just leave. Why are you asking? What has happened?"

"I make the mistake. Do not worry."

"Don't worry? You've got to be kidding." She told him about the tape. "I am worried, Russ. It seems like a psycho move to take my daughter, send a picture of her happily playing, but not to ask for ransom."

"Your neighbor, where was he when this video arrived?"

"He was in the garden. I'd asked him to meet me there."

"So he could have placed the video on the table, then gone back outside. It is possible, no?"

"No! I mean, yes, of course it's possible. But it didn't happen. Tim didn't take Aimee."

"Are you so sure?" Russ sat down again, but this time on the edge of the sofa, next to her chair. "Your oh so kind neighbor, he is recovering from burns, yes?"

She nodded.

"Even so." Russ's voice dropped. "He got these burns in an accident when his wife died. She was pregnant with his child."

"I know all this. He told me."

"Indeed." Russ's black eyes snapped. "Did he also tell you he underwent psychiatric care? Did your oh so kind friend mention that he was ordered to stay away from the children's ward in the hospital because he removed a child from her room without authorization?"

"No." Shelby stared at him as the niggling doubting voice grew louder. "He didn't tell me that," she whispered, her gaze flying to the trash basket where she'd tossed the hair.

"Your Tim Austen was fascinated with the little Aimee, yes? He spent much time with her?"

"Yes, he did. But he never hurt her. Not once. He told her stories, they played games. That's all."

"Perhaps that is not all. Perhaps he had another reason for becoming so friendly, like a kindly father. Perhaps he has her secreted away. The doctors tell me that in such a tragedy sometimes the mind plays tricks and substitutes another child for the one that died."

"But the police searched his house."

"If he took her, I do not think he would keep her at his house. It is too close here for one thing."

"What you're saying scares me." But he could be right. What if Russ was right? "I found a hair on his jacket this evening. A long blond one. It could have been Aimee's."

"Did you keep it?"

"Yes. Why?"

"Get it." When she didn't immediately move, he burst to his feet, paced in front of her. "Please, Shelby. We must know the truth. I will take this blond hair to the lab, have it analyzed along with one from the little Aimee's hairbrush. We will see the truth."

"Know the truth," she corrected absently. "But Russ, it could have fallen there any of the times Aimee was at his place." A thought occurred. "Except that I know she spilled chocolate on that particular jacket. She told me last week that she made a big mess and that we should pay for the dry cleaning."

"So the hair would not still be there, or it would show signs of the cleaning process." He tilted back on his heels, waiting for her to move.

Shelby rose, walked to the desk and picked out the hair from the trash basket. She placed it inside an envelope, handed it to him.

"I'll have to get one of hers from her room."

"I shall wait." Russ remained where he was, his eyes on her.

Shelby hurried up the stairs, into Aimee's room.

"Please, Lord, don't let it be Tim. Please make those hairs different. Please." She lifted several strands from the hot pink hairbrush and carried them back down the stairs. "Not Tim," she whispered before she pushed open the den door.

Russ was standing where she'd left him. Shelby placed the hairs inside another envelope, marked it as Aimee's with the date and time. Then she licked it shut.

"Can you take it in right away?"

"Of course. This cannot wait. But for now it would be best if you kept silent about the hair. If he has taken her, he might be afraid that he will be found out. We do not want him to run or we may never find the little Aimee." His gaze narrowed. "You must play the part now, Shelby. The grieving mother must show no change in her relationship to her kindly neighbor. For the child's sake you must be very careful."

"I know." She walked with him to the front door. "Please tell them to hurry. And don't say where the other hair came from. I don't want anyone to know. Ask the lab to phone me directly as soon as the results are in. Then I'll decide what to do."

"As you wish." Russ bent, brushed her cheek with his cold lips. "Do not worry, Shelby. We will find her."

"Yes." She closed the door quickly, then stood beside a window watching as he drove away. *Please don't let it be Tim.*

The prayer seemed weak, rather silly. What did it matter why Tim had taken her? What mattered was getting Aimee back.

Shelby waited half an hour before she phoned the lab.

"How long for the DNA tests on those hairs Russ brought in?" she asked.

"I've got a machine down. Can't start till tomorrow morning at the earliest."

She left instructions to be notified immediately then hung up and climbed the stairs once more. Back on the balcony she peered into the night sky, searching for some sign of hope.

"Who can I trust?" she whispered when there was no reassuring sign.

I'm here. I love you. I will never leave you.

Tim had talked about God, about Him using the darkest hours to teach us things we needed to learn. How could he have done that if he'd taken Aimee?

"Please help me. I'm so afraid."

Only believe.

"I finished it, Shelby." Tim stood at the end of the patio watching her, admiring the way the morning sun glinted off her fair head. His joy in the morning faded to a frown as she whirled around and stared at him, eyes wide with shock—and something else.

"Pardon?" The sound grated harsh and painful from her throat. Her eyes were red. She'd been weeping.

"What's wrong? Did something happen last night?" He waited for her to explain while trying to suppress the gnawing feeling that something wasn't quite right. He couldn't stop himself from touching her shoulder but she jerked away as if she'd been burned. Tim stepped backward. Something was very wrong. "Will you tell me, please?"

"Nothing to tell," she whispered as one hand dashed across

her face, removing the streaks the tears had left. "Just having a bad moment."

Remembering Grant again. Frustration chewed at Tim. He understood, knew that the lost feeling would never really go away, that it would only lessen as life moved in and demanded that she go on. But he could help, if she'd let him.

"What did you say?" She peered at him. "What's finished?"

"Aimee's book of stories. That's what I'm calling it. It's actually been done for a while," he admitted. "Last night I did a final proofreading, got them ready for mailing. I guess I was simply putting off sending them."

"Why now?"

The harsh note in her voice made him frown, but then he realized she might think he didn't believe Aimee was coming back. He hurried to explain.

"After talking to you about the past some things jelled for me. I finally accepted that I'm not in control, that things can happen in an instant that make you wish you'd acted instead of procrastinating." He motioned to a chair, waited till she was seated, then flopped down beside her. "I'd always wanted to do that book. I think when Aimee got me started it made me think of Sara and the baby. Maybe I was waiting for my daughter to arrive, maybe I hadn't really accepted their deaths. I don't know."

"I see." She'd turned fully around to face him head-on. As she met his gaze a small pleat marred her smooth forehead. "But now…?"

"The stories have become Aimee's, Shelby. Last night as I read them over I could almost hear that breathless little giggle she gives just before she bursts out laughing." He thought he saw some flicker of hope wash across her face before she glanced away. "I thought of the verse we were talking about. You know, about things working together? It's found in Romans 8:28–29. It starts out 'We know.' That's when I realized that our hope as Christians isn't based on positive thinking, on optimism or anything like that. Our hope is a certainty because it's based on truth—God is in control and He loves us." Tim closed his eyes, tried to assemble the rush of words that wanted to spill out.

"Nothing about Aimee's disappearance is part of fate or chance. It's like history—His story. He's pulling the strings, He's in charge and that verse assures us that everything that happens to us is simply a vehicle for Him to use. See what I mean?"

"Sort of."

"God makes it all work together, so there can't be random acts. Everything that happens becomes part of the process to help us become more like His son." He shook his head. "That's the part I didn't get—how could losing my daughter be part of His plan to work things together for the good of me just because I am His child. I still don't know how it will all come out, but I've decided to trust Him, to rest in the knowledge that He will work it through. When Aimee comes home I'll be able to tell her our stories have gone to a publisher. Hearing from them is something we can both look forward to, to see how God will work it out."

"You think she will come home then?"

Shelby's soft query made him frown. How could she doubt? What had happened?

"I *know* she'll come home. She has to."

"Why?" Her eyes turned the color of glacial ice water, shimmering aqua with deeper glints of green. "What makes you so positive?"

Tim struggled to explain the certainty he felt inside.

"Because you love her, because this is her home." Shelby

still stared at him. "Because I love her and because I'm trusting that God, who loves her more than either of us, will work this out," he finally admitted. *For the good of His children.* Tim stared at his useless hand which couldn't even make a fist. *According to His purpose,* he reminded himself. *His, not mine.*

For a moment he toyed with telling her he had a date for surgery, that his operations would take place in one month. But his trust was newly built and he was afraid that he'd blurt out that he needed her and Aimee to be there when he woke up.

No. Not now. Better to wait, to be there for her. Talk about yourself later.

"It's a matter of faith."

"Thank you for trying to encourage me, Tim." Shelby seemed oddly preoccupied, as if she hadn't heard everything he'd said. After a few minutes she motioned to the coffeepot sitting on a wicker table between them. "Would you like a cup?"

"If you have time. I want to talk about Daniel's idea."

"Daniel?" She looked confused.

"You know—about this Marta Krakow. I was thinking about his plan to disguise himself. What if he went as a feeble old pastor coming to see his former parishioner one last time before he retires? That way you could go along—as his personal nurse. You know, make sure he doesn't overtax himself, that kind of thing."

"It's a good idea, but what if something happens?"

"That's where I come in." Tim watched her eyes flare, knew she was surprised.

"You?"

Excitement rippled through him. Finally he would be able to do something to help her.

"Yes, me. I have to go in for a peel tomorrow morning, a

sort of exfoliation to get rid of scar tissue. After that proce-dure I'm always in bandages for a couple of days to prevent infection. No one will recognize me. I can wait outside in the car and if anything goes wrong I'll alert police, call 911 or something. Or if you and Daniel aren't out by a certain time I'll call Natalie."

"It might work," she mused, but a hint of skepticism underlay her soft voice. "I'll have to discuss it with Daniel, get his input. We'll need to work out the details."

"Yes." He waited, watched. Shelby kept looking at him as if she expected him to say something more, but he didn't know what that was. He'd offered, it was up to her to accept or deny his offer.

"I'll discuss it with Daniel and let you know this evening, shall I?"

"Fine." He rose, his coffee cup untouched. "You have to get to work so I'll leave." Tim walked to the end of the deck, paused, then turned.

"We know that God causes everything to work together for the good of those who love God and are called according to His purpose."

He quoted softly. "*All* things, Shelby. Hang on to that."

"Yes." Her whisper was so quiet he almost didn't hear it.

On the other side of the hedge he paused, then whispered a plea for help. Not for himself, though he hated the skin peels every bit as much as Aimee hated brussels sprouts. Instead he prayed for Shelby, for the Spirit of God to comfort her, to keep her.

"It's a good plan, Shelby. I don't understand your reserva-tions. I thought you trusted Tim."

She had. That was the problem.

"I heard from the lab this morning, Daniel. The hair I pulled off Tim's jacket was a perfect match for the one I took from Aimee's hairbrush. Even though I know that there was a stain on the jacket and it isn't there anymore, even though the jacket had to have been cleaned to get that spot out, the blond hair I found shows no trace of having gone through any cleaning process. There was no residue on it."

"Meaning?" He pulled off his glasses to stare at her.

"Tim has been with her recently. Otherwise where did the hair come from?" It gave Shelby no pleasure to say it. Of all people, she trusted Tim the most. Being with him, pouring out her hopes and fears, hearing him talk about God—she'd wanted so badly to believe he was true.

"I don't think you're right, Shelby. In my opinion, he's an honest decent man. Why would he take her? Where would he put her?"

"I don't know." She'd gone over it a thousand times last night. Nothing made sense anymore.

"Well, if you're that concerned, I'll ask Callie to tail him for a while." He made the call, then leaned back in his chair, his amber-gold eyes concerned. "You care about him, don't you?"

"I don't want to. I feel like a traitor allowing these feelings to creep in," she admitted with a sigh. She leaned over to peer through the glass. Someone, a young girl with blue hair that stuck straight up, was leaving the building. "I loved Grant," she whispered.

"I know that. And he loved you. But Grant is gone." Daniel's voice softened. "Can I say something personal?"

"Why not? We've known each other a long time."

"Yes." He paused, took a deep breath. "I think you're afraid of what you're beginning to feel for Tim. But Shelby, Grant would never expect you to spend the rest of your life alone. The man was all about life and living. That's why he loved to watch the roses bloom. Don't you remember?"

"I guess I've forgotten." She thought she'd remembered every detail, but now Shelby wondered if her memories weren't skewed by all that had happened in the past few days. "Remind me, Daniel."

"A zest for life, for what *could* happen—he was always open to the possibility that something wonderful was just around the corner and he wanted to be ready to grab it. Grant always reenergized people around him with that attitude." He stared across the room as if he saw something Shelby couldn't. "I remember he once said your grandmother taught him that nobody has tomorrow."

"Tim said something like that this morning."

"Smart man. Grant once told me that what we get is today to live in. We can plan and dream, but today is when we live. He said every time he looked at the roses, he was reminded that they blossom and then they're gone. He said roses don't worry about tomorrow—"

"'They just bloom today.'" She repeated the familiar words, the memory strong, alive. "I'd forgotten that."

"I guess we all got bogged down in how he died and forgot how he lived." Daniel slid on his glasses. "Don't get sucked into the past, Shel. What you two had was wonderful, but that doesn't mean you can't or shouldn't love again and Grant would be the first to tell you that. From what I've seen, Tim really cares for you and Aimee. You've just said you care about him. Don't let go of what you feel because of something Russ said. If you care about this man, fight for him."

"You think there might be some other reason why Aimee's hair was on his jacket?"

"At this point I'd just be guessing and you've had enough

of supposition and maybes. I think you should ask Tim about it."

"No." Fear hardened inside her.

"Shelby, you're tearing yourself up with these doubts. You're judging without hearing what he might say. That's not fair to Tim. I don't think you're being fair to yourself, either."

She looked away from his steady stare. "Surely he wouldn't offer to come along, to help us…if he was involved? Wouldn't he try to find out about the egg from Marta himself?"

"That's the thing about doubting someone, Shel. You can twist things a thousand ways." Daniel's gaze narrowed. "Are you making this into some kind of a test? Is that how you'll judge him?"

"Yes." She crossed her arms across her chest. "If everything goes fine and Tim doesn't ask us what we learned I'll know he's not part of it."

Daniel shook his head. "Me, Russ, Tim. You used to have more faith in people," he muttered, his face sad.

"I used to have my daughter at home," she snapped back. Instead of making her feel better, the words only made her hurt more. Friends, enemies. It was so hard to know who to trust. "I don't want to talk about this anymore. Let's decide what we're going to do and when."

"Tomorrow evening," Daniel said, scribbling notes on his yellow legal pad. "They eat early in those places. I've already made a phone call, had someone case the place. Medications are administered around eight. Keeps the residents quiet through the night so the staff are free," he explained.

"How did you find that out—no." Shelby held up her hand. "Never mind. I'd rather not know. So what do we do?"

"We ask to visit Marta, intercept her medication and hope she comes out of her drug-induced state long enough to tell us something."

"That's it? That's our wonderful plan?" Shelby sighed. "It could take hours for her to become lucid enough to talk to."

"It could. But I don't know of any other way to do it. Until she's wide-awake, we'll have to hide. With the patients tanked on medication the staff usually only have to make rounds once during the evening, unless there is a disturbance. Marta isn't being treated for anything so stopping the medication should be no problem." Tiny lines fanned out around Daniel's eyes. He smiled as Shelby raised one eyebrow.

"Trust me, I just know these things. There's a fire escape near her room. If we have to get out fast we can use that. Tim will be waiting so we can make a quick getaway if we need to."

"Quick getaway? Why would we need that?" This was sounding less and less like a good idea.

"We don't know that Marta *isn't* senile. She's been in that home for several months. I haven't been able to learn who signed her in, but given the circumstances of her stay there, I'd guess someone doesn't want her out wandering around. I'm fairly certain that someone doesn't want anyone talking to her, either." He tented his fingers, his stare intent. "It's all a guessing game until we get there, Shelby. That's when we'll be able to judge the situation. If you'd rather not go I can ask Callie or Samantha to—"

"I'm going, Daniel. Don't even think about it." She rose from her chair, determination gripping her anew. "I will be there. If this Marta can talk, I have a few questions for her. About Grant."

"She might not be able to give you the answers you want."

"I have to try. You know that."

Daniel nodded, though he still looked troubled. "Do you want me to talk to Tim, let him know what we've discussed?"

Shelby considered it, then shook her head.

"No. I'll do that. I want to see his face when I tell him, but

I also want to make it perfectly clear that he is not to inter-
fere with our plans. What about Russ?"

"He's out for the next two days. Tracking an item that was
delayed in Mexico. I'd rather he finish that."

It sounded perfectly plausible, but beneath the words Shelby
sensed that even if Russ had been available for this mission,
Daniel would have found another excuse to keep him out.

"You were just talking to me about trust," she murmured,
watching him from between her lashes. "What about you?"

"You know I've always been a skeptic, Shel. Trust is pretty
hard earned for me and instinct tells me Tim is okay. But I
think it is prudent to keep things to ourselves until we hear
what this woman has to say." Daniel turned away, ostensibly
to take some incoming sheets from the fax machine.

Shelby rose. "I've got some things to do and I'd better scare
up a nurse's uniform if I'm going to play my part. Anything
else?"

"Not for now. I'll make a few more inquiries just to ease
my mind about policies and procedures at Sunset Nursing
Home. I want as much information as I can get before we set
foot inside the place."

Shelby left him to it, returned to her office. Part of her
wanted to charge over there, kidnap Marta and run. The other
part wanted to forget about the whole ridiculous thing. There
was no telling what they'd learn from the woman, or where
her answers would lead them. Yes, she wanted to know what
had driven Grant to complete this mission, but what would
learning that help?

He was gone, no longer a part of her life. She'd have to
move on when Aimee came home.

When—not if.

TWELVE

Shelby slid out of the car, bent to help Daniel with his cane, just as a good nurse would.

"I'll be here waiting," Tim promised, his smile for her alone. "Daniel pointed out her room. I can see it from here. If anything goes wrong, turn the lights off and on twice. I'll think of some distraction."

"Thanks," Daniel murmured, leaning heavily on his cane. He took a few doddery steps toward the entrance door.

"Shelby?"

She leaned inside, stared into Tim's eyes, dark and mysterious against the whiteness of his bandages. "Yes?"

"I'll be praying."

He'd passed her test, hadn't asked questions or demanded to know more than Daniel had told him. She should be able to trust him. But some niggling doubt still lingered. She couldn't deal with it now.

"Thanks." Shelby nodded, then hurried to catch up to Daniel whom she wouldn't have recognized if she'd met him on the street.

"Here we go," he murmured as the automatic door opened to allow them inside.

Visitors mingled in the common room and throughout the

hallways. Shelby could tell they were visitors because they weren't old or infirm, and because they didn't wear uniforms. One burly man dressed in white pants and a white shirt with a name tag that read Burt stood behind a desk eyeing everyone.

"Room 139," Daniel whispered for her ears alone. "Down this hall."

They were almost at the door when loud thumping foot-steps sounded behind them. "Hey!"

Shelby kept her head down. *Let Daniel handle it,* she told herself.

"Where are you going?"

In a feeble voice Daniel explained that he'd come to say goodbye to his former parishioner.

"I'm not long for this world, you see. Not many days now, but I convinced my nurse that I had to see Marta Krakow, to say goodbye before I pass." He hacked out a rheumy cough that sounded terminal. "My nurse spoke to your supervisor who said Marta sleeps a lot. That's all right. So do I." He turned that into a gasping chuckle.

Shelby patted his back, held her fingers against his wrist and watched her watch as if she knew what she was doing.

"We'll just sit with her a moment," Daniel rumbled.

"You spoke to a supervisor?" Burt's hand tightened on the doorknob as if he'd bar them from entry. "I had no notice of this."

Time for officialdom to take over.

"In all my years, I've never worked in a home where the supervisor had to explain to staff about visitors," Shelby informed him scathingly. She shoved the massive glasses back onto her nose and demanded, "Are you trying to stop us? Because I can make a call—" She whipped a cell phone out of her pocket and flipped it open.

"There's no need to phone. Go ahead and visit, but you

don't have much time. Visiting hours end at eight." Burt clearly didn't like it but he wasn't going to argue.

"The way you're acting this place sounds like a jail, not a care facility." Shelby ran one fingertip along the chair rail, stared at it. "And not a very clean or well-run one, at that. I wonder when the last inspection was?"

Daniel hacked his way through another chest-wrenching cough, covering his face with a massive handkerchief. "I…must…sit," he gasped.

"Excuse us." Shelby grasped his arm and pretended to ease him toward Marta's door. "Do you mind?" she snapped, glaring at Burt's fingers on the doorknob.

"Lady, with that attitude, it's a good thing you don't work here." Burt glared at her.

"It certainly is," she responded, hardening the edge of scorn in her voice. "I'd have you out on your ear for being so rude to a weary old man who just wants to say goodbye to a woman he once knew." Shelby deliberately stepped on his toe as she helped a frail Daniel into the room. The door whooshed closed behind them.

"Remind me not to get you angry at me," Daniel chuckled, then turned his attention to the small woman lying in bed. "Are you Marta Krakow?" he asked softly.

"Yes." She frowned at Shelby. "You're going to give me the medicine again, aren't you?"

"No." Shelby thought quickly. "They haven't brought it yet?" Marta shook her head. "Do they give it to you every night?"

"They are traitors. They do not understand." Tears formed at the corners of her sad, wrinkled eyes. "I wish to be free."

"That's why we're here, Marta. To help you get free. But it might take a while. Can you rest now? Would you like to sleep?"

"That's all I do. Sleep and dream. Some dreams are good. I see them then. Oh, the laughter! I can hear it."

The old woman's eyes were open but she was rambling. Shelby wrapped her hand around the other woman's and let her babble, knowing they wouldn't have long. The PA announcement was made a few minutes later—visiting hours were over.

"I arranged a dry run last night," Daniel told her in a soft whisper. "They'll wait a few minutes then the meds cart will come out. I'm going to switch bottles."

"You can't! You'll be seen. I'm the one dressed as a nurse," she hissed when he looked as if he'd ignore her. "Let me do it, Daniel."

He finally agreed, told her which medication to change. "From what I could discover, only two others are getting the same medication and they're treated before Marta."

"Fine. We'll wait till that's been administered, then do the switch." Shelby slipped the tiny bottle into her pocket, then waited. She wasn't certain how long she waited before Daniel beckoned.

"Be careful," he whispered as she slipped through the doorway.

She darted toward the staff lounge, found one of the lab jackets she'd seen many of the others wearing. From the back, at least, she'd look as if she belonged. Around the corner she could see Burt standing by the front door. One or two stragglers still remained. Good, that would keep him busy.

When the medications nurse went into the room across from Marta's, Shelby quickly walked to the tray, found the bottle Daniel had described and replaced it with the one she carried. Then she slipped back inside the room.

"Done." She glanced at the bed. "Is she all right?"

"I think so. Easy now." He moved to support Marta who sat straight up in bed. "Maybe some water?"

Shelby walked into the bathroom, filled a glass.

"How are you, my dear?" she heard Daniel croak in his disguise voice.

Shelby froze.

"It's been so long since I've seen you, Marta. I'm sorry you've been ill. That's what happens to us old codgers, I guess."

"Time's up, old fella. You'll have to leave." Burt stood in the doorway, surveying the room. "Where's your nurse?"

Daniel coughed long and hard and loudly. "She went to get the car," he gasped. "I can't walk far. It would be so much quicker if there was a wheelchair—"

"Stay here. I'll get one." Burt left.

"You'll have to go with him now." Shelby stepped out of the bathroom, wondering what next. "He'll be suspicious if you disappear."

"Doesn't matter. I've got the fire door propped open. I can get back inside."

"But the alarm—" Shelby swallowed the comment when she spotted his grin. Daniel was a detail man. There would be no alarm. "What about me?"

"Hide in this closet and wait."

He shoved her inside and closed the door as Burt's voice echoed down the hall.

"What is the matter?" The wobbly voice brimmed with anxiety that Shelby longed to ease. But she had to remain hidden.

"Everything is fine, Marta. Just relax." Daniel's normal voice was reassuring. "We're going to be friends, you and I."

"Friends?"

"Very good friends, my dearest Marta. But I must leave now." Daniel bent over, brushed her cheek. When he spoke again his voice had changed. "Rest well. We'll meet again, dear. This I know."

"She's ninety-three. Don't suppose she's got that much

longer," Burt muttered. Shelby heard a clunk, Daniel's grunt. "Sorry about that. Hope I didn't hurt you. Where's your nurse?"

Daniel's mumble got fainter. She waited a few moments, pulled out her cell phone and dialed Tim.

"Daniel's on his way out. Alone. Keep the car by the front door till he gets in. He'll tell you the rest." At the moment she was very glad Tim was there.

Her hand was on the door when she heard a noise. Just eased the door open a fraction, saw the nurse.

"How are you tonight, Marta? Here's your pill. It should help you sleep."

"Visitors," Marta mumbled, trying to look around.

"They're all gone home now. It's time for bed." Her job finished, the nurse quickly left the room.

Moments later the door opened again. Burt's burly figure was outlined. He glanced around the room, checked the bathroom, then left. After that silence reigned. Shelby checked her watch. Eight forty-five. Where was Daniel?

A doctor walked in a few minutes later, called her name. If he hadn't spoken, Shelby wouldn't have known it was Daniel. "Has she said anything?" he asked as she emerged from her hiding place.

"No." She laid her hand on the frail shoulder, pressed gently. "Marta? Can you hear me?"

"Of course. I am not deaf." Marta's eyes flew open.

"Are you all right?"

"Yes. But soon I will grow sleepy. Always they give me the medicine. I am not sick. Why do they do this?"

"I don't know." She smiled as the old woman sighed, leaned back against her pillows. "Have you been in this place a long time?"

"Everything is mixed up. I can't remember."

"That's okay. Don't worry." She tried to think of other reassuring things but they weren't needed, for Marta had nodded off. "Now what?" she asked Daniel.

"Now we wait for the old drug to wear off. I was told she would be coming out of it around midnight." Daniel pulled a small testament out of his pocket and began to read it, pausing frequently to whisper something.

Shelby prayed, too, though she wasn't sure what she was asking for. All she really wanted was her daughter back. She'd lost everything she loved, she couldn't lose Aimee, too. Tim had promised he'd help them find Marta but Shelby didn't understand why. He must be in pain after his procedure this morning. It couldn't be pleasant to sit in that car and not know what was happening inside.

Yet he'd volunteered, even insisted they not call someone else. Surely that meant something?

"Can you understand that?" Daniel murmured as Marta began to speak.

"No." Shelby leaned over the woman, tried to gently wake her. "Marta? Can you hear me?"

"Sacha and Mikka, they haven't come, Mama. Why don't they come?"

"Marta, what are you saying?"

The elderly woman blinked awake, stared at them. "Who are you?" she whispered fearfully.

"Friends. We've come to help." Shelby glanced at Daniel who nodded for her to continue. "I think you might have met my husband, Marta. His name was Grant. Grant Kincaid."

"Ah, Grant. He wanted to know about my sisters."

"Your sisters?" Wondering where this trail would lead, Shelby thought quickly. "I wonder if you'd also tell me about them? Grant never got to explain about your sisters before he died."

"Oh, I'm sorry. I did not know." Marta reached out to cover Shelby's hands with her frail one. "He was such a lovely man. So kind. I met him when I was living in my other place. It was much nicer than this. Gardens, flowers. We talked about the roses he grew."

"And you told him about your sisters."

"Yes. Sacha and Mikka. I never saw them again you know. We were separated so we could travel without being discovered. We were supposed to meet in Austria. Mama and I waited and waited, but they never came. Then we heard that Papa had died and we lost hope. They were so small, you see. Such tiny girls. I was only five years old myself."

"Why did you have to leave?" Daniel asked.

"Because of the revolution, of course. It was only a matter of time until we were all killed. Papa insisted we leave so one very dark night Mama and I left with only the clothes on our backs, a small suitcase and a little bit of money. I remember how cold my feet got walking, walking. I thought we would never get there."

"You told Grant all this," Shelby asked, waiting for Daniel's next move.

"Yes. But he wanted to know about after."

"After?"

Marta nodded. "When I was older my mother tried to get our land back, but we had no papers to prove we owned it. Papa had been bringing those with Sacha and Mikka. So many times we tried, but they had taken it all and without the papers…" She shrugged. "Mama grew weary. I looked after her as best I could. I did many jobs but she grew sicker. When she died, I had to move. After a while I came to Canada. I met a nice soldier in the war and I wanted to marry him. Life got much better when I moved here." She licked her lips, moved her head back against the pillow. "Until my Robert died. I loved him so much."

"I'm sorry." Shelby didn't know what else to ask. She had plenty of questions but none of them addressed the reason they were here. An idea flickered to life. "Marta, did Grant talk to you about an egg?"

Marta frowned, her gaze slid from Shelby to Daniel, a suspicious glint in the depths. "An egg?"

"Yes. Grant left notes that I just found. In them he talks about a beautiful Fabergé egg. Do you know about it?"

Marta was silent for a long time, as if choosing her words carefully. "My Bible—it is on the stand. Please give it to me."

Daniel picked up the tattered volume, passed it to her.

"This was Mama's Bible. It is all I have left of my family. I keep it very near." She opened the cover, passed one thin bony finger over the spidery writing as tears rolled down her cheeks. Slowly with great care she slid a fingernail under the gilt-edged sheet on the back of the cover. "I will die soon. Perhaps it is better someone else knows."

Knows what? Shelby nerves screamed for relief from the tension. She shrugged, hoping to ease the knot of frustration that gripped the back of her neck. Marta's fingertips slid under the cover. Shelby froze as the edge of a paper appeared. She leaned forward to study what was on it.

"This is my family," Marta whispered, her eyes welling with tears. "We were at the winter palace and I was not happy to come in from ice skating for a picture. But Papa said he had a surprise. That was his surprise." She pointed.

Shelby saw a man and woman standing at one side of a worn black-and-white photograph. On the other were three young girls in very fancy dresses, their hair dressed in long ringlets. Between the children and their parents stood a man in full military dress that signaled his importance, but it was what he held that made her gasp.

"The egg," she whispered. "Daniel, it must be the egg."

"A Fabergé egg," Marta told them proudly. "He gave it to my father as a token of his great esteem. He said it would remind us of the happy times we'd spent with his family." She smiled as Shelby leaned closer. "People have written such terrible things about the Romanovs, but Nicholas was a wonderful loving father who cared deeply about his country."

"You mean…Czar Nicholas?" Shelby gulped when Marta nodded.

"That is why my father was killed. Because he supported the Czar. The Bolsheviks were gaining power and Papa felt we wouldn't be safe. He warned the Czar over and over but Nicholas wouldn't believe his people would betray him. Father was certain something was in the works, however, so he made plans. I left with my Mama. We were all to travel separately you see, so no one would suspect we were leaving the country. My sisters were to follow us with our nurse, and later on my father, but they never came. I thought they were all dead."

"You don't think that now?" Daniel murmured, peeking out the door to check.

"I don't know. Almost a year ago a woman wrote me. She tells me she is my niece, the daughter of Sacha. She claims my sisters were alive. Now that I was found they wished to reunite but several unusual things had happened and they are in hiding. I was to be contacted by my niece personally, but that never happened." She sighed. "I prayed very hard for help. One day I heard about this company that finds things so I telephoned. A man came to see me. Grant Kincaid. He said he would gladly help. That he would find my sisters and the egg."

"Did he speak to your niece?"

"Once, by telephone." Marta nodded. "She, too, was looking for the egg in that picture. For her mother, she said, but I don't know why. Whatever she told Grant caused him to go to Europe. When he came back the woman who claimed to be my niece had disappeared. I heard from your Grant once more, then nothing. I remembered my niece had said my sisters were in hiding. I was afraid someone would be after me, so I said nothing more. Then I was forced to move here."

As Shelby slipped the picture back in place and pressed down the cover sheet she learned that the old woman had been pushed out of the retirement home she'd lived in for years. Somehow she didn't have enough money, though Marta insisted her husband left her well provided for.

"Since I have come here, I see no one. I can't even get up long enough to walk around. Always they are giving me pills or needles. I sleep too much." She reached out to grasp Shelby's hand. "I am old, I will die soon. But first I wish very much to meet with my sisters once more. Is this possible?"

"I don't know." Shelby didn't want to give her false hope and in fact, she didn't know what to make of the story she'd been told. "But we are going to try. My husband wanted your family to be reunited and Daniel and I want that, too. The first thing we have to do is get you out of here."

"I have tried to leave. They won't let me."

"Tonight they will," Shelby told her grimly. She picked up her phone and dialed Tim. "You're still there," she marveled, glancing at her watch. "I hadn't realized it was so late."

"I'm not going anywhere without you." He was silent for a moment. "Are you ready to leave?"

"Yes, but it's not going to be easy. Just a minute." She listened as Daniel outlined his plan to make sure their path was clear. "Did you hear that? Good. Once we've got the green light from Daniel, Marta and I are breaking out. I'll flick the lights just before we leave the room."

"I'll be here, Shelby. Praying." His voice sounded so sincere. How could she doubt him?

"Thanks, Tim. I…appreciate it. See you in a bit."

"Shelby?"

"Yes?"

His voice came back soft but firm. "Remember the verse—we know all things work together for good. All things."

"I'll remember." She closed the phone.

"Okay. I'm going to do a test run. Give me five minutes to find a wheelchair and come back. Then we'll leave." Daniel brushed a kiss against Marta's parchmentlike cheek, grinned at her surprise, then stepped into the hall.

"I think you should put some warm clothes on," Shelby suggested. "Do you have any?"

"They took most of my things but I demanded they keep that." Marta pointed to the closet. A brown coat stuck out between the doors. "It's very warm."

"Good. Let's get you into it."

It seemed to take aeons to get Marta into the coat and sitting on a chair. There were no shoes in the closet so Shelby laced her own sneakers on the tiny bare feet.

"You will need your shoes."

"I'll be fine." She checked the hall, saw Daniel pushing a wheelchair toward her. "Here he comes. Don't forget your Bible." She tucked the treasured book under Marta's coat.

The wheelchair was bare inches inside the room when Burt's loud voice hailed Daniel who turned around and walked into the hall as if he had every reason to be there.

"Public health complaint," Shelby heard him say. "Food poisoning. I want you to show me the kitchen."

Shelby let the door close, then helped Marta into the chair. "All right?" she asked as she gently set her feet on the rests.

"I'm fine," Marta's surprisingly energetic response came back.

Shelby flicked the light twice, then grabbed the wheelchair handles. "Here we go."

The made it to the foyer before a big hand closed around her shoulder. "What do you think you're doing?"

"This woman wishes to leave. I'm helping her."

"Without proper authorization? I don't think so." Burt's hands forced hers off Marta's wheelchair. "Anyway she's senile. She could say anything and it wouldn't be true."

"Wouldn't it?" Anger burned deep within. Shelby faced him, her temper surging. "What about drugging? Would that be false? Or illegal confinement? I heard someone from public health here a few minutes ago. They might be interested in knowing what you're doing to this poor woman."

"Get out."

"Not without her."

"I'll carry you if I have to, but you are leaving. Now." His fingers around her arm were painful.

"Why not call the police?" she suggested. "Let them handle it."

"Not tonight." He half dragged her as far as the entry. "Get out and don't come back."

"Or what?"

"Or—" He stopped, his jaw dropping at the apparition that moved into the building.

Tim moaned and groaned, clutching his bandaged head. "It hurts," he hollered. "Give me something for the pain."

"Sir, this is not a hospital. You need to go to a hospital."

Tim acted his part perfectly, alternately wailing and yelling at the burly attendant. "Help me!"

"I'll get an ambulance," Burt told him as he reached for the phone. He gave the directions then added, "Hurry. He looks like he's going to keel over."

Shelby tried to push Marta forward, but Burt saw her move and stopped her, one hand yanking back the chair as Tim sent up another cacophony of complaint.

Afraid that the jerking would hurt Marta, or worse, upset her, Shelby tried to figure out the next step. Then she saw Daniel outside, waving. When Tim fell forward against Burt she raced through the door and out of the nursing home.

"What now?" she gasped as they crouched together in the shrubs.

"I don't know, I'm winging this." Daniel chuckled at her dark look. "You've been out of the game too long, Shelby. You've lost the thrill of the chase."

"Big thrill. And if you recall, I never was into this covert stuff. It was always you three boys." She waited for him to decide their next move.

"Ah, the good times." He pointed. "See that nurse taking Marta back to her room? When the ambulance comes, Tim will get inside, then somehow he's going to make them wait. You and I have to get back in that building and get Marta out and into the ambulance."

"Easier said than done. How do we get inside?"

"All planned for." He led the way around the building to the side door. It looked as if it was closed but by using a pocketknife Daniel soon had the door open. They crept inside, down the hall. Daniel peeked around the corner, jerked back. "Burt," he murmured. "Get down behind that settee. I'll take the palm."

They listened as the attendant passed their hiding place, his voice echoing in the silent hall. He was talking to someone on a cell phone.

"What do I do now?" He stopped just across from them, his voice furious. "Why do I have to kill her? The old girl is ninety-three. She's not going to say anything anyone will take seriously, even if she could remember. Yeah, yeah. I'll make sure. But it will cost you extra." Burt stomped down the hall, away from them.

"He's going to the medication room." Daniel waited a few moments more then beckoned Shelby to follow. Using a lock pick he opened Marta's door, urged her inside. "I'm going to cause a disturbance. When you hear it, get her out that side door."

"What kind of disturbance?"

"You'll know." He disappeared.

Shelby stared at Marta who was lying on the bed once more, her Bible clutched in her hands. Her eyes were drowsy and Shelby suspected she'd already been given a sedative.

"Me again, sweetie. This time we're out of here." The wheelchair had been shoved to one side. She lifted Marta's frail body from the bed and gently set her in it just in time to hear the fire alarm go off. "That's our cue." She threw the brown coat over Marta, grabbed her phone, called Tim. "I'm coming through the side door and I'll need help."

"I'll be there," was his steady response.

Shelby waited a few more minutes until bedlam reigned outside Marta's door. Then she pushed the chair into the hall. A nurse glanced at her. "Oh, good, you've got her. Can you get her outside? I don't know where the fire is but we've got to keep them safe."

"I'll take her," Shelby murmured and the nurse moved on, shepherding two chattering old ladies down the hall. Moving as quickly as she could, Shelby pushed the chair toward the fire escape. Strangely no one else was using that door, they were all going to the front. She shoved the metal door ajar, grinned when she saw Tim waiting. "You're here."

"I said I would be and I don't lie, Shelby."

That certainty in his voice confirmed his words. He meant it. As she watched him beckon the attendants forward to usher the old lady to the waiting ambulance, Shelby accepted that Tim was telling the truth. Later she'd ask him about the hair, but for now she believed that Tim was who he said he was—a friend.

"This is highly unusual," the ambulance driver complained.

"So is repeatedly drugging an old woman." Shelby climbed into the van, clasped Marta's hand in her own.

"Where are we supposed to take her?"

"Your place?" Tim suggested when she couldn't think of a response.

It was perfect. Shelby gave them her address, then frowned when he began to close the door. "What about you?"

"I've got to wait for Daniel."

"Okay. Be careful, Tim. I'll see you later."

Three-thirty in the morning. Shelby prayed the newshounds that had dogged her house ever since Aimee's absence would have gone home to rest. She didn't need a lot of questions about an ambulance now.

"No siren, no lights, okay guys? I promise you'll be paid whatever you normally get and then some if you make sure you don't upset my neighbors. Besides, this isn't a medical emergency. You're merely transporting."

They agreed and God answered her prayers. No one was waiting on the doorstep as they escorted Marta inside her house. Just for a moment, Shelby paused and let the peace and silence of this safe place sink in. Then Marta muttered something and she refocused.

With no bedrooms on the main floor, Shelby needed to get the weary woman upstairs. The wheelchair was no help, Shelby couldn't manage it alone. Esmeralda had gone home hours ago. She'd have to wait until Tim and Daniel came. Shelby rolled the chair to the garden room, switched on the outside lights to make sure no one was out there.

"That's Grant's garden," Marta murmured, her eyes

suddenly wide. "He talked about it so often, I could see it in my mind's eye. It's exactly as he described it."

"You and Grant must have talked a lot," she hinted. Maybe this was the moment she'd been waiting for.

"Yes. He told me all about his daughter. I would like to meet her."

"She's…away right now." Shelby swallowed the lump in her throat and pressed on. "What else did Grant talk about?"

"You." Marta's soft voice had grown faint and thready, forcing Shelby to lean in. "He said you were a beautiful woman inside and out. He loved you very much."

"I loved him, too." Hearing a noise Shelby excused herself and went to the front door. She let in Tim and Daniel. "Everything all right?"

"Piece of cake. Marta?"

"I think she's very tired. I need help to get her upstairs."

Daniel solved the problem by lifting the tiny woman in his arms and carrying her into a guest bedroom upstairs. Shelby soon had her tucked into the bed.

"Can I get you anything, Marta?" she asked, noting how the parchmentlike skin seemed devoid of all color.

"Thank you, but I feel very well. The muzzy feeling is gone. I'm just a bit tired. I'd like to sleep. Good night, my dear. And thank you for taking me away from that awful place. I've been praying that God would help me. He certainly has."

"I'll be across the hall. You've only to ring this little bell or call out and I'll come." Shelby pulled an embroidered coverlet over the blankets just in case Marta felt cold. "Sleep well."

"I shall, my dear."

Before Shelby had left the room Marta's soft whiffling snores were echoing through the silence. She walked downstairs, her mind whirling.

Tomorrow they would ask more questions about the egg. For tonight Marta was safe.

But where was Aimee?

THIRTEEN

"I should go home." Tim glanced down at Shelby as she watched Daniel leave. She turned to him and he took the opportunity to stare into her face, the love he'd kept carefully tucked inside suddenly spilling free. "You must be worn out."

"I'm fine. Just wondering if we've done the right thing spiriting her away like that. Kidnapping is serious." A tiny furrow marred her perfect forehead.

"We didn't kidnap her, we rescued her," Tim insisted. He could see that she was concerned. "She wanted to leave. If anyone asks her, I'm sure she'd rather be here than where she was."

"But this isn't a facility for seniors. I don't have a doctor handy if something happens."

"Neither do they. They have to call one." His finger wrapped around hers. "She's okay, Shel. In the morning we'll find out the rest of her story, but for now just try to relax."

"I'm not sure I'll ever be able to do that again." She obeyed the slight tug on her hand, followed him into the living room and sank into the settee. "I can't stop thinking about Aimee. Where is she? Why haven't I heard anything? The questions go round and round in my head and there's never an answer."

He sat down beside her, wrapped his arm around her

shoulder and hugged her against his side, his lips against her hair as she rested her head on his shoulder. His face felt tight and sore, and he was supposed to be resting, but nothing could have moved Tim from her side, not now.

"I'm so sorry you had to go through this," he whispered, then called himself an idiot for not knowing how to comfort her. But Shelby didn't seem annoyed. After several moments, she shifted away from him. A cool draft brushed over his un-bandaged skin, emphasizing the differences he could not overcome. Shelby still loved her dead husband.

"In a way, I'm glad I did go through it." Her forefinger grazed his chin. "It's hard to tell what you're thinking with all these bandages on. Never mind. Anyway, I was thinking that if I hadn't met Marta I wouldn't have known some of the things she told me about Grant. It helps somehow, to be able to share our memories. Perhaps tomorrow we'll talk some more."

Tim couldn't take any more. Somehow he had to shake her out of the past. Even if it hurt.

"I know you must miss Grant, I know it's especially hard now with Aimee missing, but you didn't die, Shelby. You still have your life ahead of you. You have so much to look forward to." He paused, noticing the way her eyes blazed, her lips tightened.

"What are you saying—that I should forget him?"

"No! But Grant wouldn't want you to keep weeping for him, to only find joy in what happened yesterday. He'd want you to live today and tomorrow, to look ahead, to think of your future. Yours and Aimee's. I'd like to be part of that future, Shelby. I'd like to watch Aimee grow up, to share the joy of raising her with you."

"What are you saying?" She frowned at him and that's when Tim knew he'd made a mistake. But there was no going back now.

"I'm in love with you, Shelby." He tried to smile as her face tightened into a white mask. The hurt he felt at her shock exceeded the pain of his damaged face.

"But—"

"I have been for a while. I don't want to replace Grant, or usurp any feelings you have for him. I want us to have something special of our own, something—a life we build together. A future we share."

"We can't. I can't."

"Can't?" he murmured. "Or won't?"

"Either. Both." She marched over to stare out the floor-to-ceiling windows into the night.

"I know my timing is lousy, that you're worried about Aimee and Marta, that things at work aren't going the way you want." He moved to stand behind her, wanting to reach out yet sensing the chill. "I'm not asking you to decide tonight or tomorrow. I just wanted—needed to tell you how I feel."

"Why?" She whirled around, her face an expressionless picture of serene beauty.

Marble. Like a statue he'd display in a museum. But behind that she hid something else, something she hadn't shared with him. What?

"I asked you a question."

"Sorry." Tim blinked, tried to focus. "What did you ask?"

"Why do you need to tell me how you feel? Why now? Why tonight?"

"Because I want to know." She was hinting at something he didn't understand. "What's wrong with you? Why are you acting like this?"

She sneered. "I should be the one asking that, don't you think?" She stepped away from him, shoved open the glass door and stepped outside.

Tim followed, unable to assess what was going on in her head. The darkness didn't help.

"Talk to me, Shelby."

"I don't think so." She shook her head. "There's been enough talk tonight. Go home, Tim. Get some rest. You must need it after your surgery today."

Suddenly he got it.

"It's the scars, isn't it? You can't bear them."

She stopped him with a look. "I'm not that shallow. Go home. Please?"

Shelby Kincaid could have asked him anything and he'd have given it to her. But to leave, to walk away without knowing how she felt, if there was a chance for him—that was the hardest thing of all.

"You're sure?" He hoped, prayed, felt despair when she nodded. "Very well, I'll leave. Good night, Shelby."

"Goodbye," she whispered, the sound so faint he almost didn't catch it. But her meaning was clear.

As he trod across the pebbled path, stepped through the hedge and onto his own porch, Tim's feet grew heavier until finally he couldn't move. Instead he sank into the big wicker chair that had come with the house, leaned back and stared at the stars.

"Help us," he prayed silently.

Sleep was impossible. At four-thirty Shelby pulled on her gardening clothes and after a quick check on the sleeping Marta walked out into the rose garden to gather a few rosebuds for the old lady's room.

Soon it would be summer. The days were already lengthening, the sun beginning to creep over the skyline coloring the eastern horizon with a wash of rosy pinks that reminded her of Aimee's pictures.

Shelby dashed away the tears that would have formed,

grabbed a pair of gardening gloves from the potting shed, and repeated the prayer that she'd already said a thousand times before.

"Please keep Aimee safe, God. Please bring her home."

She caught a glimpse of Tim's house and deliberately turned her back on it. She would not think of him now. She refused even to allow his words to replay in her mind. But a few disobedient brain cells would not cooperate.

I'm in love with you, Shelby.

Would someone who loved you steal your daughter? Would he keep her hidden even when he knew your heart was breaking?

Sighing, Shelby pushed it all out of her mind to wander through Grant's rose garden, trying to remember the past happy days when life had seemed so simple. But the pictures were faded, no longer as sharp as they'd once been. The familiar sense of betrayal washed over her. Now she could barely remember the man who'd planted this garden, certainly couldn't hear his voice in her mind. How faithful was that?

The sun was fully risen now, the birds' cheery songs filling the morning. Shelby shrugged off the past. There were things to do, jobs that she needed to attend. In that Tim was right, life did go on. She concentrated on choosing exactly the right roses for Marta. Grant's bushes had never looked more lushly alive, tiny colored buds covering almost every one, some open, most only partially revealing their beauty. When she came to Deep Secret, she buried her face in its lush fragrance and thought of Grant.

"I want that egg."

Shelby froze, felt the prod of something against her back and knew she had to remain still.

"What egg?"

"Don't play games with me." The voice was disguised—

a rasping gravel tone that gave her no hints to its owner. "I want the Fabergé egg. If you want to see your daughter again you'd better do as I say."

This person had Aimee! Shelby stared at the ground, assimilating information. He was taller than her by several inches. She hadn't unlocked the front door so he must have had some other way to get through the fence to the garden. From the corner of her eye she could see the tip of a boot, a thick, heavy covering that made her think of the military. And that smell!

She lifted her head, breathed it in, then realized that floral scent had to be the roses.

"Is she all right? Is Aimee hurt?"

"Not yet. Now where is the egg?"

"I—I don't have it."

"Another of your clever little games, I suppose. It will do no good."

"I'm not playing any game." She thought quickly. "I haven't got it. If I had time, I could find it, though."

"Time is one thing you're out of. If you don't bring that egg with you to your office tonight at nine, your child will be dead before midnight."

"But I tell you, I don't have the egg!"

"Then find it. Isn't that what you do?" Faint scoffing in that remark. "Tonight, your office. Nine o'clock. If I see police she dies."

She was about to turn around when a shove from behind landed her on her face, the scratchy thorns of the rosebush piercing her skin. Shelby scrambled up, glanced all around, but saw no one. She hurried through the house, yanked open the front door and stopped short. Daniel stood there.

"Your face!" he exclaimed, reaching out to touch her cheek. His hand came away smeared with blood. "What happened?"

She glanced down the street, then laid a hand on his arm

and dragged him inside, automatically noting that he wore the scuffed and battered loafers he favored. No military boots. There was no way he'd had time to change.

"Shelby?" A frown marred his good looks as he stared at her. One finger shoved his glasses up on his nose. "What's wrong?"

Before she could say anything Esmeralda walked into the room. "Oh, you're up. Been mucking with those rosebushes again, haven't you? Well, you can take a break now. I'll bring some coffee. On that patio?"

That was a good place to tell Daniel what had happened without Esmeralda overhearing. Shelby nodded her thanks then led the way. By the time they were seated, Esmeralda had a tray with two big mugs of steaming coffee, some fresh muffins and a pot of apricot jam on the table.

"Couldn't sleep," the housekeeper explained. "Just felt I needed to be here. I'll get to work cleaning up." She harrumphed a sigh. "Notice our policemen are gone. Good! Messy bunch of men."

"Maybe you could hold off on the vacuum a bit, Esmeralda." Quickly Shelby explained about the old woman upstairs. "I don't want to disturb her and if she calls out, I'd like someone to be there. Can you handle that?"

"Why the poor thing! I'll go sit right beside her bed and wait till she wakes."

"Just one thing. Did you see anyone in the garden a few minutes ago?"

"Didn't see anybody anywhere. I was getting this coffee made in the kitchen." Esmeralda gave Shelby a funny look then bustled from the room and thumped up the stairs.

Shelby took a sip of her coffee, noticed the crushed rosebuds sprayed over the earth around the bush. Marta's roses were ruined.

"You're stalling. Explain."

"I was in the garden just before you arrived. A man came up behind me, demanded I give him the egg." She told him the rest, every detail of it. "Here I've been suspecting Tim. But this person must be the real kidnapper. He said he'd kill Aimee if I wasn't at my office at nine, with the egg."

"You suspected me of taking Aimee?" Tim stomped around the corner of the house and across the deck. "You actually thought I would do something like that to you, Shelby?"

"Yes," she admitted on a whisper, aware as she watched his eyes of how deeply she'd hurt him with her mistrust. "Because of the hair."

"What hair?" Tim raised one eyebrow.

Briefly Shelby explained about the hair from his jacket, how Russ had taken it for testing, how the DNA had matched Aimee's. "What else could I think?" she whispered.

"You could have asked me, you could have trusted me." He closed his eyes, sagged against the wall. "You could have believed that I would never do anything to hurt either you or Aimee. You could have believed in me, Shelby."

"I'm sorry," she apologized. How wrong she'd been. Though she hadn't used it much lately, she'd always had a hunch about people. Why hadn't she been able to discern the truth about Tim? "It just seemed…odd."

"You could have asked. Maybe that hair came off another of my jackets. Maybe I picked it up off your sofa. Who knows? There could be a thousand explanations. But you never even gave me the benefit of a doubt."

"Let it go, Tim. Right now we've got to work out some kind of a plan to catch this guy and get Aimee back," Daniel muttered. "And we're not calling the police this time."

"Why not?" Tim demanded. "Have you begun to believe me that something isn't quite right about Natalie? Or I am the only suspect here?"

Shame washed over her. Shelby couldn't look at him.

"I believed you a couple of days ago, Tim. That's why I started doing some digging. Then this morning I got a call from my source at the police department. That's what brought me here." Daniel stared straight at Shelby. "Natalie resigned, left her job and is nowhere to be found."

"What?" Shelby couldn't believe it. "But what about the investigation? What about Aimee?"

"She left no notes, nothing. The file is empty. The police understood that you'd asked to be left alone."

Tim sat with his arms crossed over his chest. Shelby knew what he was thinking. Why hadn't she suspected Natalie? "I'm so sorry," she whispered.

"You can't blame yourself." Tim leaned forward, touched her hand, then quickly drew away. "There's no time for re-criminations. We have to decide what to do now."

"All right but maybe we should get Russ working on learning about Natalie." Shelby tried to remember. "He had his own suspicions about her a while back."

"I'll call him, ask him to get to work. In the meantime I'm going to have some special surveillance cameras set up in your office, Shelby." Daniel's face was set in an angry glare. "We are going to catch this person. Once he's inside Finders, he's on my turf. I guarantee he will not get away. Not as long as I can stop it."

"Thanks, Daniel." She hugged him, watched him leave, aware that Tim remained silent.

"Do you want me to go?" he asked at last.

"No." She took a deep breath. "I can't make my suspicions go away, Tim. I know now that I was wrong, that I made a mistake. And I'm sorry I didn't ask you to explain. Can you forgive me?"

He studied her for a long moment, then sighed. "It hurts,"

he murmured. "You actually suspected that I could do this despicable thing. In a way I can understand that you're frantic about Aimee, but…this is me, Shelby. I thought that you were a friend. I thought you knew how much I care about you and your daughter. I would never—"

"I know." Tears threatened but she gulped them away. There were things to do. Either he forgave her or he didn't, but she had to prepare for tonight. "I can't undo it, Tim. All I can say is that I'm sorry."

He shrugged, finally nodded.

"I know I'm asking a lot but if you don't mind, I'd appreciate it if you'd stay and pray with me. We're going to need God's help tonight." She paused, stared into his eyes. "If you don't mind," she whispered, pleading silently for his help.

After a long moment he answered. "I don't mind."

"I'm really sorry. I don't have any explanation, Tim. It just seemed that things kept coming up that pointed to your involvement."

"And you had so many doubts." He cleared his throat. "Maybe I shouldn't say this, but isn't that at the root of everything? You started doubting all of us when you stopped believing in your ability to handle whatever life gives you. But you're strong, Shelby. You have a tough inner core that has seen you through losing your parents, caring for a sick and elderly grandmother, running a company, even raising your child with all the love and devotion you could give. You've accomplished so much and yet you're afraid to trust yourself, afraid to be hurt."

"I'm not afraid." Why did he have to go into this now?

"I think you are. I think that's why you can't let yourself admit that you care for me. You're afraid to allow yourself to care. What I don't understand is why." He leaned forward, stared into her eyes. "I didn't steal Aimee, Shelby. Somewhere inside you must know that. I love you."

"I can't…" She stretched out her hand as if that would stop him from repeating those words.

"You don't have to be afraid of love, Shelby. Your love would be safe with me."

She shook her head as the truth bubbled out. "I will never be safe again. Don't you understand that?"

"No. Why don't you tell me," he encouraged quietly.

In spite of herself, she let it all spill out.

"Grandmother was the only one I had when my parents died. She had several strokes but she hung on, clung to life because she knew how much I needed her." She gulped away the tears. "When she died it hurt so much, but I had Grant and Aimee. Then Grant died and it was all up to me. I was supposed to run this company but I couldn't, I didn't dare leave Aimee because I knew that if I wasn't very careful, if I didn't watch out for her, I'd lose her, too. And then I'd have no one. I'd be all alone. Just like I was all those years ago in the car when my parents died and nobody came, nobody got me. Nobody cared."

She couldn't stop the tears, couldn't stem the tide of pain and loneliness that had built up into a wall of fear for far too long.

"Somebody cared, Shelby." Tim knelt in front of her, his bandaged face inches from hers.

"You didn't even know me then." His hands closed around hers, warm, comforting and rock solid.

"No. But He did. God knew you. He knew what was going to happen. He knew that you'd need Him to lean on, to depend on, to get you through the hardest times when there was nobody else. So He waited."

"What do you mean?"

"God waited for you to call upon Him. That's how He is. He won't push His way in, He'll stand back until you ask Him for help." He reached up to wipe away her tears. "He will be there to support you, to listen, to hear, every time you call. The thing is, you have to call on Him, Shelby. You have to *ask* for His help."

"I've prayed," she told him angrily.

"Yes." Tim nodded, a faint smile curling his lips. "You've prayed for Grant to come back, for Aimee to come back, haven't you? You've prayed for it to all go away. But have you prayed that He would help you bear it, get you through it? And then have you trusted that God would do what He promised and never let you down?"

"I don't—"

"Shelby, haven't you tried to do it all on your own? To manage the pain, to stuff it down, brooding on it whenever the memories got too strong, but never facing it head-on."

"I guess."

"That's not trust," he whispered, his voice so soft in the morning stillness. "Trust is learning that God does what is best, that whatever happens He will work it out to benefit us. Maybe not in the way that we think, but to our benefit. Trust is staying strong in the knowledge that He loves us enough to let us hurt sometimes. Trust is saying 'I don't know what You have planned, God, but whatever it is, whatever happens, I'll still trust that You know best.'"

She gulped down the fear. "Blind faith?"

"It's the only way."

"But what if—" She licked her lips but could not say the words aloud. The fear they engendered cut through to her very soul.

"What if God let Aimee die?"

"Yes, what if, Shelby? What if the very worst thing happens and you never see your daughter alive again?"

She recoiled, pushed him away. "Don't say that!"

"You have to say it, have to understand what all of this is

about." Tim rose, stepped away from her. "The thing you have to decide before you go to Finders to meet whoever is behind this is whether or not you're going to trust God. No matter what."

FOURTEEN

She was so scared.

Even though he'd finished praying aloud, in his mind Tim kept a steady stream of words barraging Heaven as he watched her staring into space. If only he could think of a subject she could discuss which would help ease the tenseness that had fallen. He needn't have worried.

The doorbell rang and Shelby returned to the patio with Russ, who was talking about Natalie.

"It would seem she has left town."

"Do you think she took Aimee?"

Panic filled Shelby's face. Tim reached out, took her hand and squeezed. She offered him a grateful smile.

"I do not think so. Her landlady said she drove away with only two suitcases."

Tim felt Russ's glance at their clasped hands, saw surprise flare his eyes. Before he could say anything the doorbell rang again. This time it was Daniel.

He and Russ traded glares, but mercifully neither argued. Daniel mentioned papers which needed Shelby's signature. Russ informed them both he'd be out of touch for a few days while he tried to track Natalie.

"I have a small lead which I must follow immediately.

If she has the little Aimee, she will pay," he promised grimly.

"Thank you, Russ. I truly appreciate all you've done." Shelby reached up to hug him.

"You are welcome. Just remain strong. The end to this nightmare, it will come soon."

A noise from upstairs interrupted their goodbye. Tim glanced at Shelby.

"I'll go speak with your guest," he murmured.

"Ah, the guest. I wondered why it is you do not come in to Finders today, Shelby. The visitors keep you away, eh?"

To Tim's mind, Russ sounded as if he were chastising Shelby. He didn't like that.

"Shelby's been pulled through a wringer," he muttered wishing the other man would just leave. "I would think that between you and Daniel, Finders would be on safe ground while she takes a break."

"Of course." Russ gave him an arch look then turned toward the door. "I must go."

Daniel came downstairs in time to answer his phone. Tim decided to check on Marta, who had been dreaming. He comforted her then left the very capable Esmeralda in charge of a promised sponge bath. When he came down, only Shelby was waiting.

"Daniel's in the study talking to Igor about the security cameras," she explained. "Let's go back to the patio, see if the coffee is still warm."

She was nervous with him. Tim searched for a neutral topic, saw the rosebush. He stood, walked over to it and fingered one of the tight, almost black buds.

"This is such a strange color," he murmured. "I was trying to describe it to my surgeon yesterday. He'd never heard of Deep Secret."

"I don't wonder." Shelby laughed. "Those aren't any official names, at least I don't think so. They're Grant's names, for special bushes he put in this area. I'm not all that knowledgeable about roses but the ones around this section all have funny names. Look." She rose, pointed to the others as she named them. "That's Incognito. That's Enigma, Moonlight, Shadow, Clandestine. They're all strange."

"What are strange?" Daniel asked as he emerged from the house.

"I'm telling Tim about the names Grant chose for his roses." She wandered back over the path and Tim followed. "Now where are those papers you wanted signed?"

But the papers fell in a scattering across the ground as Daniel stared at the nameplate in front of Deep Secret.

"When was this planted, Shelby?" he asked, his voice higher pitched than normal.

"The day Grant died." She cleared her throat, continued. "At least I think so. Aimee would know. They were out here for hours preparing the ground. Why?"

"Can you get me a shovel?" he asked.

A call from upstairs twigged at Tim. "I promised I'd carry Marta down if she ate the muffin Esmeralda was trying to stuff into her," he explained. "I'll be right back."

"Are you sure it won't be too much?" Shelby glanced at Daniel as if to ask for help, but the other man was fingering the leaves of Deep Secret.

"I'll be fine."

By the time he'd carried the tiny woman onto the patio and installed her in a lounger, Daniel was on his knees in the rose garden carefully digging up the bush.

"You won't know this, Shel, but Grant and I used to have this code when we first started in covert ops." His voice grew quieter as he lifted the bush free and set it aside. "We used all of the names he has here—Incognito, Enigma, Clandestine. Each one had a special meaning. Deep Secret always described a buried object."

"How come you never thought of this before?" Tim asked.

"Because I never had the nameplates attached until this spring," Shelby explained. "I wanted the horticultural people to take over the place and before they visited I made every effort to make it look good. I had the signs made to replace Grant's little sticks. I doubt if Daniel ever saw the name before."

"I wish I had." He bent over, felt around with the tip of the shovel. The clunk was loud. They all heard it. With a deep breath he reached into the hole and drew up a metal box. "Oh, Grant," he murmured. "If only you'd told me."

"What is it?" Shelby waited until he set the box on the step and pried open the tight-fitting lid. Another box lay inside. "It's completely dry," she whispered.

"Yes. Grant had the exterior box specially made. I saw an invoice for it but didn't understand what it was for." Daniel lifted the top of the second box. "I thought so."

A beautiful gold filigree egg lay inside, tiny jewels adorning it. Marta squealed, then reached forward and picked up the delicate thing.

"It is mine," she whispered as tears rolled down her parchmentlike cheeks. "It is the gift from Czar Nicholas. Let me see." She began exploring the egg with her fingers, pressing the delicate work here and there.

Afraid she'd damage the fragile item Tim thought to reach out and take it from her, but Shelby saw his intention and shook her head. "Wait."

Like over-taut elastic they waited; one moment stretched into the next as Marta kept her fingers moving over the expensive bauble.

"Perhaps it isn't hers," Tim murmured. But Marta glared at him.

"It belonged to my family," she insisted. "I will prove it." At that moment the top of the egg suddenly released exposing a family crest.

"Romanov," Daniel murmured. "There's an inscription below. It's in Russian."

"For Andrei Kostov," Marta murmured. "For his friendship. From Nicholas." She rubbed her finger over the letters tenderly. "Ah, Papa. I miss you still."

Tim saw tears in Shelby's eyes and felt his own prickle.

"It's very beautiful, Marta," Shelby murmured. "This is what Grant found for you?"

Marta shook her head. "Not for me," she murmured. "For my sisters. Look." She touched the side of the egg and the bottom slid free. On a bed of velvet lay three tiny gold bracelets. "Look inside," she whispered. "You will see the names."

Shelby picked up one, read the name. "Sacha. This one says Mikka. This one says Marta. You and your sisters."

"Yes." She handed the egg to Shelby in exchange for the bracelets which she clasped to her bosom, eyes closed.

The reverence of the moment was overwhelming. Tim knew they all felt it. But there were so many questions.

"Shelby, I don't understand why this person that stopped you in the garden wants it," he murmured. "It's worth a lot, of course. But why this particular egg? Why lock up Marta for it? Nothing makes sense."

Shelby hushed him as Daniel hunkered down in front of the old lady.

"You hired us to do a job, Marta. And we haven't completed it yet. We must find your sisters. To do that I will need the egg and the bracelets, just for a little while. Would that be all right?"

At first she held the golden bands tight against her cheek, her eyes wide, full of fear.

"Remember Grant's promise to you, Marta?" Shelby, too, knelt in front of her. "We always finish the job, no matter how long it takes. Let us finish it, find out who did this and why. Let us help you find your sisters. Please?"

Finally she nodded. Her gaze held Shelby's as she spoke so softly Tim had to lean in to hear.

"Your Grant said that even if he couldn't finish it, you would. He said if I couldn't trust anyone else, I could trust you. I will trust."

Tim's words. Shelby twisted slightly, found him behind her, watching. She nodded then turned back to the old lady.

"I promise we won't let you down," she murmured. She gently lifted away the bracelets, put them back inside the egg then carried it toward him.

He could hardly believe the whispered words he heard next.

"I trust you, Tim. If you want to help us, we'd welcome anything you can offer."

She trusted him!

While Esmeralda took care of Marta, he followed Shelby and Daniel into the den, relieved that at last he might have a chance to prove himself, bandages notwithstanding.

Shelby entered Finders, Inc. through the main door, conscious of the shadows that accompanied every move. He already knew she was coming, why try to hide it. She rode upstairs in the elevator, eyes alert for any movement within the building. Nothing.

At two minutes before nine she unlocked her office door and stepped inside, aware that the camera transmitted every move to Daniel, who was watching somewhere in the building. The phone rang.

"Yes?"

"Go to the warehouse, the eastern door."

"But you didn't say the warehouse, or the east door," she repeated for Daniel's benefit. "You said my office."

"Do it. You have six minutes." The line went dead.

"It's not the same voice," she murmured, as she hung up the phone, picked up the bag holding the black velvet box that housed the egg.

Now what? They'd all expected the exchange to be made in her office. Daniel would not have prepared the eastern section of the warehouse. It was seldom used with only a few security cameras to cover a large area.

And it was where Grant had died.

Feathers of worry tickled up her backbone. She'd be alone there. No one could save her if the kidnapper started another fire. Daniel's plans hadn't included that. Suddenly her nightmare became real. She was truly alone, without backup, preparing to face who knew what.

I know.

God. He knew it all. He would help her deal with whatever lay ahead if she only asked. She wasn't alone. He was there.

As she rode down, then raced through the hallways to the warehouse, Shelby prayed as she never had. Not for her own safety, not even for Aimee's. This time she prayed for the strength to do whatever He would have her do that would make this work together for good.

The warehouse seemed eerily silent. As she walked past the many vaults and cubicles, she couldn't help but replay the night of Grant's death. She'd walked here, smelled the acrid smoke as she tried to understand that she'd never see him again. Now Shelby clung to her control by repeating Tim's verse over and over.

"We *know* that God causes everything to work together for the good of those who love God and are called according to His purpose."

She waited, lips moving silently as she repeated the phrases over and over. After a moment she set the satchel down, lifted the velvet box free and set it on a nearby crate.

"I'm here," she hollered. "Come on."

Nothing.

Shelby stared at her watch as five, ten, fifteen minutes passed. She reached out to lift the box. Her hand froze as a voice called her name.

"Hello, Shelby. I see you followed instructions."

"Russ?" Shock held her immobile. Something dark and sinister glimmered in his hand—a gun? She saw him shift it to his other hand, though it stayed trained on her while he opened the box and examined the egg. A soft noise…she blinked. He knew how to open it!

"How did you—What are you doing here, Russ?"

"Retrieving something."

"The egg is Marta's. It was her father's." Anger broke free propelling Shelby forward as the truth rammed home. "You took my daughter! I want her back, Russ. Now."

"So impatient." Russ nodded. "Yes, it will be much easier for me if the little Aimee goes home to her Mama. Such a handful." A hateful mocking grin twisted his lips. "She will return, my dear Shelby. By tomorrow morning."

Shelby slid her hand into her pants pocket, closed her fingers around her cell phone and pressed the key that would automatically dial Tim's number. She raised her voice to cover the ringing.

"After you've left the country with the egg? I don't think so, Russ. I'm not waiting. I want to know where she is and I want to know now." She turned the phone outward, hoping

Tim would not hang up until he heard the pertinent details. "Where is my daughter, Russ?"

"I have told you she is safe, but if you must know the location, that is no problem." He gave an address in a residential area.

"But that's—"

"Where you once lived with your parents, yes? You see how good an agent I am. Nothing escapes me. Unlike Daniel. And you."

His smug expression made her fingers curl but Shelby remained silent.

"It is ironic, isn't it, Shelby? Your parents died but mine are still asking things of me."

"I don't know what you're talking about," she told him, praying desperately that Tim had heard the location. She didn't dare repeat the address but maybe… "Why would you take Aimee to my childhood home? Why would you do any of this? Are you crazy?"

"I am the top operative at Finders, Inc., Shelby. I assure you I am not in the least crazy." His eyes glowed like black onyx, dared her to argue. His voice hardened to a stilted staccato. "Be assured I have planned everything to achieve maximum results."

"Why?" she whispered. A new truth dawned. "You killed Grant."

"Yes. Regrettable, but necessary."

Shock held her immobile for several moments. Then the tears seeped from the corners of her eyes. Shelby could not believe what she was hearing.

"How could killing him be necessary? He was your friend, Russ. You'd backed each other up a hundred times before. He trusted you like a brother. What could possibly be a good enough reason to kill your best friend?"

Russ's hard jaw clenched but he never looked away from her.

"Some things go beyond friendship. Grant had to die

before everything was ruined. As it was, I waited too long. He caused too many problems."

"What was ruined?" She slapped her hands on her hips, frustration eating at her soul. "This is unbelievable and I demand an explanation."

"You demand?" Russ grabbed her arm and yanked her nearer, held his gun to her temple. "You are not in a position to demand, my dear Shelby. Let us only say that the past is the worst enemy a man can have."

"Let's not say that, Russ." She stood straight and tall, anger killing any fear she might have felt. She jerked her arm free, planted it on her hip. "You killed my husband, stole my child's father, ruined our lives and used my resources to do it. Offering me some cryptic line about the past isn't going to cut it. Tell me why."

"You are so blind. *Your* misery, *your* unhappiness. Compared to what is at stake it is not so much." He stepped forward, clicked the hammer of the gun back, pressed it tighter against her temple, though he made no move to touch her otherwise. "You have no idea what drives us to kill."

"You're right," she agreed. "I don't have any idea what could compel you to kill a man who loved you like a brother. But I do know that Grant would never have done that to you."

"Be quiet! You know nothing. It is time for me to go." Russ turned away, the gun dropping to his side. He set the egg on a crate.

"You're not going anywhere." Daniel appeared from behind a stack of boxes, a revolver in his hand. "Did you really think I would simply let you walk away, Russ? You are many things but I don't remember stupid being one of them."

"Ah, the faithful dog follows on the heels of his love. Do you never get weary of playing the hero, Daniel?"

Daniel lifted an eyebrow in enquiry. "What are you babbling about now?"

"Your secret love. Shelby," Russ prodded when Daniel stared at him. "Tell the truth, you have been in love with her for years."

"You're insane! She was the wife of my friend. I love her like a sister, Russ. Nothing more."

"That is why you run to her house so frequently, on matters you yourself could decide?" Russ shook his head. "I do not think so."

"I don't care what you think. The truth is I was hoping Shelby would come back to work." Daniel glanced at her. "Please don't misunderstand, Shel. I loved being able to help when you needed me, but the company isn't the same without you there. I don't have your way with people, I'm a loner, used to hiding. You have to come back, Shel. Finders needs you at the helm. Your vision, your insight."

"So touching."

Suddenly Shelby was aware that Russ had kept moving the whole time. Now he was in a position where he could shoot Daniel and easily make his escape. She reached for the egg.

"Aren't you forgetting something, Russ?" She held the egg in her outstretched hand. "Wasn't this what your murder and kidnapping was all about?"

"Bring it over here." He pointed his gun directly at her head.

"You shoot her, I shoot you," Daniel reminded him, his own aim steady, lethal. "Either way, you're not walking out of here. Walk toward me, Shelby." Something crashed in the back of the warehouse and Daniel's stare wavered, giving Russ enough time to dart forward, grab her arm. "Shelby stays here."

"I don't think so." A new voice. Tim. "Not until the truth

of these papers comes out. You might as well let her go. You'll never get away."

Tim! Relief flooded her until she remembered.

Where was Aimee?

FIFTEEN

"Don't worry, Shelby. Your faith in me wasn't misplaced. I passed on your message," he murmured low enough that only she could hear. "The police are on their way to get Aimee as we speak."

"Thank you." The relief she felt at seeing him, at hearing those words was like a wave that snuck up and swamped you when you weren't expecting to swim.

"Stop whispering. What is this about papers?"

"These." Tim stretched out his arm but didn't move from his position, forcing Russ to step forward enough to get a closer look at the sheets.

He blanched, stepped back, his hold on her arm still strong. "Where did you get this?"

"More importantly, what did you do with the diary they came from, the one you stole from Grant Kincaid?" Tim demanded. "It was a diary, wasn't it? The personal record of someone who lived in the past."

"So you say. It is your story," Russ muttered, all the while his eyes were darting around the room, searching for an escape.

"Very well. Then I shall tell it." He turned to Shelby. "After we found those pages and you made copies, I sent them to some friends. Tonight I received a very interesting phone call. I don't believe Russ killed Grant for the egg. Russ killed Grant because someone told him he had to. I think it was his grandfather."

Russ muttered with growing anger. "You do not know my grandfather, such a man is beyond your knowledge. You know nothing except the workings of a museum. What kind of boring life is that?"

"A handy one, as it turns out," Tim told him. "You might be surprised to know that I did my doctoral studies on the extensive Romanov fortune and its disappearance after the Bolshevik revolution of 1917. One of the revolution ringleaders frequently mentioned in the newspapers of the time was a young hothead of seventeen name Ruskava. Turns out that was his given name. Surname Carpolski." Tim nodded at Russ. "I see you know it." He glanced at Shelby. "Russ Carson is named for his grandfather."

"But Russ holds American and French passports," Shelby exclaimed.

"Yes. He lived there for many years with his maternal grandmother, hence his flawless French. But he was born in Russia. I believe an investigation would reveal that he never truly gave up his Russian citizenship."

"You do not know anything about me," Russ sneered, his fingers pinching tighter around Shelby's arm.

"I know more than you think," Tim told him, mouth tipped in a smile brimming with confidence. "Those pages struck a chord with some people in Russia, people who remember Carpolski the czarist very well. They also remember Ruskava, the revolutionist who so vocally opposed Czar Nicholas's plan to send more forces to the war."

"I get it. So your grandfather had a foot in both camps." Daniel wore a stunned expression. "I'm ashamed I never put it together."

"Many before you have not." Tim looked more closely at Daniel. "Does the name Carpolski not ring any bells for you now, Daniel?"

"Actually it does. But I thought he'd retired." Daniel glanced at Shelby. "If we are talking about the same man, he was supposed to be out of Russian politics. I assumed he'd passed away."

"Not yet. But he is retired, after a fashion. He could afford to hide out in his palace since his father expropriated the land, money and property that should have belonged to Marta's family and was never required to give it back." Tim's voice hardened. "The Carpolskis were peasants, they never had the means to make their own fortune so they stole from others."

"Lies!" Russ raged, his face a dark red.

"Ruskava's son changed his name and took over where his father had left off. Boris Vardeyava has been a revered and active participant in the movers and shakers of Russia for some time. He took on the veneer of a civilized businessman and gained the approval of those who could help him achieve his father's dream of becoming the most powerful man in Russia. That's where Marta's sisters came in."

Shelby glanced at Russ. His face was frozen, empty of expression. Except for his eyes, which burned with hatred. She knew everything Tim was saying was true.

"Marta's sisters found out just who Boris was and petitioned to have their family home, plus their father's art collection which Boris has hanging in his home at Minsk, by the way, returned to them. They had the egg which was part of the proof they intended to use. A detective hired by the sisters had learned that Marta had moved to America after the Second World War. Marta's niece was dispatched to follow the only lead they had."

"But where is the niece?" Daniel asked. "I haven't been able to find a trace of her."

"You see?" Russ said with a smirk. "It is typical of him, no? He cannot even find a missing person. I told you I was the better man."

"Where did you put her?" She knew he'd done it, the smug testament of his snide grin said it all.

"Safely tucked away in a place where those with delusions can't harm others."

"I feel like I never knew you, Russ. You stole my daughter, you had Marta drugged, you locked up this woman you don't even know. Why?"

"Why?" He barked out a laugh. "Even now you don't understand?"

"His father is about to announce his intention to run for president, Shelby." Tim smiled at her surprise. "Papa can't allow the old disgraces to be made public. It wouldn't do for the Russian people to know that the man they credit as an honorable man has based his stolen world on a tissue of lies, that his secure standing and business reputation are based on schemes which defrauded three feeble old women of their rightful inheritance. The egg would have sealed their case, provided the icing on the cake, so to speak."

"So you're carrying on the family tradition. Killing Grant as your grandfather killed Marta's father." Daniel's eyes widened as he spoke, his gaze centered on Russ. "The missing items from the warehouse—you took those. You had to. The book would have added to Marta's sisters' case, so I understand that. But the diamond brooch, the gold coin, the lamp? Why?"

Russ remained stubbornly silent.

"I might be able to clarify," Tim offered. "The day I saw a photo of the brooch, I thought it seemed familiar, but I couldn't think why. I've been racking my brain these past few days because something about it kept chewing at me. On the Internet news this afternoon there was an article about a diamond brooch about to go up for auction. I e-mailed the auction house. This is what they sent." He pulled out his picture phone, pressed a button, then held it out so Shelby could see. "I'm almost certain it's the same as the brooch in the photo you showed me. I have compared it to my research and can tell you it was one of those from the collection of the wife of Czar Nicholas."

The ugliness of evil crept into the room, silenced them all. Shelby tried to make it all fit, but one puzzle piece didn't work.

"But Grant, Russ," she whispered, staring at the man she'd trusted so implicitly. "Why kill Grant?"

"Because he figured it out. Am I right, Russ?" Daniel's disgust was obvious. "Your allegiance to your father and grand-father couldn't compete with the guy who dragged you out of a prisoner of war camp in Afghanistan or any of the other times Grant saved your life. He got too close, he would have insisted the egg be returned to its rightful owners. In fact he was probably in the process of doing that. You had to shut him up."

From the corner of her eye Shelby could see Tim inching his way nearer. She wanted to tell him to stay away but was afraid the motion might attract Russ's attention so she remained still.

"This is all a fantasy you've created, Daniel. Something to cover your own shortcomings. For all we know you stole the brooch this *friend* of Shelby's is talking about." He glared at Tim, waved with his gun. "Forget about the hero's rescue, or she dies."

Shelby ignored the interplay between the two. Her attention remained riveted on Russs.

"So…what? You're saying you didn't do it? That you didn't kill my husband, your best friend?" She couldn't believe he would try to deny it now, after confessing.

"Who are you going to believe, Shelby? A man who carried the hair of your daughter on his jacket? I found her, you know. He had her hidden away and I found her, took her to safety. You ask her, you'll see that Uncle Russ never harmed a hair on her head."

"Yes, let's talk about the DNA of that hair."

Shelby suddenly realized that Tim had removed his bandages. Even now, with all it's redness and puffy swelling, the damage he'd suffered couldn't hide his fury.

"I think maybe good ol' Russ pulled a little switcheroo." Tim took another step forward, his gaze locked on Russ. "You took the hair Shelby gave you that came from my jacket and deliberately replaced it with one that you took from Aimee. Didn't you?"

"This is a silly child's game you play, curator." Russ didn't bother to hide his scorn. "What do you know of DNA?"

"Not a lot. But your man in the lab does and he says the root from the hair marked as coming from my jacket was too fresh, that it had been recently pulled from Aimee's scalp. By you."

Shelby's heart sank at the look on Russ's face.

"The computer downloads from Finders, Aimee, Grant—you were behind all of it, weren't you, Russ? My trusted friend, a man I thought would honor Grant's memory. Instead you dishonor him with your lies and deceit." Shelby could hardly believe it herself, but it had to be true. Nothing else made sense.

"This is ridiculous. I will not stand here and be slandered by these stupid men." Russ began backing toward the loading dock, dragging Shelby with him. "Daniel was never clever enough to run Finders, Inc. I've proven that over and over. But you don't wish your decision challenged. So when he has a failure, you blame it on me."

"It's over, Russ. Don't be stupid!" Tim moved nearer, grabbed her arm. "Let Shelby go. What good will it do to hurt her, too? You can't possibly believe you'll get away with this?"

The buzzer that signaled a delivery at the warehouse door rang through the cavernous area startling everyone. A small smile played at the corner of Russ's mouth.

"Won't I?" He drew Shelby along, undid the door locks and pressed the opener. "I believe you are wrong on that score, curator. Which only shows how foolish you really are."

"You are the foolish one!" Natalie stood framed in the doorway, flanked on either side by police. "I should never have let you talk me into this ridiculous scheme."

"Drop your weapon!" The order came from somewhere behind Natalie.

Shelby squinted into the brilliant lights, trying to see who was behind them, but Russ jerked her against him like a shield.

"I do not think so, gentlemen. If you shoot, Mrs. Kincaid dies. A tragic things, yes? The death of one so young and beautiful, with a small child left alone. Now back off."

To Shelby it was as if the words emerged in slow motion. Fear rose from a terrified spot deep inside. She almost gagged as the image of Aimee sitting alone in their empty home played out in her mind.

Dear God, I know that You are there, that You can bring good out of bad, bring blessing and joy from pain. I trust You. I believe in You.

The cold steel metal of Russ's gun butt rested against her temple and for a moment, one split second, the fear returned. But then a gentle peace flooded her heart and she knew, *knew* that God was in control.

"Drop your guns or she dies." When none of the officers complied, Russ shrugged. "Fine. I am sorry, Shelby." He cocked his gun.

"No!" With one giant leap Tim yanked Shelby away and launched himself at Russ.

A crack echoed through the room. Tim crumpled to the ground as blood pooled around his head. His poor, damaged face went slack, his eyes closed and he sagged to the floor.

Now! The voice was loud, clear, insistent.

Shelby swiveled, shot her foot out at Russ's midsection and felled him with one kick. The gun flew out of his hand, landed on the floor. Daniel grabbed it, signaled the police officers to come.

As policemen rushed into the building Shelby collapsed on the floor beside Tim, tried to stem the flow of blood with her hands.

"Call an ambulance," she begged, "please call an ambulance. He's bleeding."

"We've got one waiting, ma'am," someone told her, gently easing her out of the way. "Let them do their job now."

Within minutes Tim was rolled into the ambulance. Shelby begged to go along but wasn't allowed.

Please don't let him die, God. Please!

When the lights had faded from view, Shelby glanced around and saw Russ standing sullenly in the shadows. She walked over to him.

"Was it worth it?" she asked angrily. "Murdering Grant, kidnapping Aimee, drugging Marta, incarcerating her niece, shooting Tim—was it all worth it just to keep the generations of lies from your family hidden?"

"You have no proof I killed Grant," was all he said.

"I do." Daniel stepped forward. "After the investigation was over, I had the old system taken down and a new one installed. I've recently had several experts examine it. They all concur. The suppression system was rigged to delay before activation. You needed Grant to die before anyone would even know he was there."

"It's a story."

"No. The lab found fingerprints on two pipes. Yours. You could have had no other reason to touch the system, Russ. You deliberately killed him. The one man who would have given his life willingly if you'd asked."

The accused man remained silent.

"Who's the stupid one now?" Daniel murmured.

"He is." Natalie stepped forward. "He said it was a trick to play on you, Mrs. Kincaid. A game that had to be real in every detail. But I do not like this game. I am not a babysitter."

"Turns out her name is Natasha, not Natalie. And her credentials are fake. Probably engineered by him." The cop who'd protected Shelby's front door for days stepped forward. "I started asking questions when she took me off duty. No way that happens in a case like this with that video coming in when it did. My Sergeant got Internal Investigations going."

"I'm glad you did check. Thank you very much." Shelby struggled to ask the question she was most afraid of. "Is my daughter—"

"Safe and sound, ma'am. Eating those excellent cookies your housekeeper makes. They were giggling when I left. Probably planning another surprise."

"Thank you." Shelby was glad of Daniel's hand under her arm, supporting her, caring for her. *Thank You, God. Please take care of Tim.*

"I would never have hurt the petite Aimee," Russ muttered, glaring at the cop. "Nor you, Shelby. I care for both of you." His eyes beamed hate at Daniel. "It is his fault this happened."

"Excuse me? You care for me?" Incredulity swamped her. "That's some caring, Russ." She shook her head, glared at him. "Want to explain how you murdering my husband and shooting my friend could possibly be Daniel's fault?"

"Still you don't see." Russ sighed. "As long as you stayed away from Finders, I had a chance to find the egg and even if I didn't, nothing more would have happened. The ladies could prove nothing without it. But Daniel had to involve you in his questions. You began to poke around, research Grant's old cases. I couldn't have that. My duty was and is always to my family. If I could have stopped the niece from making her journey to this country, I would have. But I was notified too late. After that it was necessity that drove me."

Natasha muttered something in Russian.

"Pardon?" Shelby nodded at her, encouraging her to voice her opinion in a language they could all understand.

"He makes it sound so noble—to kidnap an old lady, to drug her so much she can't tell what day it is. The kind Russ. So thoughtful." She scorned him. "Is that why you gave the order to that stupid man to kill her with an overdose—because you loved your family so much? What about *her* family? What about the little girl and that stupid video to torture her mother? What about the niece you have locked up in The Bleich Institute under a false name?"

"Shut up, you stupid woman! What an imbecile you have turned out to be. To make such a fuss about pulling a strand of hair from a child's head—it is ridiculous."

"And you with your lies and secrets—are they not ridiculous? Killing a man you once told me was like your brother—this is the action of a sane man? It is you who are stupid. The truth always comes out."

Russ's face grew cold and hard. "I should have killed you," he murmured.

"You could not."

"Oh yes?" In a split second he'd grabbed an officer's gun. He fought to free himself, took aim. A shot rang out. The entire room went motionless.

Russ reached toward Shelby, then paused as if frozen.

"So sorry," he whispered. Then he collapsed onto the warehouse floor. Police rushed forward.

"He's dead," an officer told her moments later.

Daniel supported her as she sagged, knees weak, staring at the man who'd brought so much pain into her life. Behind him the police were forcing Natalie out of the building and into a police cruiser. It was all such a waste.

"Come on, Shelby. Be strong."

Daniel's words reminded her that this was not over. Not yet.

"Aimee," she whispered. "I must see Aimee. Then Tim."

"Go with the police, Shelby. I'll handle things here. Take the egg with you." He squeezed her arm. "Don't worry, I'll make sure the niece is released tonight. Maybe we'll bring her to see Marta tomorrow."

"Yes, of course." She wrapped her arms around him and hugged him tightly. "Thank you, Daniel. Thank you for being my friend."

"Your best friend. And don't forget it." He hugged her back, then chucked her on the chin. "Keep the faith," he murmured as his lips brushed her cheek.

"I'm trying," she whispered back.

The officers helped her off the warehouse deck to the platform below, then into a police cruiser. Soon she was flying through the city, lights flashing, siren wailing.

"The chief said to get you home ASAP. This is an emergency," they told her as they roared into her drive.

"Thank you." She climbed out, stood at the front door. "I'll have to make a statement, won't I?"

"Yes, ma'am. But that can wait. Go be with your daughter now." Officer Dan grinned. "The happy times are the ones you have to savor."

"Yes, they surely are." Shelby let herself in the front door, heard the soft murmur of Marta's voice. She eased the door closed and stood, content to wait for the reunion she'd longed for. It was not long in coming—that joyful, bubbling giggle from the kitchen quickly melted her heart and sent a spear of pure joy racing through her body.

"I'm home," she called.

"Mommy!" Aimee raced through the house and launched herself into Shelby's arms. "I missed you so much."

Her heart sang praises as she snuggled her darling child close and reveled in her soft weight.

"I missed you, too, sweetheart." She held her back, checked her face, her limbs through the wash of tears that would not stop. "I love you so much, Aimee. So very much. Are you all right?"

"She's perfect," Esmeralda murmured as tears streamed down her cheeks. "Absolutely perfect."

"Did you like the game, Mommy?"

Shelby carried her child to the kitchen, set her down on a stool, wondering what had happened to her child during the horrible days of her absence. Marta was there, bright eyed and alert. She tilted her cheek up for Shelby's kiss, her smile happy as she gathered the velvet box containing the egg into her hands.

"What game?" she asked, accepting the cup of tea Esmeralda handed her.

"Our hide-and-seek game, silly." Aimee clapped her hands together, her little face alight with excitement. "Uncle Russ said you were so good at games that we had to hide really well, but you must have guessed or the people wouldn't have found me. Uncle Russ said that when they found me the game would be all finished."

"Did he?" In some part of her heart Shelby was grateful to Russ for making Aimee believe her abduction was all part of a joke on her mother. Clearly her daughter had not been traumatized, had no notion of what Russ was really up to. "Who looked after you when Russ couldn't be there?"

"A pretty lady called Natalie. And a man. But he was grumpy." Her nose wrinkled. "He didn't even know how to play Chutes and Ladders!"

"Huh." So there was someone else involved. She wondered if they would ever know who.

"Did you like the video, Mommy?" Aimee's eyes sparkled with fun. "Uncle Russ said I was a very good actress."

"Yes, you were. I liked it very much."

The doorbell rang. Shelby found her favorite police officer and a woman she'd never met standing on the doorstep.

"Mr. McCullough said we were to stop by. Apparently this lady is to meet someone you have staying here."

"You're Marta's niece," Shelby exclaimed.

"Great-niece, actually. Is she here?"

"Yes. Come in. You, too, officer." She led them into the kitchen. The younger woman gathered the fragile old lady in her arms as both began to weep. Shelby couldn't suppress her own tears as Marta's niece began to talk about the two sisters and how they longed to be reunited with the one they'd been searching for. Together they examined the Fabergé egg.

Shelby stepped closer to the officer, lowered her voice. "How's Tim?" she asked.

He shrugged. "Sorry. I don't know."

"Uncle Russ said you'd want to ask me lots of questions when I got home. Aren't you going to ask me?" Aimee demanded. "And who are those ladies? Esmeralda said the lady in the wheelchair is your friend."

"Yes, she is," Shelby assured her. "And the other lady is her niece. I'll explain later."

"Okay. But what about the game?"

"You and I are going to talk about the game later, too, sweetheart. After I get used to having you home again."

"It was so much fun. Except I missed you, Mommy. And I missed Mr. Tim." She glanced around, obviously disappointed. "I thought he would come over to see me as soon as I got home, but he didn't. Can I go see him?"

"Honey, it's really late."

"Mr. Tim won't be sleeping." Aimee's bottom lip jutted out.

Shelby knew Aimee wasn't going to be put off, no matter how much she danced around the truth. She'd been hoping to visit the hospital after Aimee went to bed but now saw how foolish that was. She sought for the best words as she crouched down in front of her daughter, kept her voice low so she wouldn't interrupt the two ladies.

"Aimee, honey, listen. About Tim—he couldn't come over tonight, sweetheart. Not even though I know he wants to very much. You see, he's in the hospital."

"Oh. Did he have another operation?" Aimee whispered, her eyes worried.

"Sort of. I thought I'd go check on him as soon as I tuck you into bed."

"I don't want to go to bed." Aimee shook her head. "I want to go with you, Mommy."

"Maybe tomorrow, honey. Visiting hours are over for today."

"But if Mr. Tim hurts I can tell him the stories and he'll feel better. I told them to Uncle Russ. He liked the one about the little girl whose name was Anastasia. You remember—she was a princess until some bad men took away her palace. Uncle Russ likes that one. He says I'm just like Anastasia."

A vague memory of Anastasia, the fabled Romanov daughter who some thought had escaped her family's execution, flickered through Shelby's mind. She'd have to ask Tim about that. If…when he was better.

"Russ liked that story especially?"

"Yes, he did." Aimee's bright head cocked to one side, glossy strands bright against her blue sweater. To Shelby she resembled an inquisitive bluebird faintly troubled by what had happened. "I think Uncle Russ was sick, Mommy. Sometimes when he was sleeping he would start yelling. Maybe he had a pain."

A big pain, in the pit of his heart. Someday she'd tell Aimee the whole story. But not tonight. Tonight was for rejoicing. Her daughter was home.

"I promise I'll take you to see Tim tomorrow, darling."

"Okay. The phone's ringing, Mommy."

"So it is. Hello?"

"Mrs. Kincaid, this is Nurse Tara Tobin at City General. A Mr. Daniel McCullough asked me to call you."

Dread crawled over Shelby's nerves. Her fingers squeezed around the phone, clung to it as if it were a lifeline. *Please don't let it happen,* she prayed. *Not again.*

"Yes?" she whispered, never more aware of the ever-present specter of fear than now. "What did Daniel want you to tell me?"

"To come immediately, if you could." The nurse offered nothing else.

Come now? It could only be bad news. Shelby sucked in a breath of oxygen, cleared her throat hoping her voice would come out steady.

"Please tell Mr. McCullough I'll be there shortly. And thank you, Nurse. I appreciate the call."

As she turned away from the phone and caught sight of

Aimee's curious look, Shelby steeled herself for what was to come. Couldn't God have given her a few minutes of joy with her child before He let this happen?

...causes everything to work together... Tim's chiding voice echoed through her mind.

"Mama? Who was that?"

"That was the hospital, darling. Tim is there. Uncle Daniel's with him. He wants us to come and see Tim. Right away."

"But it's nighttime, Mama. You told me you can't visit people in hospitals at night."

"Not usually, Aimee. But this is a special occasion." She crouched down, met her daughter's stare. "Tim is very sick. I don't think he'll be able to talk to us but we can sit with him, tell him we're praying for him."

Aimee absorbed that, then frowned. "Is he going to see God like Daddy did? 'Cause I don't want him to."

Me, neither. But no one had consulted her, asked for her input.

"I don't know, darling. Let's just go and find out for ourselves."

But as she drove toward the hospital Shelby couldn't shake the feeling that she'd gotten the only gift she was going to get tonight. Aimee was safe and sound—because of Tim.

Now Tim was going to die.

And it was all her fault.

SIXTEEN

The hush of the hospital felt ominous.

Shelby checked with admitting, then led Aimee onto the elevator, then through the halls to the room where Tim was housed.

"I'm scared, Mommy."

So am I. Shelby gathered the tiny hand a little tighter as she forced down her apprehension.

"It's okay, sweetie. Remember how we prayed? God is going to take care of Tim."

Please, God? Shelby squeezed her eyes closed in a quick unspoken prayer, then pushed open the door.

The bed was empty.

"Mr. Tim isn't here, Mommy."

A rush of tears clogged her throat as the knowledge hit home like a sledgehammer.

She loved him.

It wasn't a betrayal of Grant, as she'd thought, and condemned herself for. This was a new love, a different love, one that made her feel alive and able to think about the future when she stopped being afraid.

She hadn't wanted to love again, hadn't wanted to risk the possibility of losing another part of her heart, of losing another person she cared about. And yet somehow the tender beginnings of a new love had taken root and flourished during the past weeks she'd come to know the man next door.

"Mommy?"

"Yes?" She stared down at her daughter, dazed as the knowledge flooded her soul.

"Where's Mr. Tim?"

"He's in the operating room, Aimee." Daniel stood in the doorway grinning. He bent over and scooped up the hurtling body into his arms, hugging her as he pressed a kiss against her hair. "Boy, it's good to have you back, punkin."

"Uncle Daniel, didn't you know about the game?" Aimee leaned back to study his face. "Didn't Mommy tell you?"

"Yes, sweetie, she did. But I'm glad it's over. I missed you."

"I missed you, too. Is Mr. Tim having another operation on his face? Because he told me that they don't do those at night." Trust Aimee to dot all the *I*'s and cross all the *T*'s.

"No, they don't usually." Daniel sank into a nearby chair with an apologetic look at Shelby. "But the thing is, Tim was kind of sick and the doctors wanted to make him better as soon as they could. So they decided to operate right away."

"Oh." Aimee wiggled off his knee, walked over to tug on her mother's pant leg. "I think I'll pray for Mr. Tim."

"You do that, honey. You can sit right beside his bed and talk to God about it. I'll be just outside talking to Uncle Daniel. Okay?"

Aimee nodded and tugged a chair beside the bed. She closed her eyes, then her lips began to move in a silent prayer. Daniel escorted Shelby outside the room, closed the door.

"What's wrong?" she demanded.

"They're afraid the bullet damaged his optic nerve. They had to go in right away or risk further damage."

"His sight?" She could hardly bear to hear it. Hadn't he suffered enough? Wasn't it time for God to help?

"They don't know, Shelby. He could lose one eye."

"Oh, no!" She felt herself sagging and was grateful for Daniel's strong arms that reached out and supported her. "If only I hadn't let him come."

"You couldn't have stopped him. He wanted to be there, to tell Russ what he'd learned, to unmask him. He wanted to do it for you."

"But—"

"No buts, Shel. It's done. Tim knew what he was doing, knew the risk he took. When he jumped in front of you, he understood what that meant. But he wanted it that way." Daniel's husky voice compelled her to listen. "Do you think it would have been easier for him to watch you be shot? He loves you, he has for a long time."

"He told me that," she whispered, remembering. "I wouldn't listen. I had all these feelings but I couldn't let Grant go."

"So you made yourself feel guilty. You're not guilty, Shel. God has blessed you with love again." Daniel shook his head, his amber eyes brimming with compassion. "Grant is in Heaven. You promised to love him till death parted you and that's what you did. But now you have to let go. You have to live. Sometimes that's the hardest part."

"I should have told Tim. I should have let him know that I cared, that I was afraid to love."

"Tim has faith, Shelby. A stronger faith than I've seen in some time. He believes God is in charge, that He knows what He is doing. I don't think you not saying the words in return is going to affect him. He knows what his hope is built on."

"I hope you're right. I just wish I'd told him what I felt." She glanced into the room, saw Aimee leaning against the side of the bed, her head resting on her arms as she slept. "I got a gift today, Daniel. A blessed, precious gift."

"Yes, you did." He walked into the room, lifted the child into his arms, smiled when she draped one arm over his shoulder and whispered his name. "You want to stay here, Shel. I can see the longing in your eyes. I'll take Aimee home, ask Esmeralda to put her to bed."

"Will you, please?" She tried to smile past the tears clogging her throat. "Thank you, Daniel. You're the best friend a girl could ever have."

"And don't you forget it!" He chuckled at her blink of surprise. "Say good-night to your daughter, Shel. Then go the chapel and duke it out with God."

"Like I can control God," she muttered as she leaned to kiss Aimee's silky cheek.

"No, you can't," he agreed. "But you can talk to Him, ask Him to help you find the peace He gives, thank Him for the opportunity He gave you to meet a man willing to do anything he could for you."

"Yes. I don't know why He did that, but I'm glad He did." She couldn't say anything else so she walked down the hall with Daniel. At the elevator he paused, one foot holding the door open.

"There's a little plaque on the back wall of the chapel, Shel. Look at it, will you? For me?"

"Sure." She touched his cheek. "Thank you. I love you."

"I love you, too, Shel. Have some trust."

"I'll try." She waited till the elevator closed on them, then asked a nurse for directions to the chapel. It was a small room, hidden from the normal bustle of the hospital. Backlit stained glass windows and low lighting made it a peaceful sanctuary.

Shelby glanced around the room, remembered Daniel's request.

Be still and know that I am God.

She sat on a pew, stared at the front of the chapel where white roses sat beneath a cross. What did it mean?

Be still. Stop fussing and fuming. Rest. Relax. Be at peace.

It sounded wonderful. But how was she supposed to do that with Tim so close to losing his sight?

Know. There was a certainty to that word that did away with hoping and guessing and trying to convince oneself. She'd heard it before—in the verse Tim had used over and over. *For we know.* No questions to be asked here. Know meant that it was indisputable, sure, certain.

Know that I am God. What did that mean?

Be certain, I am God. I've got it all under control. Forget trying to help, I'm in charge.

Shelby leaned back in her seat, closed her eyes. If only she could rest in that. But what if—what if—what if …

She sat up straight as the light pierced her soul with truth.

That was the point! No matter what, God had a plan that could accommodate anything people threw into it. An injustice that had been perpetuated for years, a woman kidnapped and incarcerated against her will, another drugged, a child abducted, a husband taken too early—He'd woven them all together to cause something good. Three sisters reunited after many years, a cheat and a liar brought to justice, a child returned home.

Little by little the jigsaw began to make sense. She didn't know why it had to be that way, but there was no denying that God had taken what men ruined and turned it into something wonderful.

Except for Tim. How could his injury turn out to be for good?

It didn't matter. Shelby almost shouted as the truth dawned in her heart. It truly didn't matter how or why—God would work His way and turn it into good.

Because He was God. Because He loved His children. Because God causes everything to work together for the good of those who love God and are called according to His purpose for them.

. It wasn't random, chance or freakish that Tim had been injured. Somehow it was all part of the plan. And all she had to do was trust that God would make it work out.

After all, He'd done it with Aimee.

Shelby whispered a prayer of thanksgiving then rose from her seat. She could hardly wait for Tim to come back to his room so she could tell him what she'd learned, to tell him that she loved him. The guilt, the doubt—it had all dissipated in the knowledge that she was safe in God's plan.

But when she got back to Tim's room, a No Visitors sign hung on the door.

Shelby shrugged, seated herself on the bench beside the door. She could wait while God worked it all out.

He knew every sound, every smell, every voice, though he could see nothing. Tim lay on his bed silently recording them all. Nurse Ratchet—that's what he called her privately—had just finished changing his bandages. Now he felt the familiar prick of a needle in his arm to dull the persistent agony that seemed to drag at him ever since he'd realized he might never see again.

"Drink," she ordered, slipping a straw between his lips.

He drank, a tiny sip of the sickly sweet soft drink she was convinced he enjoyed.

"There we are. All ready for visitors."

"No visitors," he muttered, trying to free his mouth of the straw. "I told you before."

"That was then. You're much better now. I'll just tidy up a bit."

In a moment she'd let Shelby in. He knew she'd been waiting outside for almost a week, hour after hour, day after day. He'd hoped she might take the hint and forget about him, but it looked as though he'd have to tell her straight.

"There we are. Come along in, Mrs. Kincaid. Mr. Austen is doing well today."

"Thank you."

He heard Shelby's soft tread into the room, felt her presence beside the bed and knew she was staring at him.

"Hello, Tim."

He kept his head turned away, refused to acknowledge her presence.

"How are you?"

Oh, lovely, thanks. And you?

"I wanted to tell you how sorry I am about the gunshot. And how grateful." Her voice died away, then returned softer, more intimate. "You saved my life. I'll never forget that."

Tim wanted her to forget it, to go on with her life and pretend that he'd never been in it.

"Aimee and I came to visit yesterday. She was disappointed not to see you."

Aimee. In spite of himself, his mouth curved into a faint grin. She was such a bundle of spirited delight. He was going to miss her. A lot.

"Maybe I could bring her by tomorrow. She really wants to talk to you about something, though she wouldn't tell me what it was."

"Not tomorrow. I won't be here." He broke his own vow of silence.

"They're releasing you? But that's wonderful!"

"Yeah. Fantastic." Except that he wouldn't be going home. The powers-that-be had decided to go ahead with the surgery on his face. To Tim the scar tissue's encroaching obstruction seemed irrelevant given he wasn't likely to see out of that eye again anyway but the doctors ignored his opinion.

She said something else but he didn't catch what it was. The drug had begun its numbing work. He struggled against it, knowing it was imperative that he tell her now.

"Don't come back here, Shelby. Don't try to see me. Just tell Aimee goodbye then get on with your lives." His tongue felt fuzzy, uncontrollable. He couldn't make it say what he wanted. Anyway, he couldn't quite remember what he wanted to say.

"You can't mean that, Tim!"

Just for a moment he wished he could see Shelby's eyes, those expressive windows to her soul. But why prolong the torture? She loved Grant. It was as simple as that.

"Leave," he managed to say, surprised by how forceful he made it sound. "Leave me alone."

Shelby said nothing, though he waited and waited. Finally it became too much to hang on as he realized she must have left. With a soft sigh, he gave in to the powerful drugs as his brain played its usual refrain—if only…

Two weeks later.

"Mommy! There's someone over at Mr. Tim's house." Aimee grabbed at her hand, dragged her away from the rose garden. "Come and see."

"Honey, we shouldn't be spying. If Tim wanted to see us, he knows where we live."

But Aimee would not be appeased and Shelby found herself peering through the hole in the hedge like a six-year-old. Unfortunately, she could see almost nothing.

"I'm going to see him."

Before Shelby could stop her, Aimee had rushed through the opening and was racing up the stairs. Shelby longed to follow but Tim's words kept echoing through her brain. *Leave me alone.*

He'd been very clear. She would not go against his wishes.

Aimee appeared, her face sad. "It's not him," she muttered. "It's some people who are moving things. Mr. Tim's not going to live there anymore."

"I'm sorry, honey. I know you loved him."

"The man said Mr. Tim is in the hospital. A different hospital than ours. He's getting another operation today."

A memory fluttered through Shelby's mind—of Tim saying how he hated waking up after surgery, of feeling alone. Suddenly it didn't matter that he'd sent her away, that he'd asked to be left alone. She made up her mind in an instant.

When Tim Austen woke up after this surgery she was going to be right there. After that she would do whatever he wanted.

"Come on, sweetheart. You and I are going to talk to that man."

"Why?"

"We're going to visit Tim."

Aimee squealed with delight then led the way through the hedge.

Shelby wasn't quite so delighted. She longed to see him again, to tell him what was in her heart, the things she'd realized. But all that would be up to him. For now she'd have to be content just to be there.

Whatever happened.

SEVENTEEN

The pain was excruciating.

Tim tried to bury himself in the darkness again but failed as another stab of sheer agony clawed at him.

"We're here, Tim. Aimee and I are here."

Hallucinations, too? Well, why should he be surprised. Nothing about this process was easy.

Something warm, familiar curled around his hand. It took several moments to puzzle out what it was. A hand, a child's hand.

"Pretty powerful drug," he muttered, or thought he did. At least he could still pretend.

"The nurse says it's time for you to wake up, Tim. Can you do that?"

His eyes were bandaged, he couldn't see. There was no miracle for him. He was scarred and ugly and now he was blind. He lifted his unattached hand to his face, stopped just short of the bandages.

"Open your eyes, Tim. I need to talk to you and I can't be sure you'll hear me if you've got your eyes closed."

"Go 'way." The haunting dream was becoming too real, probably because he wanted it so much.

"Like you went away and left me?" A laugh. "Not a chance,

buddy. I'm staying right here until you open those peepers. I've got something to say and I'm not leaving until I've said it."

The voice was too firm, too full of that trembly laughter to be anything but real. Shelby? Here? But he'd specifically told no one.

"Come on, Tim. You can't quit now. Don't you remember?

> We know that God causes everything to work together for the good of those who love God and are called according to His purpose for them.

Isn't that what you've been trying to hammer into my head for the past month?"

Everything he owned hurt. New pain waited in the wings to take over where the last stabbing agony left off. But this time as the anesthetic wore off—even though he knew what he'd have to endure in the next few days—he felt a flicker of something new. Something like hope.

"I won't be able to stay long," she whispered so close to his ear he could feel her breath. "I've got to go to Austria this afternoon. Marta's sister fell so her daughter flew home to be with her. There may not be much time for them to be reunited so we're flying out tonight." Her fingers touched his hair so lightly, a tender gentle brush. "Daniel did some smooth talking and Marta has a visitor's visa that will allow her to stay up to a year. She's so excited you wouldn't believe it."

"He's not listening, Mommy. Mr. Tim doesn't hear you." The fingers holding his hand slackened. Before they could pull away he squeezed. "He's waking up," Aimee's voice trilled. "He pinched me!"

"Yes. Come on, Tim. I know it hurts. As soon as you're awake, they'll give you something. Just please, wake up. Now. I'll have to leave soon and there's so much I need to tell you."

The lead weights holding his eyes closed would not move though he desperately wanted to look at Shelby once more before she abandoned him.

"All the time they were operating, all the time I waited to get in your room, even after, when you sent me away…I hung on, Tim. I kept praying, trusting, believing that God would somehow work it out. Are you going to just lie there?"

Waves of pain engulfed him but he fought to lift his eyelids. Maybe there'd be a shadow, a glimmer of light, something that he could hang on to. Something that would help him know that he wasn't alone. She didn't love him, he'd accepted that. But maybe with time, after more surgeries, maybe—

There was a whispered consultation in the background. He heard Shelby say "No." The door closed.

"Tim Austen, if you don't open your eyes and look at me, I'm going to walk out of this room and never come back."

That's what he'd told her to do before. But she was here anyway. She was stubborn, proud. She probably wouldn't come back.

Summoning every vestige of strength he could find, Tim forced one eyelid to lift. He could see—nothing!

"Good. Guess I'm going to have to be very firm with you from now on," Shelby chuckled.

"Don't worry if things are a little hazy. They'll straighten out in a minute. Just keep working to open your eyes." A doctor—he couldn't remember the name—spoke from his other side.

He was right. First there were shadows, faint blurry ones. Then he saw bits of light, dim but slowly getting clearer. He forced the other eyelid to lift just the slightest, found the light too bright and quickly closed both.

"Come on, darling. You can do it."

Darling? Who was she talking to? Tim wanted to see so he stuffed back the pain as best he could and concentrated on blinking until his vision began to clear. It wasn't easy. The room seemed overly bright but he could discern figures. One with bright blond hair piled high on her head, curls tumbling everywhere. A matching head, smaller, tucked against her waist. Aimee's hair was pulled into two neat ponytails.

"Shelby?" he whispered, unable to believe what he thought he saw. He blinked again, over and over, willing her face to come into view, relieved when it finally did.

"It's me, Tim." She stared at him. It was then he saw the tears. Her face was wet with them.

"Why are you crying?" he murmured, glad for the prick of the needle that would ease the throbbing that threatened to swamp him.

"Because I love you." She touched her forefinger to her lips, then brushed it against his. And strangely that didn't hurt at all. "Don't ask me how or when. I just do. I love everything about you. I don't care if you can't see me, I don't care if you're mad at me for coming when you said not to. I don't care how it looks to the rest of the world. I love you."

"Me, too," Aimee crowed.

Little by little the cloudiness dissipated until he could see them perfectly, the two most precious people in his life. The morphine was creeping through his veins now, slowly dulling his senses so that he felt as if he was being rolled in cotton wool.

"Please don't go anywhere until I get back, Tim. Please." She leaned over, met his stare. "You see, I have this idea that I think, I hope you might be interested in."

There were a thousand things he wanted to say, but only one word emerged. "Sleepy."

"Yes," she laughed, tears edging her voice. "I imagine you are. Sleep, my darling. Know that you're in my head and my heart and I love you terribly."

"Love you, too," he managed. Felt the fingers tighten. "Aimee, too. Make sure...come back."

"Always," she promised.

If she said anything else Tim didn't hear it. His eyelids wouldn't stay open and his brain begged for relief. He let go, one phrase clinging to the nether regions of his mind. She loved him.

Shelby grabbed the nearest taxi and gave her address.

"There's a twenty in there for you if we don't dawdle."

The taxi driver chuckled. "Got something special at home, huh?"

She leaned back against the seat, fought off the apprehension that had clung ever since she'd boarded the plane. "I hope so," she whispered.

She'd phoned Aimee every night of the two weeks she'd been away. At first her daughter had given her details of her visits with Esmeralda to Tim and Shelby had lapped them up as if she'd been starved.

But for the past two days Aimee had been strangely uncommunicative. Shelby had a hunch it was because Tim had told her he would not be moving back to his home next door. Somehow she'd known that he wouldn't believe her proclamation of love, that he'd put it down to a drug-induced hallucination or something like that. As if!

By the time the taxi pulled up at her front door, she was a bundle of nerves.

"You go ahead, ma'am," the driver encouraged. "I'll bring the bags."

"Thanks." Shelby hurried in the door. "I'm home," she

called as she dropped her things and hurried toward the kitchen. But there was no one there.

"I'm out here, Mommy," Aimee's voice called. "Come and see what I'm doing."

Shelby waited until the taxi driver had hauled in her bag. She paid him then closed the door wondering why her daughter still hadn't appeared.

As she moved through the room she couldn't see any light coming from the patio. What was going on?

A faint flicker drew her attention. She saw Esmeralda rocking on a wicker chair. Across from her, Aimee sat perched on a knee. Tim's knee.

"Hello, Shelby."

She stared at him, unable to believe what she was seeing. He sat on a lounger looking perfectly normal except for the thin layer of gauze still covering his face.

"Aimee and I are talking about a new book that's going to be published."

"It's my book! Mr. Tim named it for me, Mommy. *Aimee's Book of Stories* it's going to be called. Because I helped." She scooted off Tim's knee, hurried over to peer up at her mother. "Are you sick, Mommy? 'Cause you look funny."

"I feel funny, too. I missed you, sweetie."

"I know." Aimee wrapped her arms around her neck and hugged her. "But you're back now, right?"

"Yes. But beginning next week I'm going back to work at Finders, Inc. Is that all right with you?"

"Oh, yes. After all, I'm going to camp for two weeks and Mr. Tim's going to take me fishing and Esmeralda says I need to help her with some stuff. I'm going to be very busy, Mommy."

Shelby hid her smile, content to hold her child for a few moments more before she grew up. She explained about

Marta and her sisters, the happy reunion they'd shared and how they'd all admired the egg. But all the time she kept wondering why Tim was here, in her house.

A silence fell on the patio, a peaceful one as the stars came out overhead, each one adding another dimension to the velvet sky. Esmeralda rose.

"The little one's asleep," she murmured. "I'll take her up and put her to bed."

"Thank you. For everything." Shelby watched them leave, wondering what she would say to the silent man. "How are you, Tim?" she asked when they'd left the room.

"Nervous." His face lay in shadow and she couldn't read his eyes.

"Nervous? Why?"

"I'm afraid I've made a mistake."

She would have said something then but he held up his hand.

"When I was coming out of the anesthetic after the operation I thought I heard you say something. I've been living on tenterhooks ever since, wondering if I was dreaming, if you meant it, if I should be here."

She wanted to make it easier for him so she pointed to the rose garden.

"Can you walk?"

"Of course." He rose, followed her to the bush where Grant's Deep Secret had been replanted and now bloomed.

"In the hospital you said you loved me," he murmured. "But you have no idea how the surgeries will turn out. The scars aren't pretty. Most people stare. I look nothing like Grant."

"Who wants you to?" She leaned over, cradled a black red bud between her fingers. "Do you see this?"

"Shelby, I don't want to talk about roses."

"I do. Because they remind me of you. You remind me of

this rosebud, crunched up tight, afraid that your scars will drive people away when really those scars are just another step toward a new part of your life." She turned, gently cupped his face in her hands. "I've never known anyone more beautiful inside and out than you, Tim Austen. I've doubted you, said harsh things to you, I even thought you'd kidnapped my daughter. And yet you kept coming back."

His hands slipped around her waist. "I had to," he whispered. "I love you."

"Then why won't you believe I love you, too?" she asked just as softly. "I don't care how many more surgeries there are ahead, except that I want to be there with you. I don't care about the scars. To me they're badges of honor. They testify to your commitment to those you care about. That's what I value about you the most—you always do the right thing, no matter what. That you would stop that bullet…" Tears rose to her eyes and she leaned her head against his shoulder until she could regain her control.

"You're the kind of hero every woman wants, the kind who sticks by her no matter what, the kind she can count on to be there in a pinch." She tipped her head near his ear and whispered, "The kind who hears her heart instead of the words and silly things she says when she's upset."

There were other things she wanted to say but he stopped her very effectively. With his lips on hers and his arms holding her fast, Shelby couldn't remember her well-rehearsed little speech. She could only praise God that He had so marvelously worked things out for her good.

"I love you very much, Shelby Kincaid."

"I love you back," she whispered against his lips.

"Hey, you guys are kissing!" They glanced upward, found Aimee leaning out her window, a huge grin on her face. "Does this mean I get to have three daddies?"

"Three?" Tim stared at Shelby. "Something you forgot to mention, darling?"

Shelby made a face at him, then called out.

"You're supposed to be in bed, young lady. Asleep." But she didn't want Aimee asleep. She wanted her to share in their happiness. "Maybe you'd better come down here and tell us what you mean about three daddies."

They cuddled on the love seat, Aimee on Tim's knee, wrapped in his strong arm while his other encircled Shelby.

"So what's with the three daddies thing?" he asked her.

"Well, my one daddy is in Heaven. He's with my other daddy, God. I'm glad cause Mommy says Heaven is nice. That's two. But I think it would be really nice here if I could have a daddy who would stay with me. You have to have a daddy to show you how to fish," she explained. "I think I'd really like to learn to fish." Her golden head flopped onto his shoulder. "Why can't I have you for my daddy, Tim?"

"Aimee, you know that I love you very much. But I couldn't possibly be your daddy unless your mommy asked me to." A grin teased his lips into a smile as Shelby stared at him.

"You'll ask him, won't you, Mommy?"

Shelby glared at Tim, smiled at her daughter and offered the standard mother-response. "We'll see."

Two months later Aimee did see as her mother tossed the bridal bouquet she'd made from the last of the beautiful black buds of Deep Secret over one shoulder straight into Daniel McCullough's arms.

"Uncle Daniel! You caught the flowers." Aimee frowned at him. "You're not getting married. Are you?"

Shelby left them to discuss it, drew Tim with her deeper into the garden, into the center of the arbor.

"You don't want to move from here, do you?" he asked, his finger tracing the slim line of her neck.

"I'll live wherever you want," she told him quietly. "I've experienced joy, sorrow, love, and loss in this house. But most of all I've learned that God is in charge of the future and that whatever happens He'll make it work together for our good. It's the people that matter in my life, not the house."

"All the same, if you don't mind, I think we should stay put for now." He counted the reasons on his fingers. "It's Aimee's home. She loves having her friends come over to the pool. Grant's roses have drawn interest from around the world. You love it here and now so do I. Besides, Esmeralda is determined to remain in control of this place. She's already asked me about buying my place next door. I dare not challenge her."

"But that's not the real reason." She frowned. "Are you regretting your decision to come on board with Finders, Inc.?"

"Not at all." He grinned, kissed her cheek. "I love working with you."

"Then what's behind your decision to live here." She felt a sudden gnawing low in her stomach, a return of the fear and worry against which she'd fought for so long. Shelby pushed it away. *I know* she reminded herself.

Tim's eyes were dancing and his face had come alive.

"I found a room, Shelby. In the basement. It's full of wonderful things. You've probably seen all of them many times, but to me they're a treasure chest of history come to life. It's going to take me years and several books to make up stories about them."

"My grandmother's treasure trove. She'd be so happy to know you appreciate her collections. I'm glad you think it will take years to sort through." She stood on tiptoe to hug him, then whispered, "Because that's what we've got."

Tim grinned.

"Years and years of unwrapping the future and learning

what God has in store, just as the buds of Deep Secret unfold to display a flower no one believed could be grown. I can hardly wait."

* * * * *

*Look for the next riveting FINDERS, INC. book,
SILENT ENEMY in September 2006,
only from Love Inspired Suspense!*

Dear Reader,

Welcome to Finders, Inc.—a place dedicated to finding the truth. The idea for this series grew after a return visit to a city I particularly love, Victoria, British Columbia. While I was sitting in the hotel lobby, a woman stopped in, tossed off a cryptic comment then disappeared. And my story wheels started turning.

Shelby Kincaid is my kind of heroine. She's tough, strong and competent. But she's also vulnerable in her love for her only child. As I imagined the pain and terror of a mother whose child is missing, I was drawn to thoughts of God and His suffering when we refuse to walk with Him, to obey His rules. Our human love pales against His. There is no greater love than the Father for His beloved creations, His precious children.

I hope you'll return for another visit to Finders. Until then I wish you contentment with whatever state you're in, courage to deal with the future and most of all love—without it we are nothing.

Blessings,

QUESTIONS FOR DISCUSSION

1. Loss comes to everyone sooner or later. Discuss some losses you've experienced, how you dealt with them and the way your perspective on life has been altered because of them.

2. Imagine you were offered ten minutes to talk face-to-face with God about anything, and there's just half an hour to prepare for this meeting. Share some of the things you'd ask, or you may wish to make private notes. Share the feelings you believe you'd have at the end of your ten minutes with God. Would the answers you receive be enough or would you need to keep talking?

3. When her daughter disappeared, Shelby began to suspect her friends, those she'd always trusted most. In several cases she was wrong and could have done irreparable damage to her relationships. Discuss how our own feelings often make us suspect others of less-than-pure motives.

4. Like Tim, many folks with physical problems feel ostracized by other adults but relate well to small children who seem to see past their difficulty. Take an honest survey of your group to discover what makes us look away. Then think of ways we can train ourselves to focus less on physical appearance.

5. In the story the characters uncover a buried object that helps solve many puzzles. The object, like truth, is not immediately apparent but must be dug up first. Discuss truths people try to avoid and why.

6. Russ's actions were motivated by his family, because he loved and cared about them. Suggest ways children, grown or small, may try to cover for or protect their family members and how this can harm their relationship with others and with God.

7. We all love happy endings, but sometimes God doesn't send them until we're well past our prime of life. Consider Marta and the length of time she waited to reunite with her family, the lost years they could have shared. What are some ways you deal with prayers not yet answered?

8. Pause for a moment and reflect back over your own personal life. Think of times God used something you thought was a problem to bring resolution or peace to your situation. Share successes and difficulties in your life to gain a new perspective through another's eyes.

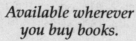

2 Love Inspired novels and a mystery gift... Absolutely FREE!

Visit

www.LoveInspiredBooks.com

for your two FREE books, sent directly to you!

BONUS: Choose between regular print or our NEW larger print format!

There's no catch! You're under no obligation to buy anything. We charge nothing—ZERO—for your first shipment. And you don't have to make any minimum number of purchases.

You'll like the convenience of home delivery at our special discount prices, and you'll love your free subscription to Steeple Hill News, our members-only newsletter.

We hope that after receiving your free books, you'll want to remain a subscriber. But the choice is yours—to continue or cancel, anytime at all! So why not take us up on our invitation, with no risk of any kind!

Love Inspired

THE FAMILY MAN

BY
IRENE
HANNON

Davis Landing

**Nothing is stronger
than a family's love.**

Hiring her old flame
wasn't easy for magazine
editor Amy Hamilton, but
Bryan Healey was the best
writer for the job. Yet
working closely with the
widowed single dad—and
getting to know his adorable
son—made Amy want this
family man to be hers!

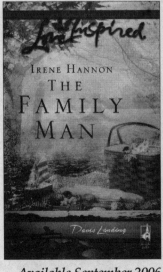

*Available September 2006
wherever you buy books.*

Steeple
Hill®

www.SteepleHill.com

LITFM